Darkest
Before Dawn

By
Arlene Brathwaite

BRATHWAITE PUBLISHING

www.brathwaitepublishing.com

Books by Arlene Brathwaite are published by

Brathwaite Publishing
P.O. Box 38205
Albany, New York 12203

This book was printed in the United States of America.

ACKNOWLEDGMENTS

It's 2011 and Brathwaite Publishing is growing in numbers and accomplishments with each year that passes. This year we are bringing on a few new authors, and we're opening Albany's first official urban book café called The Book Club. We are hanging tough in an industry that will run you over if you stand still. So, we here at Brathwaite Publishing are steady moving, and are steady coming up with stories that will keep our fans demanding more.

The fans drive us, but it's the support of fellow comrades in the book industry that guide us and keep us focused. People such as; Anthony Whyte, Erick S. Gray, Jason Claiborne, Shannon Holmes, Wahida Clarke, Nakea Murray and K'wan Foye. Thank you Locksie, English Ruler and SiStar Tea of ARC Book Club Inc. for your support and constructive criticism. English, you really came through for us on the editing tip. Thank you.

A special thanks to Jonathan Johnson of Brand Concepts for the book covers. Their works are fresh and eye catching.

And a very special thanks to all the readers and supporters who motivate us to give them the glued-to-the-seat, can't-go-to-sleep-til-I-finish-this-last-page reads. Those are the kinds of stories that we're known for, and that's not going to change. Thank you so much for your support and we hope to see you at future events, and at The Book Club.

CHAPTER 1

*F*riday night, Westside, Manhattan, drizzle dampened the deserted streets. The driver of the Cadillac CTS piloted the glacial-blue coupe through the wet night like a NASCAR driver.

The driver made a hairpin turn into the underground garage of the club known as The Bank. Before The Bank was a club, it was a bank. Lowe, its owner, figured that if he called his club The Bank, the name would attract the ballers, the divas, the gangsters, and anyone else who was about getting that paper— he was right.

The two bouncers posted on either side of the private elevator perked up when the Caddy came to a screeching halt in its reserved parking space.

Both men stared at the stiletto-heeled Givenchy sandals as they made contact with the pavement, then their eyes traveled up the tone legs that were in them. A copper-complexioned woman stood her full height of five foot six inches. She had dark brown eyes set in a walnut face framed by beautiful braids. She smoothed out her black Ralph Lauren dress that stopped mid thigh. Bending at the waist, she reached into her car and retrieved her purse. The men gawked at the woman's perfectly round behind. They quickly averted their gazes as she stood back up. Getting busted lusting over the boss's wife was grounds for automatic dismissal and a thorough ass whipping.

"Good evening, Mrs. Jones," Lou, the bouncer on the right said, as Julisa approached.

"Good evening, Lou," she responded in kind. Lou looked like a black sumo wrestler. The suit he was wearing fitted him like a strait jacket.

"Good evening, Mrs. Jones," Cash, the bouncer on the left said.

"Good evening, Cash," she responded. Cash was tall and lean like a basketball player. Cash's suit fell on him just right. "Quiet night gentlemen?"

"No Ma'am," Lou said. "Since Obama won the presidency, folks have been partying nonstop."

"More money for us, right Cash?" Julisa asked.

"More money for you and Lowe, Ma'am."

"Good answer." Julisa began reaching in her purse.

Cash quickly pulled out his elevator key. "I got it Mrs. Jones." He stuck his key into the lock; the door opened immediately.

"Thank you, Cash."

"Not a problem, Ma'am."

Julisa stepped in. The elevator opened onto a secluded corridor.

"Good evening, Mrs. Jones," Bono, the bouncer posted in the corridor said.

"Good evening, Bono, where's Lowe?"

"VIP room."

"Thanks." Julisa sashayed down the corridor and through the sound proof glass doors. The club was pulsating with music, sweat, and young bodies in heat. The crowd was jumping, literally. Men and women were pumping their fists in the air, screaming Obama's name. Julisa continued heading to the VIP room.

"Julisa!" Lowe called out when he saw her. He was rocking his customary fitted cap pulled low, white tank top, and blue jeans. He was sitting with his entourage of lackeys.

Julisa walked up to him and sat on his lap. "How many drinks have you had?" she asked, twisting his cap backwards.

"Two."

"You're such a liar."

"What he meant to say was he stopped counting at two," Trent, Lowe's right hand man said.

"Yeah, that's what I meant to say," Lowe said, winking at Trent.

"Trent's always bailing your sorry ass out."

"That's why he's my ace, boon, coon." Lowe held his fist out.

Trent banged it with his.

Julisa shook her head.

"C'mon, baby." Lowe kissed her on the cheek. "We're just having a few drinks." Julisa shot him a look full of attitude. Lowe dug into his pocket and pulled out a wad of twenties. "What's that charity you're raising money for? Kids Living with AIDS or something?"

"Don't try and buy your way out of this."

He handed her a stack of twenties and then looked at his entourage. They dug deep and came out with tens and twenties. They passed the pile of bills to Lowe, who in turn, handed it to Julisa. "There, we did our good deed for the night."

Julisa folded the cash and placed it inside her purse. "We need to talk."

"Now? I'm with my boys."

"They'll be here when you get back."

"Go ahead," Trent said. "That big ass wedding band is cramping our style anyway."

Julisa led Lowe by the hand to his office.

"This better be important," Lowe said.

"Make sure we're not disturbed," Julisa said to Bono.

"Yes, Mrs. Jones."

"Keep up the good work, Bono," Lowe said, pounding his fist against Bono's.

"I will, sir."

"What's so important?" Lowe asked, as they entered his office.

"You haven't been home in two days."

"I've been here the whole time; you know that. Trent and I had some shit to take care of."

"The type of shit I don't want to know about?"

"Yes."

Julisa slid her hand inside his jeans and began playing with him. "You missed me?"

Julisa felt him stiffening in her hand. Lowe removed her hand and pulled her to him. He stuck his tongue in her mouth and started kissing her hard. Then he slowly opened the front of her dress, and sucked on her nipples.

"You haven't been home to handle your business," Julisa moaned. "I had to handle it for you."

Lowe licked her nipple. "I'm about to handle my business right now."

Julisa unbuttoned his pants and stroked him until she felt precum on her fingers. "I want you in my mouth."

Lowe watched her as she sank to her knees. He closed his eyes, anticipating her hot tongue licking up and down the sides of his throbbing shaft. Julisa squeezed his balls. He moaned. Her grip tightened. Lowe winced. He looked down and saw her staring up at him with fire in her eyes.

"What?"

She stood up and smacked him.

"What the fuck?"

She grabbed a handful of his boxers and showed him the smudges of lipstick. "I hate your fucking guts."

"You need to chill."

"Chill? Are you serious?"

"Look, shit's been hectic; I was stressed out."

"Stressed out?" Julisa said dumbfounded. "Imagine you going down on me and finding another man's cum stains in my panties, and I say, chill, shit's been hectic; I was stressed out."

"Julisa, don't even play like that."

"Who said I'm playing? You can get your dick sucked whenever and by whomever and I'm supposed to be all right with that?"

"You act like I'm fucking these bitches."

"Bitches? You mean to tell me there's more than one?"

"You bugging, right now. Go home and I'll see you when I get there."

"I'm not going anywhere."

"Fine. Stay here; I'll go home. I don't have time for this." Lowe left the office.

Julisa folded her arms and fumed. Finally, she snatched up her purse and took off after him. "Where'd he go?" she asked Bono.

"To the garage."

Julisa got to the garage just in time to see Lowe's Escalade turning out into the street. She got into her car and took off after him. She got caught at a stoplight. She spotted Lowe down the block stuck at a stoplight, as well. Her eyes widened when she saw a shadow detach itself from the curb and run up on the side of Lowe's truck. The hooded figure yanked his door open and fired two shots into the SUV.

Julisa screamed and stomped on the gas pedal. She watched the figure pull Lowe out of the truck and fling him to the ground. The carjacker hopped into the Escalade and peeled off. Julisa skidded in front of her husband's body and jumped out of her car.

"Lowe!" She fell to her knees and cradled his head in her arms. "You're going to be all right, baby." She screamed when he started coughing up blood. "Somebody help me!"

Dawn stared at her husband as he slept. She slid the covers off of his naked body. She didn't worry too much about waking him; Dante was a hard sleeper. He had broad shoulders, a wide chest, and a thin waist. She traced his full dark lips with her tongue and then ran her finger down alongside his neck. Dante stirred, but didn't wake. Dawn continued outlining his pecs and then the deep grooves in his six-pack.

"Damn, you fine," she whispered.

Dante was Dawn's dream come true. He was educated, fine, and had an insatiable appetite for pleasing her in every way imaginable.

She traced his pubic hair down to his soft penis. It was huge even when limp. She caressed it and watched it grow. She bit down on her tongue when she felt herself getting moist. Her hungry eyes shot up to Dante's as he stirred again.

"Dawn?" he moaned in his sleep.

Dawn gathered her nightgown around her waist and gently mounted him. She eased down on his shaft, inch by pleasurable inch. She stifled a groan when she had all nine inches of him inside her. She rode him slowly for a good ten seconds before he woke up, wiping sleep out of his eyes.

"You awake?" she whispered.

"I am now," he mumbled.

"Good." She squeezed her walls around his stiff muscle and rode him like he was a bucking bronco.

Dante tried turning her over to get on top, but she refused. He tried again, but she wasn't giving up her position. "You're a control freak, you know that?" he said in between moans.

"Hush and enjoy the ride." Dawn arched her back when she felt him swelling inside her. Dante's eyes rolled to the back of his head as his body spasmed. Dawn couldn't hold back her orgasm anymore once she felt him shooting his hot fluid against her walls. When she no longer felt him twitching inside of her, she stopped riding him and laid her head on his chest.

Dante rubbed her back. "When did you get in?"

"About fifteen minutes ago."

Dante looked at the clock. "It's almost nine o'clock. You're getting home later and later."

"I'm doing the work of three secretaries now. My boss fired another one this morning."

"And Bush tried to convince us that we weren't in a recession. He's so full of it."

Dawn lifted her head off of his chest. "Are we going to be all right? We worked so hard to get this house, our cars—"

"Hey," Dante said, cupping her face between his hands. "We're going to be just fine. We got money in the bank just in case things get rough and... David told me that the bosses are considering me for a promotion."

Dawn's eyes lit up. "He told you that?"

"He sure did."

"Oh my God, that's wonderful." She kissed him long and hard. She moaned when she felt him growing inside her again. Dante rolled her over before she had a chance to fight for the top position.

"My turn to drive."

Dawn placed her legs up on his shoulders. "Drive it all the way home, daddy."

The following afternoon, Dawn strolled into the Ritz Carlton Lounge in Battery Park, wearing black slacks and a simple black sweater. Dawn had brown eyes, high cheekbones, and full lips. She had long legs, plenty of breasts, and a heart-shaped rump, all of which she kept hidden under baggy clothing.

"Dawn!" Julisa waved her over.

"Hey, girl." Dawn gave her a hug before sitting down across from her. "How you holding up?"

"I'm getting better."

"Any change in Lowe's condition?"

"He's still in a coma. The doctors were able to remove the bullets and stop the internal bleeding..." she started to tear up. Dawn put her hand on top of hers. "I saw everything. When the guy walked off the curb, my mind was telling me to honk my horn to warn Lowe, but my body wouldn't respond. And then this shadow of a person opened the truck door and shot him. I can't lose him, Dawn. I don't know what I'll do without him."

"You're not going to lose him. Lowe's a fighter, he'll pull through, you'll see."

"Thank you for being my best friend."

"I should be thanking you. If it weren't for you, I'd probably be in the Feds doing a life bid."

Julisa chuckled. "You were the only girl in school that I knew back in Charlotte who wanted to be a drug dealer's ride or die bitch."

Both of them started laughing.

"Now look at you." Julisa continued. "All grown up, and you went in the opposite direction. You got yourself a fine, college educated, Wall Street fella."

"Who would've thought?"

"And who would've thought I would wind up marrying Lowe."

Dawn rubbed the back of Julisa's hand. "Lowe's a good man."

"Lowe's into everything that I used to stand against."

"The important thing is he takes care of you and he doesn't involve you in his bullshit." Dawn waved the server over. "I'll have a turkey and cheese sandwich."

The server looked at Julisa.

"Nothing for me."

"She'll have a turkey and cheese sandwich, as well," Dawn said, eyeing Julisa. "You have to eat something."

"So, what's good with you and Dante?"

"We're doing well. His firm is giving him a promotion."

"That's good. What about your job? They don't believe in giving secretaries promotions?"

"Shit, I'm lucky I still have a job, with the way this recession is hitting us."

"Well, if there's anything you need from me—"

"Dante and I are going to be okay." Dawn turned her attention to the gentleman sitting a few tables away. Every time she looked in his direction, she would catch him staring at her. She rolled her eyes when he got up from his table and started walking their way. "Oh God, here we go."

"What?" Julisa said.

"Good afternoon, ladies." He sat his slinky frame down and tugged at the huge diamond stud in his ear.

"Um, excuse me," Dawn started. "No one gave you permission to sit down."

"He's cool," Julisa said.

"The name's Trent. You must be Dawn."

"And who are you again?" Dawn asked.

"I'm a friend of Lowe and Julisa, so I guess that makes me your friend, too." He smiled, flashing his platinum grille.

Dawn studied the different color diamonds in his grille, the platinum chains dangling from his neck, and the platinum rings decorating his fingers. "Friends? You don't even know me."

"Then, give me a chance to."

"Why did you even come over here?" Julisa had an attitude. "You were supposed to stay at your table."

"I just came by to say hi." He winked at Dawn. "Hi."

The server returned with their sandwiches. Dawn pushed hers to the side.

"I lost my appetite."

"Bye, Trent," Julisa said.

He stood up. "I'll be in the car." He looked at Dawn. "Nice meeting you."

"Whatever," she mumbled, waving him off. "What's that all about?" she said to Julisa.

"Girl, please. He's not letting me go anywhere without protection. He's not buying that carjacking story."

"He thinks somebody put a hit on Lowe?"

"He doesn't know shit. He's just speculating. You know how niggas are with their conspiracy theories." Julisa slid Dawn's sandwich back in front of her. "Eat."

"My half hour break is about up."

Julisa looked at her watch. "I'm going to the hospital to sit with Lowe."

"Everything's going to be fine, you'll see."

As they stood to leave, Dawn noticed three men getting up from their tables as well. "Damn, Julisa, it's like that?"

Julisa looked at the security detail Trent put on her. "I told you. Niggas and their conspiracy theories."

Dawn hugged her before heading back to work. Trent watched Dawn sling her tote bag over her shoulder. Unbeknown to her, she walked right in front of his parked car as she stepped off the curb to cross the street.

"I definitely want to get to know you," he whispered to himself, as he watched her hips roll.

Julisa opened the passenger side door and got in. "This has got to stop," she said, slamming the door.

"Lowe will kill me if anything happened to you."

"Nothing's going to happen to me. Lowe was carjacked. Stop making it more than what it was." She punched him in the arm. "And stop staring at my friend's ass, she not on your level."

"Well, maybe it's time for her to upgrade."

"Nah, baby, fucking with you would be a step down for her."

"Damn, it's like that?" Trent squinted trying to see where Dawn went, but he lost her in the crowd.

CHAPTER 2

*D*awn turned off the highway. She looked at the dash-
board. It was 9:30 pm. She then looked at the gas gauge
and sighed. With gas at $4.79 a gallon, it cost her close to
$70.00 to fill her tank up on the way to work this morning.
Now, the needle was just above half a tank.

She turned onto her quiet street and pulled into her driveway. When she walked into the house, she picked up the
remote and turned on the TV.

"The Dow fell 427 below 8,000 for the first time in five
years," the newscaster announced.

That can't be good. She changed the channel. "Governor
Paterson is proposing to slash $2 billion from state spending
which will cut into aid to public schools and health care,"
another newscaster said.

Dawn turned off the TV, and headed upstairs. Dante was
asleep. His clothes crumpled up by the foot of the bed, and a
bottle of Tylenol was on his nightstand.

Dawn undressed and took a shower. She closed her eyes as
the pulsating water massaged her back. She smiled as she
thought of Trent's cocky, hood rich, ass. Seven years ago she
would've been all over him like hot sweat. She thought of her
ride or die days with Ray, a drug dealer on the come up in
Charlotte. She was in the passenger side of his Camaro driving

from Charlotte to New York. Shit turned sour when a State Trooper hit his sirens. Ray thought he could outrun him in his souped up muscle car. He turned a routine traffic stop into a high-speed chase, spanning two states. He finally turned off into New Jersey and ended up crashing into a telephone pole. When Dawn regained consciousness, State Troopers had the car surrounded with their guns trained on her. The driver's side door was wide open and Ray was nowhere in sight.

The Troopers found a 9mm handgun under the driver's seat and a pound of weed in the trunk. Because, Dawn wouldn't "snitch" her man out, she was charged with everything from reckless endangerment to drug trafficking. While Ray left her in jail to rot, Julisa stepped up and hired a hotshot lawyer who got the case thrown out on several technicalities. Dawn's ride or die days were over.

She toweled off and slid into bed next to Dante. She draped his arm over her chest and kissed his fingers one by one. "I love you," she whispered, and then thanked God for the life He'd given her.

The next morning, Dawn rolled over and realized the bed was empty. "Dante?"

He peeked out of the bathroom. "I didn't mean to wake you."

"Come back to bed."

"I wish I could." He walked out the bathroom, straightening his tie. "The bosses called for an emergency meeting this morning."

"Is everything okay?" Dawn looked worried.

"Investors are starting to panic. The Dow dropped, the NASDAQ   dropped and the price of oil shot back up to a hundred and twenty dollars a barrel."

"What does that mean for us?"

"It means go back to sleep, we're fine." He pecked her on the cheek.

"Let me fix you something to eat."

He grabbed his keys off the dresser. "Don't have time. See you tonight. Love you."

"I love you too."

Dawn was sitting at her desk when her boss, Mr. Morgan walked by. "Dawn I need to see you in my office."

Dawn's heart started racing. She could feel all eyes on her. *God, please don't do this to me.* The closer she got to Mr. Morgan's office, the madder she was becoming. *This fucking bastard, I can't believe he's firing me. I've been here longer than any of these secretaries.* She cleared her throat as she walked into the office.

"Have a seat, Dawn."

"I'll stand." *Fuck that. If you're going to fire me, I want to be standing.*

Mr. Morgan sighed. "Dawn there's going to be more cuts."

"You're firing me?"

"No, I'm not firing you, but your item number has been eliminated."

"Eliminated?"

"I was told this morning that I'm only allowed five full-time item numbers. Yours was the sixth."

"I don't understand. You're not firing me, but my item number has been eliminated."

"I have a part-time item number available, so—"

"Part-time?"

"It's the best I can do, right now."

"The best you can do is keep me full-time and make one of those secretaries, who just started working here part-time."

"I don't make the decisions, I'm just the asshole who has to do the dirty work. I wish—"

Dawn held her hand up. "Don't even say it." She walked out, and sat at her desk. She picked up her cell phone and noticed that Julisa had texted her. She wanted to meet her at their usual bench in Battery Park in ten minutes to discuss something important. Dawn grabbed her jacket and headed to the elevator. Right about now, she needed some fresh air.

Dawn sat on the park bench, massaging the back of her neck when she heard a voice from behind.

"Smoothie?"

She turned around and looked at the cup in Trent's hand. "Where's Julisa?"

"She's not coming. I'm the one who texted you." Dawn stood up.

"Hold on a minute," he said, stepping in front of her.

"I don't have time to play games with you."

"This isn't a game, I really need to talk to you."

"We don't have anything to talk about." Dawn tried to move past him.

Trent held his ground. "Look, I know you don't know me, you may not even like me, but on the serious tip, I really need to talk to you about Julisa. Just give me ten minutes." He held the smoothie out to her.

Dawn took it from him and sat down. "Ten minutes."

Trent sat down. "I know you and Julisa have been friends for a very long time. Lowe and I have a long history, as well. I'll do anything for him, which means, I'll do anything for Julisa. Feel me?"

"I'm listening."

"Here's my dilemma. Since Lowe's been in a coma, certain people have been testing the waters."

"Testing the waters? I don't know what that means," Dawn said, becoming impatient.

"It means they are doing shit that they wouldn't dare do if Lowe wasn't comatose."

"Shit like what?"

"Like being late with payments. Some not even making payments."

"What does this have to do with Julisa?"

"It's understood by all that until Lowe is back with us, she's in charge."

Dawn snorted. "I hardly think Julisa's going to get involved with Lowe's shady enterprise. She's only concerned with the club."

"That's where the dilemma lies. When I tell her about Lowe's other *enterprises*, she brushes me off, and tells me that she doesn't want anything to do with them. Now, if I just ran off and handled this situation on my own, it will look like I'm usurping her authority."

Dawn shot him a puzzled look. "Her authority?"

"Whether she wants to accept it or not, she's running The Bank, the good and the bad of it. So, if she doesn't hold a meeting with Lowe's people, and give me the go-ahead in front of them to handle this business, the Streets are going to sense weakness. And—"

"And *certain* people will try and take over Lowe's business."

"Including The Bank."

Dawn sipped on the smoothie. "So, you want me to talk to Julisa, convince her to have a meeting, and give *you* the green light at this meeting to handle your business, by any means necessary."

"Exactly."

Dawn stood.

Trent stood as well. "So, I can count on you?"

Dawn tossed the rest of the smoothie into a nearby trash can. "Do me a favor."

"Anything."

"Don't ever contact me, again."

"Wha… wait, I thought you understood."

"You're the one who needs to understand. Julisa's my friend. I would never disrespect our friendship by trying to convince her to do something that may send her to prison."

"Prison?"

"You want her to stand up in a room full of witnesses and tell you to go handle your business by any means necessary? What if one of the people in attendance is working with the Feds? What if he is a Fed?"

Trent smiled. "You have a vivid imagination. None of our people are working with the Feds nor is anyone of them a Fed."

Dawn tugged on his jacket collar, bringing his ear to her lips and whispered. "If you believe that, then you're dumber than I thought." She spun on him and headed back to work.

"I'm tired of the bureaucracy bullshit at my job," Dawn said to Julisa as they sat on their bench in Battery Park the next day. "Obama better represent the working folk, because the Higher Ups don't give a damn about us."

"I can't believe you told your boss that he should've made one of those other secretaries part-time."

"You know I don't bite my tongue."

"So what are you going to do?"

"What choice do I have?"

"You tell Dante yet?"

Dawn shook her head. "I was going to tell him last night, but he looked stressed about something. He went straight to bed. I'm going to tell him tonight." Dawn took a bite of her sandwich. "You been to the hospital lately?"

Julisa sighed. "This morning. Nothing's changed. Lowe's just laying there like a corpse."

"Don't say that."

"It's true. I squeeze his hand, pinch his fingers, and he doesn't even flinch."

Dawn looked over Julisa's shoulder. "I see you still have your three shadows."

"I can't even go into a public bathroom without them checking it out first."

"Where's Trent?"

"He said he had a couple of things to do."

"I don't know how to tell you this, so I'm just going to tell you."

"Tell me what?"

"Trent came to see me yesterday."

"What?"

"Actually, he texted me from your phone, which is why I thought it was you, but he was here at the park instead of you."

"That snake. I was wondering why he wanted to borrow my BlackBerry. He knows you're married."

"He didn't meet with me to try and get with me."

Julisa stared at her in confusion. "Then why would he want to meet with you?"

"He's concerned with the side of Lowe's business that you don't want to deal with."

"Why would he come to you about that?"

"He wanted me to convince you to put him in charge of Lowe's shady dealings until he comes out of the coma."

"I don't give a damn what he does, just as long as he doesn't bring that shit to the club."

"According to him, it's not that simple. Lowe's people see you as the shot caller, so Trent can't do anything without your okay."

"I'm not okaying shit," Julisa said, becoming upset. "I can't believe he came to you with this. Wait until I see him. And he actually thought you could convince me to do some crazy shit like that?"

"That's what he thought." Dawn shrugged.

Julisa crossed her legs and lowered her voice. "Do you think I'm in any danger?"

"I don't know. What if what happened to Lowe wasn't a carjacking?"

"So, what should I do? Should I have this meeting that Trent keeps riding me about?"

"If I were in your shoes, I wouldn't."

"Well, if you were in my shoes, what would you do?" Julisa's voice became tense.

"I don't know what I would do."

"Dawn, don't do this to me."

"What do you want me to say?"

"Anything, but I don't know."

Dawn saw the look of desperation in Julisa's eyes, but Dawn would never forgive herself if something happened to Julisa because she took her advice. "How 'bout this, focus on the club. I'm sure the other stuff will work itself out."

"And if it doesn't?"

"Then, we'll cross that bridge together when we get there." Dawn sipped her soda. "So, how's business at the club?"

"Better than ever."

"Even with this recession?"

"Are you kidding? People are always looking for a place to escape from their problems. What better place than The Bank where you can drink, dance, and be entertained?"

"Shit, maybe I need to come down there."

"Speaking of which, when are you and Dante coming through again?"

"Girl, you know my man is a square. He doesn't hang out unless it's a special occasion."

Both women stopped talking when Julisa's cell phone rang. "Hello?"

"Julisa, where are you?" Trent asked.

"I'm having lunch with Dawn."

"I need you to meet me, right away."

"Now? Are you serious?"

"Yes." He gave her the address of a Midtown Manhattan building.

"What's going on?" Julisa asked, after writing down the address.

"Just get here, immediately, okay?"

Julisa sucked her teeth. "I'm on my way." She hung up. "I have to go," she said to Dawn.

"Business?" Dawn asked with an inquisitive look.

"I believe so."

"Well, go handle your business."

"And you go handle yours. I don't think Dante will take you being part-time, too hard. At least you'll be home more."

A half hour later, Julisa walked into the Midtown office building. Trent paced the lobby waiting for her. When he saw her, he led her to the row of elevators.

"What's this about, Trent?"

The elevator doors opened and they stepped in. Trent pressed the button for the twenty fifth floor. "You're about to meet one of Lowe's associates."

"If this doesn't have anything to do with the club—"

"It has everything to do with the club."

They stepped off the elevator, and headed down the corridor to the last office on the right. When they entered, the receptionist led them straight in.

"Good afternoon, Julisa," the man from behind the desk said. He stood up and walked toward her. He was brown skinned, clean-shaven, all the way up to his baldhead. He wore a tailor-made, dark blue suit. He shook her hand. "I'm Mr. Green."

Julisa looked around the decorative suite. "I'm not sure why I'm here."

"Have a seat," Mr. Green said, as he walked to the countertop mounted on the wall. "May I offer you a cup of coffee or tea?"

"No thank you." Julisa sat down.

Mr. Green fixed himself a cup of tea, and then sat behind his desk. "First off, I'm sorry about Lowe. My prayers go out to you and your family."

"Thank you."

Mr. Green cut his eyes at Trent and then looked back at Julisa. "Trent tells me that he will be overseeing things for the time being. Is that true?"

"No, that's not true," Julisa said, looking at Trent.

Mr. Green looked at Trent as he sipped his tea.

Trent smiled nervously and looked at Julisa. "He's not talking about the club."

Mr. Green placed his teacup back on its saucer. "Trent, give us a minute, will you?"

"Mr. Green—"

"Wait outside." Mr. Green's words were smooth and even, unlike the jagged vein forming on the top of his baldhead.

"I'll be right outside," Trent said to Julisa.

When he left, Mr. Green spoke. "Julisa, I'm going to be blunt with you, because there's too much at stake for me to sugar coat my words."

Julisa shifted in her chair.

"Lowe and I had an understanding. I'm the brain and he's the brawn. He keeps the money pouring in and I clean it up, and make it legal."

"I'm not involved with Lowe's other activities, I'm only concerned with running The Bank."

"I own The Bank, Julisa."

"What?"

"I own The Bank. So, I decide who's going to run it and who's not."

"Lowe never told me about you or that you owned any parts of The Bank."

"Maybe he didn't deem it necessary, but whatever his reasons may have been, they're irrelevant, right now. Out of respect for Lowe and all the money he has made me over the years, I'm giving you the opportunity to step up and run The Bank, and all of its operations."

"I can run The Bank, but all of the other operations…"

"This is a package deal, Julisa. Either you run it all or… I'll find someone else who can."

"Someone like Trent?"

"The only reason why Trent is still around is because of Lowe."

"I don't think I can—"

"Before you give me your final answer, take a few days to think about it. If I have to find someone else, then I will no longer need Lowe's services."

"Meaning?" Julisa shot him a challenging look.

"Meaning, when Lowe comes out of his coma, he will be looking for other means of employment."

"Are you serious?"

"You have until the end of the week to give me your answer." Mr. Green sipped his tea.

Julisa stood up. At that moment, she wished she had Dawn's backbone, because she wanted to tell Mr. Green to go fuck himself. Instead, she could only muster up the courage to slam the door as she walked out of his office.

Trent cut his conversation short with the receptionist when Julisa walked out. "What happened?" he asked, as he tried keeping up with her.

Julisa pressed the elevator button. "Since when did Mr. Green own The Bank?"

"He always owned it."

The elevator doors opened. Julisa rolled her eyes at him and stepped in. "All this time I thought Lowe owned The Bank. I can't believe this."

"What did Mr. Green say to you?"

"Basically, he wants me to fill in for Lowe. He said if I don't, he's going to find someone else to run The Bank. Without The Bank, Lowe and I will have nothing."

"You're going to hold everything down until Lowe pulls through."

"And how am I supposed to do that?"

"I'm going to help you."

Julisa looked like she was on the verge of crying. "I don't know if I can do this."

"All you have to do is gather everyone together and tell them how it's going to be."

"I don't even know how it's going to be."

Trent placed his hand on her shoulder. "All you have to do is let me put a meeting together tonight and then you tell everyone that you're putting me in charge."

Julisa squinted at him. "I put you in charge and then what?"

"Then you sit back, relax, and take the credit for a job well done."

Julisa shrugged his hand off her shoulder as the elevator doors opened. They walked in silence across the lobby and out onto the sidewalk.

"I'll think about it," Julisa said, as she headed to her car.

Trent cut in front of her. "We have to do this tonight, Julisa. The longer we put this off, the harder it's going to be to put things back in check. I'll arrange a meeting tonight, okay?"

Julisa looked at the ground.

"Julisa—"

"Okay, okay." Julisa got into her car and drove off.

CHAPTER 3

*D*awn pulled into the garage a little after eight. She dropped her head on the steering wheel. *How am I going to tell Dante that I'm part-time?* She pictured the look of shock on his face. He would automatically start calculating the amount of money they spend a month and where he could cut corners.

She sighed, knowing the first thing he would want them to do is car pool, or worse, take public transportation to work. No more weekend getaways, Broadway plays or spontaneous shopping sprees. Dawn moaned.

She entered the house through the backdoor, stopping short between the threshold of the kitchen and the living room. "Hey, what's up?"

Dante was leaning back on the couch with their monthly bills scattered all over the coffee table.

"Baby, is everything okay?"

Dante grabbed the bottle of wine off the floor and took a long swig. "I'm done."

"Done? What are you talking about?"

He swiped the bills off the coffee table.

"Okay, Dante." Dawn sat down next to him. "You're scaring me. What happened?"

"Yesterday, I was being made partner in the firm. Today, I was made a scapegoat for the millions of dollars our investors lost. And tomorrow I will be cleaning out my office."

Dawn got an instant headache. "After all these years, after all the money you made them, they fired you just like that?"

"Just like that."

"But... they just can't fire you."

Dante laughed. "They can do whatever they want."

"Well... you can just get a job with another firm."

"It doesn't work that way. When they're through crucifying me in order to appease their investors, no one is going to hire me."

"You can start your own business."

"Doing what?"

"You can be an investment consultant."

"It's not that easy. People aren't just going to hire me. They're going to want references." Dante was getting more frustrated by the second.

"You can't just give up." Dawn looked down at their bills scattered all over the floor. "What about our car payments, our mortgage?" Dante tried to take a drink from the bottle of wine, but she stopped him. "I'm not giving up my car, Dante or our house."

He handed her the bottle and stood up. "I'm heading upstairs. I'm going to take two Tylenols, and I'm going to bed."

"Bed? We need to talk about this."

"Not tonight. Too much has happened to me."

"To you? What about me?"

He stopped at the bottom of the steps and turned around. "What happened to you?"

"I got a job change."

"Are they paying you more money?"

Dawn didn't know what else to say other than, "Not really."

Dante sighed and headed upstairs.

At The Bank, Julisa sat in the office, nursing a glass of Crown Royal XR. She'd been sitting there, going over the lines Trent had given her to say at the meeting. She went over them in her head again and then took a big gulp of whiskey. She jumped when she heard the slight knock on the office door. "Yes."

"Mrs. Jones," Bono said from behind the closed door. "They're waiting for you in the conference room."

"Thank you, I'll be right there," Julisa said, as she reached into the desk drawer and pulled out a breath mint.

Julisa walked into the conference room many times in the past while Lowe conducted meetings with the same men who were seated around the table today. But when she stepped in tonight, she felt like she'd never been in there. The faces that stared at her as she headed for Lowe's seat didn't sport the same smiles and nods she used to receive when she used to walk in and sit on Lowe's lap to quickly whisper something in his ear. The faces now were stoic and tracking her every step.

As she stood in front of the chair, she wanted to collapse into it, but Trent instructed her earlier that it would be better if she spoke while standing. She cleared her throat and took a deep breath.

"Good evening."

The faces nodded.

"I asked Trent to assemble everyone here tonight, so we can all be on the same page. Lowe may be in a coma, but that doesn't mean that people can take it upon themselves to stop paying what they owe."

No one said a word.

Julisa looked over at a chunky, high yellow fellow she knew as Bigger and pointed at him. "Bigger, you're way behind in your payments, that's unacceptable."

Bigger leaned forward in his seat. "Before Lowe's untimely situation, there was a discrepancy on the amount I owed"

"Well, let me round if off for you. Bring an even sixty-five thousand to The Bank tomorrow night."

"What? Julisa—"

"Think very hard and long about what you're about to say."

He looked around the table and caught the glares directed toward him. He nodded. "I'll have it here tomorrow night."

Julisa nodded. "Starting immediately, Trent will be overseeing the day to day operations." Julisa ignored the shocked looks on some of the faces. All she was thinking about was getting out of there before her knees gave out on her. She nodded at Trent and exited the conference room. She walked back to her office, downed the rest of her whiskey, and fell back into the chair. A few moments later, there was a knock on the office door.

"What?"

Trent stepped in. "You did good."

"Don't ever ask me to do that again."

"The worst part is over."

"It better be, because if it's not, I will tell Mr. Green to take his club and shove it up his ass before I stand in front of those men again. Bigger looked like he wanted to rip my head off my shoulders."

"I'm going to take care of everything. You just focus on the legal side of The Bank, and let me worry about everything else."

Monday morning, Dawn's cell phone rang. "What's up Julisa?"

"You at your desk?"

"I'm home. I'm part-time remember? I work Tuesday, Wednesday, and Thursday this week."

"What did Dante say about you being part-time?"

"I haven't told him yet."

"You had the whole weekend to tell him; what happened?"

"He got fired from his job."

"God, no. What happened?"

"You know how these corporate execs are. They'll throw their own mothers to the wolves to save their own asses."

"Cut throat motherfuckers. Where's he now?"

"He's meeting an old colleague. He thinks that maybe he can get him a job with his firm."

"Wall Street's a dirty game."

"Yes, it is." Dawn grabbed the remote.

"So, what are you doing?"

"Watching Lifetime."

"You're really turning into a housewife, huh?"

"Never that. I called Richie this morning and asked him for my old job back at the hotel."

"No you didn't," Julisa said surprised.

"Yes, I did."

"You hated cleaning those rooms."

"I didn't hate cleaning them, I just didn't like it."

"And Richie's a pervert."

"No he's not."

"You caught him sniffing a chair you sat in."

"Well, I'll deal with a job I hate, and Richie's perverted ass to keep what Dante and I have worked so hard to get."

"I don't think Dante's going to go for it."

"I don't care what he goes for. I got to do what I got to do."

"Why don't you come work for me at the club?"

"At the club? Doing what?"

"Assistant bartender."

Dawn snorted. "I don't know anything about serving drinks."

"What's there to know? Just pour the drink into the glass, and hand it to the customer."

"I think it's a little more complicated than that, Julisa."

"The tips alone will add up to more than what you'll get at the minimum wage hotel gig."

"Sounds tempting, but—"

"But nothing. If you're going to have a second job, it's going to be here at The Bank with me."

"Dante will flip if he found out I was bartending."

"He'll flip if he found out about chair-sniffing Richie."

"You wouldn't," Dawn said.

"You know I would."

"I can't believe you're blackmailing me to work for you."

"And I can't believe I have to blackmail you to work for me."

Dawn sighed. "I'll talk to him tonight. I'll let you know what the verdict is tomorrow."

"Hell no," Dante said, as he exited the kitchen and entered the dining room with their dinner. Dawn was right on his heels.

"But Dante—"

He placed each plate down. "First, you hit me with the part-time situation at your job that you should've told me three days ago, now, you're telling me you want to bartend at The Bank."

"I'm just trying to hold us down."

Dante pounded his chest. "I'm holding us down."

"How are you holding us down without a job?"

"I should be hearing from Bobby by next week."

"The friend you had lunch with? He said he would see what he could do. That doesn't sound too promising."

"I know Bobby. He's going to come through for me."

"And if he doesn't?" Dawn asked.

Dante sat down at the table. "Sit down." Dawn didn't move. "Please." She folded her arms and sat.

Dante gently pulled one of her hands to his lips and kissed it. "You can work at The Bank."

Dawn eyed him suspiciously. "What's the catch?"

"Huh?" Dante said, as he cut into a piece of his lamb.

"Huh? You heard me."

"Why does there have to be a catch?" Dante said, refusing to look at her.

"With you, there's always a catch."

"Well, there's no catch, it's more like a condition."

"What's the condition?" Dawn stared him down.

"You can work at the club, *if* Bobby doesn't come through for me, and you can work there *until* I start bringing in a paycheck. Once I'm on someone's payroll, you will put in your two weeks' notice."

"Dante—"

"That's it, that's the deal." He started to tear into his food. "You're not eating."

"I'm not hungry."

"Fine." He bit into his lamb and moaned.

Dawn looked at her plate of roast lamb chops with cipolini onions, white beans, and escarole. It was one of her favorite dishes.

"You sure you're not hungry?" Dante asked, eyeing her.

"Positive."

He smiled when he heard her stomach growl. He finished off his lamb chops and started reaching for hers.

Dawn snatched her plate off the table. "Fuck you, Dante." She got up, plate in hand, and headed upstairs.

The house phone started ringing as soon as Dawn stepped into the bedroom. She put her plate down and looked at the caller ID. "Either you have good timing or you need to start a psychic hotline."

"So what did he say?" Julisa asked.

"He said yes."

"What's the catch?"

"There's no catch."

"With Dante, there's always a catch."

"No catch, but there's a condition."

"I knew it."

"If his friend can't get him a job in his firm, I can take the job, and I have to quit when he finally finds a job."

"Okay," Julisa said, sounding pre occupied.

"You okay?" Dawn asked.

"I'm fine."

"You don't sound fine, you sound like you've been drinking."

"I had a couple shots."

"A couple shots mean you're stressing about something. What is it?"

"Nothing I can't handle."

"Where are you?"

"I'm at a carwash."

"A carwash?" Dawn said, wondering why Julisa would be at a carwash this late.

"It's not just any carwash, it's Lowe's carwash."

"I didn't know Lowe owned a carwash."

"What a coincidence neither did I," Julisa said in a high-pitched tone.

"What are you doing drinking in a carwash at ten o'clock at night, anyway?"

"Taking care of business."

"What business?" Dawn's tone turned serious.

Trent tapped on the office window.

Julisa nodded. "I have to go. I'll call you in the morning."

"Julisa—" Dawn heard the dial tone. She sat on her bed and wondered what business Julisa could be taking care of in a carwash so late at night.

Julisa stepped out of the office. Trent was leaning against the wall. "You ready?"

"No."

"C'mon, Julisa, you don't have to say anything. All you have to do is look at my man, nod, and walk out."

Julisa's eyes started to water as she hugged herself. Trent pushed himself off the wall and pulled out a handkerchief. He dabbed at her tears.

"I can't," she said.

"This will be the last thing you have to do, I swear. The team needs to see that you can do this."

"But I can't do this, look at me. My hand is shaking."

Trent interlaced his hand with hers. "I got you." He led her by the hand into the carwash.

Julisa squeezed his hand when she saw Bigger. He'd been strung up by his wrists. One of Trent's henchmen was using him as a punching bag. Bigger grunted each time a body blow landed. The rest of Lowe's clique had ringside seats to the merciless beating.

The henchman saw Julisa and Trent out the corner of his eye and stopped delivering the blood curdling body blows and spun Bigger around toward Julisa. Bigger's eyes nearly popped out of his head when he saw her.

"J... J... Julisa, I have your money. I was going to bring it but—"

Julisa's grip tightened on Trent's hand. She looked at Trent. He kept looking at Bigger. He squeezed her hand, reminding her of what she had to do. She looked at Lowe's team. They locked eyes with her. She looked around the room before looking back at Bigger. Mr. Green's words came to her mind. She had to hold things down until Lowe came out of his coma.

"Julisa," Bigger pleaded.

Julisa looked at the henchman and nodded. He smiled and nodded back.

"No!" Bigger managed to squeal before three punches to the mouth silenced him.

Julisa snatched her hand out of Trent's and headed back to the office. She slammed the door, slid down behind it, and cried.

Dawn turned into the underground garage of The Bank. Julisa stood in front of the elevator between Cash and Lou. Dawn parked next to Julisa's Caddy and headed toward them.

"You remember Cash and Lou, right?" Julisa said to Dawn.

Dawn looked at both of them and smiled. "Of course I do."

"Good evening," both men said to Dawn.

"Gentlemen," Dawn said, as she followed Julisa into the elevator. When the doors closed, Dawn put her hand on her hips and faced Julisa. "I've been calling you for two days. Where the hell have you been?"

"Girl, I've been going through it."

"What's up?"

"Forget it," Julisa said, flipping her hand to her. "I guess Dante's friend didn't come through, huh?"

"Nope."

"So when do you want to start?"

"Tonight."

Julisa looked at Dawn's black slacks and off-the-rack blouse. "Not dressed like that you're not."

"What's wrong with what I'm wearing?"

"You look like a librarian."

Dawn removed her glasses and let her hair down. "What about now?"

"Like a librarian in heat."

Dawn was about to mush her but the elevator doors opened and she got stuck on Bono's Colgate smile. His teeth were perfectly straight and white. His dimples deeper than a deep-dish pizza. And his suit was crisp and sharp like his tapered haircut.

"Bono, this is my best friend, Dawn."

He nodded.

Dawn smiled and then followed Julisa to her office. "I don't remember seeing him here."

"He's only been working for us for a few months."

Dawn snuck a peak at him before closing the door. "I like his mannerisms."

"He's the only man in this place I haven't caught looking at my ass."

"Maybe he's gay."

"As fine as he is, that would be a sin." Julisa grabbed the wine glass off her desk and downed what was left in it.

Trent knocked and stuck his head in. He saw Dawn without her glasses and with her hair down and forgot why he came to the office.

"What is it?" Julisa asked.

"Yeah… um, I just wanted to let you know that Fifty and his peeps just walked in. He wanted me to tell you how he was sorry to hear what happened to Lowe and if you need anything, don't hesitate to ask."

"I'll be out in a minute to talk with him."

"Hi," Trent said, winking at Dawn.

"Bye," she said, waving him off.

Trent closed the door and walked off.

Dawn cut her eyes at the door and then back to Julisa. "I don't like him."

"You don't even know him. He has his annoying ways, but he's been a big help with keeping things in check."

Dawn rolled her eyes. "Whatever."

"Dawn, please," Julisa said, refilling her glass. "I'm dealing with enough stress."

Dawn took the bottle and glass from her and put them back on the desk. "Talk to me, what's going on?"

"Nothing. I'm just not used to everybody depending on me to make decisions."

"That's it?" Dawn asked, staring at Julisa.

"That's it." Julisa looked away.

"You know you can't lie to me, right?"

"Which is why I don't try to."

"So, what kind of clothes do you expect me to wear when I start working here?" Dawn said.

"Follow me." Julisa led her back down the corridor, through the soundproof doors and into The Bank where they walked up to the bar.

A woman with golden hair pared down to a brush cut was serving drinks to five people at the same time.

"Whitty," Julisa called out. Whitney, known in The Bank as Whitty, flashed Julisa her million dollar smile. She twirled the bottle of Grey Goose around her finger, like a gunslinger would his six-shooter, and slid it back into its slot under the bar. She tapped her partner, a white girl named Cassidy, to tell her she was on her own for the moment and then sashayed over to Julisa.

"What's up, Boss lady?"

"I wanted to show my girl the type of clothes she needs to wear when she's working the bar with you this weekend."

Whitty did a slow twirl. Dawn sized up the low-rise jeans that Whitty's butt filled to the max, and then noticed how her sheer blouse struggled to contain her breasts.

Dawn subtly shook her head. "I don't have anything in my closet that... expressive."

Julisa and Whitty laughed.

"Not a problem," Julisa said. "I've been dying to use my brand new Visa."

The next day, Julisa picked Dawn up after work and drove them downtown to the SoHo neighborhood. They shopped til their feet hurt.

"Time to lose the bozos," Julisa said, as they entered the Spa. Julisa's security detail couldn't follow them any farther than the waiting room.

"You know I'm not paying you back for all the stuff you bought me, right?" Dawn said, as they undressed in the changing room.

"Girl, do I look like I need you to pay me back?"

"The jeans, alone, were a buck fifty," Dawn said, still not believing the price tag.

"And you got five pair."

"You made me get five pair."

"I can't have you wearing the same pair of jeans to work. How would that make me look?"

"It's all about you, huh?"

"You better act like you didn't just meet me yesterday. It's always been about me," Julisa said, putting on a robe.

Four hours later, after a carrot-and-sesame body buff followed by a hot oil massage, manicure and pedicure, Dawn and Julisa walked out of the spa feeling brand new. Their mood quickly soured when they saw Trent leaning against his Lexus. He hopped off his car and unfolded his arms.

"Three goons following me around weren't enough?" Julisa asked with an attitude.

"I wouldn't be here if you'd answer your phone like I told you to."

Julisa looked like she was rearing up to curse him out, but she bit her tongue. "I needed some 'me' time, I didn't want to be disturbed."

"This isn't a game, Julisa. Even if you want to believe that what happened to Lowe was a random thing, you got to *act* as if it wasn't. You can't afford to be careless."

"Enough with the grade school lecture," Dawn said, staring him straight in the eyes. Julisa may have bit her tongue but she wasn't.

Trent flashed her his platinum smile. "And how are you doing, beautiful?"

"I *was* doing just fine."

"Well, how can I make you feel better?"

"Walk across a highway blindfolded."

Trent laughed out loud. "That was funny."

"I wasn't joking," Dawn said seriously.

"You're going to make it my lifetime mission to make you like me."

"You're going to need more than one lifetime to do that."

"Ouch."

Dawn turned toward Julisa. "I'll be in the car."

Trent watched her walk off. "Damn, she's a firecracker."

"Why are you here, Trent?"

He turned serious. "Those men have specific orders not to let you out of their sights for any reason."

"You know what Trent, I'm really starting to lose my patience with all this unnecessary bullshit. I'm stressed out as it is dealing with Lowe's condition and trying to keep things running smooth." She began walking. He grabbed her by the elbow. She pulled away from him. "Get the fuck off me." He grabbed her again and slammed her up against his car. His aggressiveness caught her off guard.

He blinked, catching himself. He quickly released her. "Julisa, I'm sorry, I didn't mean to..." She bounced off the car and shoved him. He grabbed her arms. "Listen to me please." She was breathing hard, but she was still. "I'm under a lot of stress, as well. Lowe's my boy, so I'm feeling it, too. My worst nightmare is him coming out of his coma and finding out that I let something happen to you. What could I possibly say to him? You know him better than me. He would kill up half of New York."

Julisa's eyes softened.

"I know I can be a hard-ass—" he started to say.

"Asshole's more like it. Can you let go of me, now?"

Trent released her. "Just do me a favor and don't make security's job any more difficult than it has to be."

Julisa sighed. "Okay."

"Thank you."

"Yeah, whatever." Julisa walked off to catch up with Dawn.

Julisa pulled up to Dawn's house. "I'll see you tomorrow night. Don't forget to come through the garage. Cash and Lou will be expecting you."

Dawn got out and gathered her shopping bags from the backseat. "See you tomorrow night."

Dante looked at the bags as Dawn stepped into the house. "You went shopping?"

"Before you flip out, I didn't spend any money, Julisa bought all of this for me."

He stared at her for a moment and then returned to the paperwork in front of him.

"What are you working on?"

"Our new budget."

Dawn dropped her bags.

Dante stared at her with a frustrated look. "I'm not in the mood, so please don't start."

"We're not in trouble yet, and already you're coming up with a budget."

"You want me to wait until we're behind in our bills before I come up with a new budget?"

"I start work at The Bank and—"

"And what? You think your two part-time jobs can pay a twenty eight hundred dollar a month mortgage, two car payments, and the utility bill? And that's not counting our insurances, phone bills, and food."

Dawn picked her bags off the floor. "Do whatever you want, I don't care anymore." She stormed upstairs.

A few moments later, Dante knocked on the bedroom door. Dawn continued to put her clothes away as if she didn't hear him. He walked up behind her and touched her shoulder. Dawn turned around and cried into his chest.

"Why is this happening to us?" she sobbed.

"It's not just happening to us," Dante said. "Believe me, I don't want to lose what we have either."

"Then why does it feel like I'm the only one fighting to keep what we have?"

"You're not the only one. I'm busting my ass trying to find a job."

"What if you can't find the kind of job you want?"

Dante gave it some thought before answering. "Then... I guess you'll have to call Richie and get him to hook me up with a job at the hotel."

Dawn looked up at him. "Stop playing."

"To keep what we have, I'll do what I got to do."

"I love you," she said hugging him tighter.

"I love you, too. But I'm going to let you know, right now. If I catch Richie sniffing a chair that I sat in, I'm going to jail for a long time."

Dawn's mouth dropped open.

"I know you didn't think Julisa could keep a secret."

"I'm going to kill her."

CHAPTER 4

*A*s Dawn cruised past The Bank, she started getting butterflies. *It's going to take me forever to remember the names of the popular drinks and probably forever and a day to remember their ingredients.* She turned into the garage and parked behind Julisa's car.

Cash reached into his pocket for his elevator key when he saw her. "Good evening, Dawn."

"Good evening, Cash."

"Good luck," Lou said, stepping to the side to allow her to enter the elevator.

"Thanks," Dawn said, as she walked past him. As the doors closed, Dawn removed her jacket and studied herself in the full-length mirrors lining the elevator walls. Her freshly pedicured toes were on display in a pair of three inch heeled Gucci sandals. Her tight jeans accentuated her shapely legs and the curvature of her bottom. She tugged at her Calvin Klein T-shirt, and no sooner than she let it go, it slowly rode back up to reveal her belly button. *Fuck it,* she thought, as she puckered up and applied her lip-gloss.

Bono greeted her when the doors opened. "Julisa's in her office."

"Thank you." Dawn eyed his crisp suit. "You're the only bouncer in this joint who wears a real tie."

"A real tie?"

"It's not a clip-on," Dawn pointed out.

Bono nodded. "You pay attention to detail, I see."

"Force of habit." She waved at him and headed to the office. She knocked on the door, and stepped in. "Girl, if you don't..." She walked over to Julisa and snatched the glass of whisky out of her hand.

"What?" Julisa slurred.

"What? I'm going to have to start taking you to A.A. meetings in a minute."

Julisa inspected Dawn's outfit. "Look at you, looking all hot and spicy. You ready to do this?"

"There's only one way to find out."

They headed down the corridor into The Bank. The dance floor was so packed that people were dancing right where they stood. The bar was mobbed with thirsty clubbers. Whitty's arms were moving so fast, she looked like she had eight arms. Dawn noticed she was working the bar alone tonight.

"What happened to the other girl?"

Julisa raised a section of the bar's countertop. "You are the other girl. Go do your thing."

Whitty spotted her and waved her over. "Hey, wassup?"

"Looks like you can use a hand?" Dawn said, shouting over the music.

"Ever work a bar before?"

"No."

"Then step back, you'll only get in the way."

Dawn stepped back and watched Whitty flip bottles, spin them on the palms of her hands, and concoct drinks she never heard of. "Not bad," she said when the crowd died down.

"Okay before we get bum rushed again, you need to know where everything is." Whitty showed her where the different liquors, vodkas, whiskies, and beers were located.

Dawn shook her head. "I'm never going to remember where everything is."

"I tell you what, start with the beers. I'll handle the rest. Once you've got them down, then we can add on the liquors, then the vodkas, and so on."

"When did you start working here?" Dawn asked.

"Two years ago."

"Two years ago? I was here last New Year's eve, I don't remember seeing you working the bar."

"I work The Vault every New Year's."

Dawn arched an eyebrow. "The Vault?"

"Julisa didn't tell you about The Vault?"

"No."

"Just then, a cluster of thirsty dancers swelled around the bar. When the crowd dissipated, Dawn sat on a stool, and sipped on a Red Bull. The club scene hadn't changed a bit. She watched a crew of women with their assets on display, ready to leave with the highest bidder. To her right, a group of men sat around a table in business attire, ties undone, jackets slung behind their chairs, just unwinding from a hard day's work. Then there was the look-at-me-I'm-getting-money crew sitting high in the VIP section. The last group she focused on was the men and women looking for the one-night stand. They slid up on the unsuspecting under the guise of innocent conversation. Two drinks and 30 minutes later, the verbal foreplay would begin. Soon after that, they would be taking their "Conversation" to a more private venue.

"Um, I knew you were holding, but damn," Trent said as he sat on a barstool next to her.

Dawn got up and walked back behind the bar.

"Hold up, let me holler at you."

"I'm on the clock," Dawn said full of attitude.

"Then take a break."

"I just took one."

"Then, take another."

"I don't think Julisa would appreciate me taking two breaks in a row."

"Julisa's not the one you have to worry about." Trent slid his Gucci frames down his nose and locked eyes with her. Tonight he traded in his hood rich gear for a more conservative look. His brown shoes, beige slacks, and beige linen shirt made him look like someone Dawn could take serious.

Dawn shot him a sour look. "Don't you have something to do?"

He leaned on the countertop. "As precious as you are, Julisa should have you in The Vault."

That was the second time someone had mentioned The Vault. Dawn made a mental note of it.

"Can I have a mango Madras?" a woman asked. Dawn spun on Trent and got back to work. She could feel his eyes violating her body. It was creeping her out, but she knew the more attention she showed him, the longer he would hang around. He finally got the hint and disappeared.

At one o'clock in the morning, Cassidy, showed up.

"It's quitting time for you, Miss," she said to Dawn.

"And it's break time for me," Whitty said, heading to the bathroom.

When Dawn got home, she opened the front door as quiet as its squeaky hinges would allow her to.

"I waited up for you," Dante said from the dining room, startling her. "How was your first night?"

"Good."

"You just up and left this afternoon without saying you were leaving or anything. And what's up with the jacket?"

"Dante, it's late, I'm tired."

"Take off the coat."

"Dante—"

"Take. Off. The coat." Dawn started to remove it. "Come closer." She sucked her teeth and stepped all the way into the dining room. She laid the coat across one of the chairs.

Dante stood up and examined her tight clothes. He walked around her like she was on an auction block. "How many phone numbers did you get tossed at you tonight, and don't lie to me."

"Ten numbers, two marriage proposals."

He sniffed her. "And you're wearing perfume?"

"And makeup," she said, pointing to her face.

"I can see that."

She tensed when she felt his hands palm her butt and pull her close to him. She was expecting him to yell at her about her tight clothes. She didn't expect to see lust in his eyes. He kissed her, sucking the tenseness out of her tongue.

"What's the catch?" she whispered as their tongues unwrapped.

"Why does there have to be a catch?" Dante said, as he ran his hand up the front of her T-shirt.

"With you, there's always a catch."

"It's more like a favor."

"I knew it."

"I feel like eating one of your pies."

"A pie? At two in the morning?"

"You know how I love your coconut cream pies."

"You want me to bake a coconut cream pie, now?"

"Please," Dante begged.

"You're crazy."

He led her into the kitchen. Dawn huffed and started to grab the ingredients from the cabinet. Dante grabbed the coconut shavings and whip cream out of the fridge. He licked his lips as he watched Dawn strut across the kitchen in her heels to turn on the oven.

He walked up behind her and turned off the oven. "The pie's already done, I just need you to help me put on the topping."

Dawn shook her head. "Okay, where is it?"

He lifted her up and sat her on the island. "You're sitting on it."

"Nah, ah, you are so nasty."

"I know I don't say it often, but I'm proud to have you as my wife. Sometimes I just—"

Dawn put her finger to his mouth. "Are you going to eat this pie or not?"

The next night Dawn got twenty numbers and five marriage proposals. Tonight she was working side by side with Cassidy.

"Whitty's off tonight?" Dawn asked.

"No, she's in The Vault."

"The Vault?"

"Oops," Cassidy said, covering her mouth.

"Oops?" Dawn said, staring Cassidy down.

Cassidy looked over Dawn's shoulder, causing Dawn to turn around. Julisa was walking toward them.

"How you holding up?" Julisa asked Dawn.

"What the hell is The Vault?" Dawn asked with her hand on her hip.

Julisa looked at Cassidy. "And you want to know why I'm so hard on you."

"Dawn's your best friend, I thought—"

"You're on your own tonight." Julisa looked at Dawn. "Follow me."

When they entered the elevator, Julisa pulled out her key and stuck it into the keyhole before hitting the button for the garage.

"Why are we going to the garage?"

When the doors opened, they weren't in the garage. They were below it. They were in the very bedrock in which the building sat upon. Dawn stepped out into the dimly lit corridor with Julisa.

"You guys keep your money in a vault down here?" Dawn asked.

"Yeah... you can say that."

As Dawn followed her, she could hear the low humming of the machinery responsible for The Vault's climate control.

Julisa stopped at a set of double doors. "Welcome to The Vault." She pushed open the doors.

Dawn stood there with her mouth hanging open. She blinked when the flash on Julisa's cell phone went off.

"I'm sorry," Julisa said laughing. "I couldn't resist... the look on your face..."

Dawn never saw anything like it in her life. The Vault was an underground club, literally. Julisa grabbed her hand and took her up a spiral stairway that led to her office. When they entered and Julisa closed the door, Dawn's ears popped. Julisa cracked a bottle of Jack Daniels and poured herself a drink. Dawn walked to the one-way mirror that reminded her of the kind in a police station interrogation room. She looked down on the scene. The dance floor was packed. Whitty was at the bar mixing drinks, and... "Is that Jay?" Dawn said in amazement. "Oh shit, I know that isn't Weezy, that *is* Weezy." She looked at Julisa. "Girl, you got some explaining to do."

"What's there to explain? It is what it is."

"Make believe I was born yesterday and tell me what I'm looking at."

"You're looking at The Vault. A club within a club. A club reserved for the cream of the crop. Those who don't want to mingle with everyday people. A place where there's no Paparazzi, stress or worries. The Vault is paradise on earth. Anything you want is here."

"Anything?" Dawn asked suspiciously.

"From A-Z."

Dawn studied the scene. The Vault looked like one big VIP room. Chairs, plush. Tabletops, illuminated onyx. Stage, fashioned like a model runway. The pole in the middle of it told Dawn that the stage wasn't just for fashion shows.

"How come you never told me about this place?" Dawn asked Julisa.

"It's a secret."

"So, why'd you bring me down here?"

"Trent thought it would be a good idea for you to work down here."

"Trent? Why am I not surprised?"

"I think it's a good idea. You get to rub elbows with some of Hollywood's famous actors, Music's most talented singers, CEO's of billion dollar companies…"

"I'm not here for that. I'm here to work, that's it."

"I'm just saying, maybe you can make the right connections, someone who knows someone who knows someone who can get Dante past the job interview."

Dawn looked back at the crowd. She saw Whitty swamped at the bar. "Fine, it looks like Whitty could use a hand."

"Go do your thing, girl," Julisa said with a wink.

On her way to the bar, Dawn tried not to look too starstruck when she passed by a few actors she recognized. She almost lost it when she saw Russell Simmons. She was just pulling herself together when a woman with racetrack curves waved her over. Dawn looked around and then pointed at herself. The woman nodded.

"Can I help you?" Dawn asked as she approached.

"What's your name?"

"Dawn."

The woman scooted over and tapped the cushion on the bench of her booth. "Have a seat, Dawn, let me holla at you."

Dawn's face turned red. "I don't get down like that."

"That's because you haven't gotten down with the right one." The woman spotted the ring on Dawn's finger. "You married?"

"Happily."

"Well then. We can kill three birds with one stone."

"How's that?" Dawn asked.

"Every man dreams of being with two women at the same time, and right now, I'm dreaming of being with you. So it's a win-win situation. Your husband lives out his fantasy, I get to have you, and you get the best of both worlds."

"If my husband has a fantasy of being with two women, a fantasy is all it will be as long as he's with me." Dawn walked off.

Whitty saw Dawn walking away from the woman and smiled. "Welcome to The Vault."

"You wouldn't believe what I just went through."

"This is The Vault, nothing surprises me anymore. I lost count of how many women Lavita-the-coochie-licker has turned out. Her tongue game is legendary."

"And how would you know?"

"That's just what I heard."

"Umm hmm."

Whitty sensed the skepticism in Dawn's response. "I'm a freak, but I have my limits."

"Honey!"

Both women turned around at the same time as a guy walked up to the bar wearing a Kool-Aid smile.

"Oh shit! I can't believe it," he said, staring at Dawn.

"Andre?" Dawn said, not believing her eyes.

"Damn, Honey, I see you still looking fine as wine." He zeroed in on her filled-to-the-brim jeans and lace blouse.

"No one has called me Honey since Charlotte."

Whitty cleared her throat.

"Andre, this is Whitty, and Whitty this is Andre."

"Hi." Whitty showed off her dimples as she slid him a drink. "Patron and Tonic, right?"

"Yes, how did you know?"

"You look like a smooth, Patron kinda fella." Andre stood at six foot, his skin the color of rust. He wore a navy-blue Prada cotton and wool suit, a color purposely chosen to emphasize his ruddy complexion and freckles. Other than the expensive wardrobe, the trimmed five o'clock shadow, and gleaming baldhead, he looked like the "Dre" Dawn remembered from back in the day.

Andre grabbed the glass of Patron and winked at Whitty. "What do I owe you?"

"Please," Whitty said waving him off. "A friend of *Honey* is *definitely* a friend of mine."

Andre nodded and then looked at Dawn. "I'm surprised no one in this town has had the smarts to wife you and treat you like a queen."

Dawn flashed her ring. "There is one, and he treats me like a queen."

"So what are you doing working here?"

"With this recession—"

Andre chuckled. "The recession is like rain, Honey, it only falls on those who can't soar above the clouds."

"Still the slick talking Andre I remember."

"Only now, I'm not just talk. Whenever you get some free time, we need to get together and catch up." He picked up his drink and headed back to his booth. Dawn watched the four women seated at his booth part like the Red Sea. When he sat in between them, they closed back around him like a clam on a pearl.

"Andre," Whitty said dreamily.

"He's all smoke and mirrors. He was broke and stunting in Charlotte. Nothing's changed," Dawn said.

"Girl, this is The Vault. No one down here is broke. You better pick up a newspaper and read about Mr. Andre Wilks, CEO of Richman Realty. The urban papers are calling him the new Donald Trump."

Dawn looked at Andre again. He caught her staring and winked. She waved politely and turned away.

Whitty elbowed her. "He damn near broke his neck, making his way over here to speak to you. And the way he was devouring you with his eyes…"

"Whitty please."

"Please my ass. You better know like I know and milk that cash cow. He throws cash around here like rice at a wedding."

"Milk, huh?"

"This is milking." Whitty pointed to the diamond bracelet on her wrist. "This is milking." She pointed to the diamond necklace around her neck.

"I'm not milking Andre or anybody else for that matter."

Whitty peeped Andre stealing glances at Dawn "Umm hmm."

"How'd you know he was a Patron kinda fella?"

"I know what everybody down here drinks, pops, shoots, smokes, and snorts."

"Damn, you in people's business like that?"

"Knowing people's business is a very lucrative business. I learnt that in college."

"College?" Dawn asked shocked.

"I have a masters in business management."

"What the hell are you doing working as a bartender?"

"A masters in a recession is about as useful as monopoly money. Besides, the money I'm making here is excellent, and I'm making connections with very influential people."

"And all this time I thought I was working with an air-head."

"Fuck you."

CHAPTER 5

*D*awn arrived home in time to catch Dante watching the news.

"The US government is prepared to lend more than 7.4 trillion on behalf of American taxpayers to rescue the financial system since the credit markets seized up 15 months ago," the newscaster said.

"How was work?" Dante asked.

Dawn stood in front of him and pulled out a wad of cash.

"Julisa cut you a check already?"

"This," Dawn said, handing him the bundle of bills, "is my tip money for the night."

Dante counted it. "Three hundred dollars? If I find out that you're doing more than bartending…"

"Shut up." She sat on his lap and kissed him.

"Between last night and tonight, you made four hundred dollars in tips alone. I might not have to find a job if you keep this up."

"No luck on finding a job?"

"Nah, I really thought Bobby would come through for me."

Dawn turned her attention to the newscaster as she went on about the collapsing of the housing and financial sectors, eroding consumer confidence, and the worst unemployment rate in 14 years. "How in the world did we wind up in a recession?"

"Greed," Dante said dryly.

"What does greed have to do with the recession?"

"There used to be a time when getting a loan was nearly impossible if you didn't have a high credit score. Banks wanted to make sure they could get their money back. Recently, a new generation of banking geeks came up with a win/win/win lending practice where they decided to be less stringent on whom they loaned money to. They started loaning money to people for cars, houses, businesses, etc, not caring if they could pay it back or not."

Dawn looked confused. "Then why would they loan them the money?"

"Their plan was simple: Loan money, securitize the loans, and then sell those securities to the idiots in Europe and China who like the idea that they could make six percent a year on one with no risk. So, people get the money they need, the geeks get their money paid back up front from investors across seas, and those investors are collecting a nice interest percentage on these loans. Thus, you have your win/win/win situation."

"Or so it seemed," Dawn said.

"Exactly, the players couldn't see past their greed. So what happens when the Joe Shmoes and Plain Janes can't afford to pay back their loans? Cars get repossessed, houses get fore-closed on, businesses shutdown, people lose jobs. This sends a ripple effect throughout the economy causing—"

"A recession," Dawn said, finishing his sentence. "When will this recession be over?"

"If the banks get back to their old way of lending money, and if Obama can get his stimulus package off the ground, I say in about five years."

"Five years?" Dawn looked depressed. "Can we survive that long?"

"If we budget wisely."

Dawn sucked her teeth.

"I'm keeping it real. Everybody has to make sacrifices if they want to survive this recession."

"Not everybody. There are people out there who aren't being affected by the recession."

"Unfortunately, we're not one of those people."

Andre's words came to her mind. *Recession is like rain; it only hits those who can't soar above the clouds.*

The following day, Dawn sat at her desk sorting through spreadsheets for her boss when her cell phone rang. "What's up, Julisa?"

"Please tell me you didn't have to work today."

"Yeah, and I'm really busy."

"I need to see you."

"I get a coffee break at ten."

"No, I need to see you now."

"Now? I just punched in, Julisa. What's wrong?" Julisa didn't answer. "Hello... Julisa?" Dawn heard ice cubes dropping into a glass. "Julisa, I know you're not drinking at eight o'clock in the morning. Since when did you start keeping liquor in the house?"

"I didn't make it home last night, I'm still at The Bank."

"What the hell is going on with you?"

Julisa started crying. "I told him that I couldn't do this."

"What are you talking about? Who's him?"

"I have to go. I'll call Trent, he'll know what to do."

"Trent?" Hearing his name made Dawn want to throw up. She grabbed her purse. "I'll be there in thirty minutes."

Julisa was waiting at the front door of the club when Dawn pulled up. She let Dawn in and quickly locked the door.

"You here by yourself?" Dawn asked.

"Yes," Julisa said, before gulping down the drink in her hand. Julisa didn't say another word until they entered her office. "I can't do this."

"Do what?"

Julisa tossed her the yesterday's paper.

Dawn quickly read the caption. "Cops pull man's body out of the Hudson River." Dawn looked up at her. "You knew him?"

"I killed him."

Dawn dropped the paper. "The article says he was shot twice in the head. You could never—"

"I didn't shoot him, but..."

Dawn sat down to stop her head from spinning. "Julisa, you need to tell me exactly what the *fuck* is going on."

"It started last week when—"

"Hold on." Dawn grabbed the bottle of whiskey off the table, poured herself a drink and downed it. "Okay... it started last week..."

"I had the meeting that Trent was pestering me about. There was a guy there I only knew as Bigger. I found out from the paper that his real name is Tyrone Johnson. Trent tells me that Bigger owes Lowe sixty-five grand, and that he stopped paying his weekly payments. He said if I didn't make him pay up in full, other people would stop paying what they owed. So I told Bigger to bring my money to The Bank the following night."

"Your money?"

"That's how Trent told me to say it."

"And let me guess," Dawn said, already knowing the answer. "Bigger didn't bring the money."

"No."

"So, you killed him?"

"No! Remember that night when I called you from the carwash?"

"Yeah."

"Trent had Bigger brought there. He told me we had to make him an example. He said they were just going to beat him up and then let him go."

"So, Trent killed him."

"When I walked in and saw Bigger strung up, I nodded to the guy who was beating him up, just like Trent told me to, now, Bigger's dead."

"Trent is using you. You may think you're running shit but you're not, he is."

"That's where you're wrong. Trent's not running shit, and neither am I. Mr. Green is."

Dawn put the glass down and drank straight from the bottle. "Who in the fuck is Mr. Green?"

"He's the hotshot money launderer who just happens to own The Bank."

"Wait; I thought Lowe owned The Bank."

"So did I until I had a meeting with Mr. Green in his plush Midtown office."

"So, Lowe works for this man?"

"Well, as Mr. Green put it, he's the brains and Lowe's the brawn."

Dawn closed her eyes, trying to make sense of what Julisa just dropped on her.

"I had no choice," Julisa wept. "He told me that if I didn't hold things down until Lowe came out of his coma, he would find someone else to run things."

"So, let him find someone else."

"Then Lowe and I would have nothing."

"You and Lowe could open up a club of your own."

"It's not that easy, Dawn."

"And this is easier?"

"You said you would help me if we ever had to cross this bridge."

"Help? What do you expect me to do?"

"Tell me what to do. You have experience in this."

"Experience? Don't even go there."

"All those criminals and drug dealers you dated back in Charlotte, I know you had to learn something from them."

Dawn stood up. "The only advice I can give you is get out before you get in too deep."

Julisa stared off into the distance. "Trent said all I would have to do is sit back and—"

"Fuck Trent, and fuck what he said."

"You got to help me with this."

"If you're asking me to do something illegal, the answer is hell no!"

"After all I did for you, this is how you repay me?"

"What?"

"You'd be doing federal time if it wasn't for me getting you that lawyer," Julisa shouted.

"I can't believe you just threw that up in my face."

"It's true."

"You're right, but best believe that's the only thing you'll ever be able to throw in my face, because I will never ask you for another thing." Dawn started to walk out.

"Dawn wait."

"Fuck you, Julisa, and I quit." She slammed the door and headed back to work.

For the next three days, Julisa rang Dawn's phone off the hook around the clock. Dante couldn't take it anymore. He grabbed her cell phone off the kitchen counter and answered it.

"What's up Julisa?"

"Hi, Dante, is Dawn there?"

"She's right here."

"Can you convince her to talk to me?"

Dante held the phone out toward Dawn. "This is childish. You two are grown ass women."

Dawn folded her arms and spoke loud enough for Julisa to hear her. "Tell Miss throwing-shit-up-in-people's-face that I'm not talking to her, and to stop calling me."

"I guess you heard that," Dante said.

"Can you tell her that I'm sorry for what I said, and I really need her to come into work tomorrow."

"I'll tell her."

"Thank you."

Dante hung up. "She said she needs you to work tomorrow night."

"I quit, I told you that."

"You just can't quit like that."

"Why not?"

"You just started last week."

"So."

"So, you have to give your employer at least two week's notice. That's workplace etiquette."

"Fuck her, fuck etiquette, and if you're taking her side…"

"Fuck me too?"

"You know what it is," Dawn said, rolling her eyes.

"Fine, don't go to work." He left the kitchen.

Later that night when Dawn headed upstairs, Dante was laying on the bed with papers spread out all around him. She walked up to the bed and started swiping them off.

"I quit and you go back to making a budget?"

Dante looked up at her. "What do you expect me to do?"

"Get a fucking job."

"I'm trying."

"Try harder, lower your standards."

"I have a bachelors and—"

"There's a girl at The Bank who has a Masters in Business Administration and she's working as a bartender."

"She's a fool."

"She's far from a fool, and she's making a thousand dollars a week, easy."

"So maybe I should put on a pair of tight ass jeans, go to The Bank tomorrow night, and mix some drinks."

"Maybe you should," Dawn said sarcastically.

"You think I can't go down there with nut prints in my pants and get some phone numbers and marriage proposals?"

Dawn started laughing.

"I'm fucking serious."

Hearing Dante curse made her laugh even harder. Dante stood up, took off his glasses, and pulled his pants up to form a nut print in the crotch of his khakis. "Don't let the glasses and clean-cut fool you. I could be a playboy."

Dawn grabbed her stomach as she started to laugh even harder. "Stop!" she said, struggling to catch her breath. "Please, no more, you win." She held on to the headboard as her knees gave out and she sat on the bed. She knocked Dante's hand from holding his pants up above his waist. "Here's the deal."

Dante chuckled. "Now you want to deal?"

"I go back to work at the club and you promise to trash that bullshit budget."

"If you renege, I swear, I will make a budget so tight—" Dante clinched his hand into a tight fist.

"Will it be tighter than this?" She leaned back and seductively opened her legs.

"I don't know anything tighter than that."

"Good answer."

CHAPTER 6

Julisa stood outside the elevator next to Bono when the doors opened. She didn't wait for Dawn to step out; she stepped in and hugged her.

"I'm so sorry. You know how I get when I'm having a nervous breakdown."

Dawn hugged her back. "Breakdown or not, the next time you throw something in my face—"

"There will never be a next time, I swear."

Dawn looked at Bono. "Ever get bored back here?"

"Bono's seen his share of excitement," Julisa said, pulling out her elevator key. "Be back in five minutes," she said to Bono as the doors closed.

As soon as Dawn entered The Vault, she noticed the entertainment on stage. A girl with a voice like Alicia Keys mesmerized the crowd with her seductive lyrics. Miss coochie-licking Lavita spotted Dawn and blew her a kiss. Dawn kept walking toward the bar as if she didn't see her.

Whitty was serving drinks and bobbing her head to the catchy hook. "What's good, Honey?"

"Don't play yourself," Dawn said, cutting her eyes at her.

"That's what Andre called you; I like it."

"Well, unlike it."

"Why'd everybody call you Honey, anyway?" Whitty smiled in anticipation for the answer.

"It wasn't everybody, only men called me that."

"Okay, why'd men call you Honey?"

"Use your imagination."

Whitty's mouth fell open. "Nah, ah."

Dawn looked up at the stage. "Who's the singer?"

"She's hot, right? That's one of Jay's up and coming stars."

"She definitely got what it takes." Dawn noticed Whitty wearing a black shirt with black slacks, and black ankle boots. "Somebody die?"

"I came straight here from a funeral."

"I was just kidding. I didn't know you actually went to someone's funeral. I'm sorry to hear that. Who died?"

"This guy I knew. We used to call him Bigger."

Dawn stopped breathing, as she remembered what Julisa said to her the other day.

"He was murdered. The police pulled his body out of the Hudson River." Whitty started to tear.

"You two were close?"

Whitty touched the necklace around her neck. "We were just friends." Whitty changed the subject. "Miss coochie-licker was asking about you. She's determined to taste some of that honey."

"The only thing she's going to taste is blood in her mouth if she keeps coming at me."

Whitty sighed when she saw Trent heading toward them. "Now, that's one funeral I would love to go to."

"Ladies," Trent said, as he stopped at the bar.

"What's up?" Dawn asked him.

He turned to Whitty. "Julisa needs to see you in her office upstairs."

"What's the problem?"

"You'll find out when you get there."

Whitty sucked her teeth. "I'll be right back," she said to Dawn, as she followed Trent out.

"Hey you," Lavita said to Dawn, as she sat at the bar.

Dawn looked at her. "What can I do for you?"

"You really want me to answer that?"

Before Dawn had a chance to verbally lash her, Lavita picked up her drink and got lost in the crowd.

"I think she's got the hots for you."

Dawn turned, surprised to see Andre. "I've been nice to her twice, there's not going to be a third."

"With the Honey I used to know, there was no twice, much less a third."

"I'm a lady now."

"Yes, you are." Andre was wearing another one of his tailor-made suits with a pair of Brasco frames, fitting to the contour of his face perfectly.

"Patron and tonic, right?" Dawn asked.

"Correct."

Dawn could feel his eyes on her as she fixed his drink.

"So, how's the married life?" He asked, pretending to make small talk in order to find a way to get her into his bed.

"Wonderful."

"Do I know him? I mean... is he from back home or..."

"No, he's from up here, Brooklyn."

"You love him?" Andre said jokingly.

"To death," Dawn answered with no hesitation.

Andre looked at the ring on her finger. "He's a very lucky man."

"Yes, he is."

"I'm sure you get at least a dozen of these a night, so please don't mix mine up with the rest." He handed her his business card. "Maybe your husband and yourself can hook up with my wife and I for dinner one night."

"Your wife? Which one of those women at your table that night was your wife?"

"C'mon, Honey... I mean Dawn, you know how I do."

"Some things never change, huh, Dre?"

Andre's BlackBerry vibrated on his hip. He unclipped it from his belt and checked the caller ID. "Then again, some things do." He answered his phone. "Talk to me, Diddy, you decided if you want the penthouse or not?" He picked up his drink and winked at Dawn before walking off.

Cassidy walked behind the bar.

"What happened to Whitty?" Dawn asked.

"I don't know. Trent just told me to come down and help you out."

Ten minutes later, Dawn looked at her watch. "Hold things down, I'll be right back."

Dawn rode the elevator up to The Bank. When the elevator doors opened, Bono held up his hand. "You shouldn't be up here, right now."

"Where's Julisa?" Dawn could feel the tension in the air.

"She's busy right now."

"Doing what?"

"Go back to work, Dawn."

She tried to walk past him, but he stopped her. "Talk to me, Bono, what's going on?"

Both of them turned toward the conference room when they heard Whitty's screams followed by slaps.

"What the hell is going on in there, Bono?"

He didn't answer.

"You need to let me by. I'll tell Julisa I kneed you in the nuts and ran past you."

Bono looked at her.

"Please, Bono, don't make me kick you in the nuts for real."

He looked toward the conference room and then back to Dawn. He stepped to the side.

Dawn ran toward the conference room when she heard flesh hitting flesh. She pushed the door open, causing Trent and Julisa to look at her in shock. The woman standing over Whitty was too focused on choking the life out of Whitty that she didn't notice Dawn running up on her. Dawn grabbed her by her long weave and yanked her off of Whitty. Trent tried to get in between them as Dawn and the woman clawed at each other.

He finally wedged himself in between them and held the woman at bay. Dawn turned to Julisa.

"What the fuck is going on?"

"How did you get in here?" Trent screamed.

"I'm going to kill you, bitch," the woman said to Dawn.

"You and what army?" Dawn responded.

"Get out of here," Trent said to Dawn.

"Fuck you," Dawn said, as she helped Whitty to her feet.

"Julisa," Trent said, wanting her to get Dawn out of the room.

Julisa held the glass of whiskey to her chest as her lips quivered.

Trent punched the wall.

Bono stepped into the conference room.

Trent shook his fist at him. "How did she get past you?"

"I hit hard," Dawn said. "Ask that skank."

The woman tried to get at her, but Trent held her back.

"Get her out of here, now!" Trent said to Bono.

"I'm not going anywhere." Dawn looked at Bono, and told him, "They got to go."

Trent laughed. "He's not going to listen to you." He looked at Bono. "I'm not going to repeat myself."

Bono looked at Julisa.

She looked at Dawn and then to Trent. "Ah… maybe you should take Tunisha home, Trent."

"What?" He started walking toward her. Bono cut in front of him. They say the eyes are the windows to the soul. The only thing Trent saw in Bono's was a bad decision. He grabbed his coat and whispered something to Tunisha. Tunisha cut her eyes at Whitty. "This isn't over, bitch."

Whitty stepped behind Dawn.

Trent cut Bono a stare and slammed the door behind him and Tunisha.

Dawn walked up to Julisa and knocked the glass out of her hand. Before Julisa could get a word out, Dawn grabbed her by the front of her shirt and slammed her against the wall. Bono started to grab her, but Julisa called him off.

"Wait outside," Julisa said to him.

Dawn let her go. She looked at the bruises on Whitty's face and neck and then looked back at Julisa. "I can't believe you."

Julisa looked at Whitty. "All you had to do was tell her."

"I can't tell her what I don't know," Whitty whined.

"She had the text messages off his phone, telling you to meet him at his place."

"Text messages? Meetings?" Dawn said confused. "Who was that woman?"

"That was Bigger's wife," Julisa said. "She was somehow able to retrieve Bigger's text messages from his phone between him and Whitty. She always believed Bigger had an apartment she didn't know about. A place where he would take his other women."

"And she believes Whitty knows where this place is?" Dawn said.

"She's positive."

Dawn stared at Whitty for a moment. "You were fucking with Bigger?"

"No, and I don't know what that bitch is talking about."

"Okay," Dawn said with a shrug.

"Okay?" Julisa said in shock. "You believe her?"

"Go home," Dawn said to Whitty.

"And make sure your ass is here an hour early tomorrow," Julisa said.

"I can't work tomorrow, look at my face."

"Don't worry, I'll stick you someplace where no one will have to look at you."

Whitty pouted and walked out.

"Before you curse me out—" Julisa started to say.

"I come in here and this Tunisha bitch is choking Whitty out. What were you thinking?"

"I was about to stop her."

"Stop her? You should've never allowed her to put her hands on her."

"Trent said—"

"You know what? I'm sick and tired of hearing what Trent said."

Julisa's bottom lip started to quiver and her hands started to shake. "I... I can't do this." She barely made it to her wastebasket before throwing up into it. She sat on the floor cross-legged and hugged the wastebasket to her chest as she started to cry. "I don't know what I was thinking."

"Julisa—"

"No, you were right. I never should've gotten involved. Once Mr. Green told me the truth about The Bank, I should've just told him to find someone else. I thought I could be strong like you and hold things down, but I'm weak. I could never be like you."

"If you're trying to get me to feel sorry for you, it's not working."

Julisa smiled. "You were always the strong one. God, I wish I had your strength."

"If you're trying to flatter me, that won't work either."

Julisa stood up and put the trash can down. She wobbled behind her desk and picked up the phone.

"Who are you calling?"

Julisa didn't answer as she waited for Mr. Green to pick up. "Just great, he's not picking up." Julisa left a message. "This is Julisa. I'm calling about our little arrangement. I'm not going to be able to follow through on it, because—"

"Julisa," Mr. Green said, as he picked up the phone.

"Yes, I was just calling to—"

"Whatever you have to tell me, I want to hear it in person."

"That won't be necessary. What I have to say isn't that long."

"Oh, but it is very necessary. I expect to see you in my office first thing Monday morning."

"But..." Julisa blinked and stared at the receiver. "The motherfucker hung up on me."

"Call him back."

Julisa called back and got his answering machine. She slammed the phone down. "He wants me to come to this office and tell him what I have to say."

"Then, that's what you'll do. You're doing the right thing. Fuck this club and fuck Mr. Green." Dawn rubbed her temples and headed toward the door.

"Where are you going?" Julisa asked.

"Home." Dawn met Bono at the elevator. "Thanks for letting me in there earlier. I hope Trent doesn't try and get at you."

Bono smiled. "The last thing Trent would want to do is get at me."

"You talk pretty tough for a guy who guards an elevator."

"Good night, Dawn."

"Good night."

Dawn woke up when she heard someone snoring. The snoring stopped. She cracked her eyes as she yawned. Dante's side of the bed was empty, so that meant... "Damn, I was snoring like that?" She sat up and faintly remembered Dante telling her about an interview. She got up, showered and got dressed. She grabbed the bottle of Tylenol and started to put it back in the drawer. That's when she saw the bills Dante placed in there last night. She put down the bottle and grabbed them up. Dante was two months behind on his car payment. The next bill was a shut off notice from the utility company stating that the full amount had to be paid by the end of the week. She stared at the bills for a moment before heading to the computer and pulling up their bank accounts. They were still in the black. She knew they had enough money tucked away to hold them over for at least six months. She was about to log out when she saw an envelope sticking out from under Dante's clipboard. Her heart fluttered when she saw FORECLOSURE NOTICE in big red letters. She dropped the envelope and frantically dialed Dante's cell phone.

"Hey beautiful," Dante said.

"Why am I staring at a foreclosure notice?"

"Baby—"

"Don't baby me, and why are you two months behind in your car payments?"

"I'm about to go into an interview in two minutes," Dante whispered into the phone.

"To hell with that interview, I'm talking about our home. And who the hell does job interviews on Sundays, anyway? I'm sending the mortgage company a check."

"No, you're not."

"Yes, I am. I'm holding a foreclosure notice in my hand."

"That notice is just a scare tactic."

"It's working. I'm sending the check."

"We don't have the money right now. Why do you think I haven't paid my car payment in two months?"

"I just looked at our bank accounts online. We have plenty of money."

"Where are you now?" Dante asked.

"Sitting in front of the computer."

"Look in the center drawer."

"What am I looking for?"

"Open the drawer, you'll see it."

Dawn opened the drawer and saw an envelope from New York City Treasurer's Office. She opened it. "I don't understand. It's saying we haven't paid property or school taxes in two years. How can that be?"

"Remember the last mortgage company we had before refinancing?"

"The one that went bankrupt?"

"Yeah, well, it seems that they weren't putting enough in escrow to satisfy the taxes owed on our property."

"They weren't... what? So we just get stuck with having to pay..." Dawn looked at the amount due, "ten thousand dollars in back taxes?"

"Yes."

"No. This isn't fair. Why do we have to pay for that mortgage company's incompetence?"

"I have to go, the secretary is waving me in. I'll call you as soon as the interview is over, okay?"

Dawn hung up. She re-read the letter and started to cry. She crumpled up the letter, threw it back in the desk drawer and slammed it shut.

A dark place in her mind lit up. A place she swore she would never go back to. "I can't go back to crime," she said in an unconvincing tone. Then she thought of how the government was just sitting back and allowing mortgage companies to charge a ridiculously high interest rate, and then just snatch away people's homes when they fell a little behind.

"These crooks aren't snatching my home. Y'all want to play the game?" Dawn wiped the tears from her eyes. "Let's play."

CHAPTER 7

*D*awn pulled up to Bono's apartment complex. According to the employee's records, he lived in apartment 3C. She walked up to the front entrance and rang the buzzer. No answer. When she saw a woman in a sweat suit and sneakers exiting the building, she tried walking past her.

"Excuse me, who you know in here?" the woman asked, blocking the entrance.

"Mark Bonneau," Dawn replied.

"Bono?"

"Yeah."

The woman studied Dawn's simple blue blouse and blue slacks. "You his parole officer of something?"

"Yes," Dawn said, as she walked past her. She rode the elevator to the third floor. She took a deep breath and then rang his bell. When no one answered, she knocked.

A woman in just a pair of panties and a T-shirt opened the door. "Can I help you?"

"I'm here to see Bono."

"And you are?"

"She's cool," Bono said, as he stepped from behind the door. He had on a pair of jeans, no shirt and no shoes. The female rolled her eyes at Dawn and headed back to the bedroom.

"What are you doing here?" There was no politeness in his voice, no sociability in his demeanor. Dawn noticed the tatts etched across his pecs, abs, and arms.

"I need to talk to you."

"I don't talk business outside of the club."

"I'm not here to talk about the club. I want to talk about your boss."

Bono studied her for a moment. "Close the door behind you." When he turned around, Dawn stared open-mouthed at the tattoo stretched across his back. It was an image of five grim reapers trying to pin down a man who was refusing to give up his soul.

The woman stepped out of the bedroom and folded her arms across her chest. "What's up?" she asked Bono, and then cut her eyes at Dawn.

Bono shot her a look that made her lose her attitude quickly. "Disappear."

The woman sucked her teeth and went back into the bedroom.

"I think this was a mistake," Dawn said.

Bono looked at the front door. "There's the door."

Dawn opened it and walked out. She headed to the elevator and pressed the call button. She sighed and thought about the ten thousand dollars in back taxes. She did an about-face and banged on Bono's door.

He opened the door, irritated.

Dawn pushed past him. "I need you to get dressed."

"I am dressed."

"I mean dressed like how I'm used to seeing you, so we can talk."

"Talk to me as is or… there's the door."

"Get dressed or—"

"Or what?" his face hardened.

"Or I will try my damnedest to whip your ass up in here in front of Miss whoever-the-fuck she is."

Bono cracked a smile.

Trent was at a traffic light, staring at Mr. Green's office building. He cut his eyes at Julisa as he waited for the light to change. Julisa sat in the passenger seat, arms folded, staring out the window. They both just came from seeing Lowe.

Julisa needed to tell him what she was about to do. She prayed to God that what she was going to tell him would shock him out of his coma. When she finished whispering in his ear, she stepped back and looked at him. Nothing changed.

Trent cleared his throat. "So, there's nothing that I can say that will convince you that this is a bad idea?"

"I'm done. You should be happy. I'm recommending that you be my replacement."

"It's not even about that, Julisa."

"Whatever," Julisa grumbled.

Trent sighed. The light turned green and he pulled into the building's parking lot.

Mr. Green sat behind his desk, sipping his tea when his receptionist escorted Julisa in.

"Have a seat, Julisa."

Julisa sat and crossed her legs to keep them from shaking.

"Now, tell me what's going on."

"Well, it's like I was saying on the phone, I can't do this anymore."

"Do what?"

"Run The Bank and the other shit you and Lowe are into."

Mr. Green sipped his tea. "Julisa, I put my trust in you. Do you know how hard it's going to be to find someone to run The Bank?"

"Trent seems like he can do a pretty good job."

"I told you before that it's on the strength of Lowe that I tolerate Trent."

"I'm sure there's someone on Lowe's team that you can work with."

"And therein lies the problem," Mr. Green said, pointing at Julisa. "I only want to work with you."

"I don't want to work with you."

Mr. Green removed his glasses and rubbed his eyes. "You sure you want to do this?"

"Positive," Julisa said, but her stiffened body communicated something else.

"If Lowe comes out of his coma, he will never forgive you."

"And I can never forgive myself if I continue trying to be someone that I'm not."

"Fine."

Julisa stood up. "That's it then."

"There's just one thing."

"What's that?"

"I will need you to hold things down until I find a replacement."

Julisa's shoulder slumped.

"It'll only be for a few weeks."

"I'm done in three weeks, whether you find a replacement or not."

Mr. Green nodded.

Bono walked out of the bedroom dressed in a pair of slacks, shoes, and a tank top. "So, what do you want to know about Julisa?" he said, as he sat at the kitchen table with Dawn.

"I don't want to talk about Julisa."

"You said—"

"I said I wanted to talk about your boss."

"That would be Julisa."

"No, it wouldn't." Dawn matched stares with him.

"Technically, I work for Lowe, but it's the same thing."

"Technically, Lowe pays your salary, but you don't work for him, either."

Bono sighed. "I don't know where you're going with this, but—"

"I know that Lowe pays you more than any other bouncer in The Bank. And according to the records, you're probably the highest paid bouncer in the five boroughs. Now, why would you get paid so much just to guard an elevator?"

"If you're trying to impress me, you're not, but if you're trying my patience..." Bono's voice dropped to a whisper, "You've succeeded."

"And what does that mean?" Dawn cried out when someone grabbed a handful of her hair and yanked her head back. She gasped when she felt a blade rest against her exposed neck.

The woman in the tank top and panties locked eyes with Dawn. "Hi."

Dawn tried to look back at Bono, but the woman's hold on her hair and the knife at her throat forced her to only stare at the woman looming over her.

Bono spoke. "I'm not the one to be playing games. So, let's just get to the point. What the *fuck* do you want?"

Dawn's eyes watered as she felt the blade threatening to sink into her flesh. "I want to meet with your boss..." Dawn's eyes began to water. "Your real boss."

Lowe's team sat around the conference table, waiting for Julisa to show. Gamble, a light-skinned pretty boy stopped playing with his cufflinks. "What's taking her so long? I got something to do."

"Something or someone?" Naji asked. Naji was a little darker than Gamble, and a lot more thuggish.

"Like I said, *something*, because the shit this woman does isn't humanly possible. The other night we went at it for three hours, and when I woke up in the middle of the night to take a piss, she was on my sofa with a cucumber she took out of my fridge and…"

"And?" Buck said. Buck wasn't the shiniest spoon in the drawer, but being smooth and debonair wasn't what got him on the team. Everyone in Manhattan knew the rule. Anytime you saw Buck, grab whom you're with and duck.

"Let's just say, I'll never look at another cucumber the same," Gamble said.

"Let me hit that when you're done," Buck said.

"Figures you wouldn't have a problem with sloppy seconds," Naji said.

"Or thirds or fourths or motherfucking fifths," Buck said.

"You aren't talking about that chick that's always trying to stick her tongue in every woman's twat, are you?" Naji asked.

"That's the one," Gamble said.

"I didn't know she liked the Mandingo," Buck said.

"And cucumbers," Naji added.

"I got a fat cucumber for her," Buck said, grabbing his crotch.

Just then, Trent walked in. He looked around the room. His eyes stopped on Gamble. "What's up?"

"We're waiting for you and Julisa."

"She's not here yet?" He turned around when the door opened. His blood pressure almost shot through the roof when he saw his worst nightmare walking straight at him in a skirt and stilettos. He was about to spazz, but Julisa, Bono, Cash, and Lou strolled in behind her.

He watched Dawn as she walked in and sat in Julisa's chair. Julisa sat next to her, while Bono, Cash, and Lou stood behind Dawn.

"Have a seat," Julisa said to Trent.

Trent stared at her with a scornful look. "What's going on?"

"Sit down and find out," Dawn said.

Trent chuckled.

"Something funny?" Bono asked.

Trent stopped smiling and reluctantly sat down.

Julisa picked up the conference phone and dialed a number. "We're all here." She pressed the speaker button and put the receiver back in the cradle.

"Gentlemen," Mr. Green said. "I called this meeting tonight to let everyone know that Julisa is doing a wonderful job holding things down until Lowe comes back to us."

The team looked at Julisa and nodded.

"I do have one problem, though. I don't feel comfortable with Trent being in charge of our day-to-day operations. So, Julisa and I have decided to place that task into the hands of the beautiful lady you see sitting before you. With that said, I'll let you get yourselves acquainted with Julisa's assistant." Mr. Green hung up.

"If anyone has a problem with what just went down, speak up now," Bono said, staring Trent in the eye.

"I have a question," Gamble said, trying to maintain his composure. "If she's taking Trent's place, what will Trent be doing?"

"Whatever I tell him to do," Dawn said. "Right, Trent?"

He smiled, and then finally responded. "Whatever you say... boss."

"Good," Dawn said. "Let's get down to business."

"Hold up," Naji said. "We don't even know your name."

Dawn looked them each in the eye before responding. "Call me Honey."

CHAPTER 8

When Julisa ended the meeting and everyone cleared out, she looked at Dawn and shook her head.

"What?" Dawn said.

"I can't believe you; just when I thought I was out of this, you drag me back in."

"I dragged you back in? You dragged me in, remember?"

"When I got a call from Mr. Green this morning telling me about the meeting you two had, I couldn't believe my ears. What changed from last night to this morning?"

"Dante's two months behind in his car payments."

Julisa shrugged. "That's not a big deal."

"I also found a foreclosure notice in his drawer."

"That's not good."

"And I found out that we owe ten thousand dollars in back taxes."

"How the fuck did that happen?"

Dawn explained the situation with the shady mortgage company.

"That's fucked up."

"Who you telling?" Dawn said, exhaling a breath full of stress.

Julisa hugged her.

"What was that for?"

"I knew you would come through for me."

"Come through for you? Didn't you just pay attention to anything I just said? I'm doing this for me, fuck you."

They both started laughing.

"All jokes aside," Julisa said. "Do you think you can do this?"

"I walked into the office of a complete stranger and convinced him to put a million dollar enterprise in my hands."

"You have to be ruthless," Julisa said.

"I can do ruthless."

"What about Dante? You're not the kind to hide things from him."

"He hid that he was two months behind in his car payments, and that we owed ten thousand in back taxes."

"He probably didn't want to stress you out."

"Well, I don't want to stress him out. As a matter of fact, you're stressing me out right now. Don't worry about me, you got something else to worry about," Dawn said, becoming irritated.

"What's that?"

Dawn walked to the door and called Bono. "Bring Whitty to the office for me, please."

He nodded. "I got you, Honey."

Down in The Vault, in the VIP section, Buck, Gamble and Naji sat at their usual table tossing back shots of vodka.

"Aye, yo," Buck said, slamming his shot glass down on the table. "What the fuck just happened?"

"We got a new boss," Naji said. "That's what happened."

"But I'm saying, wasn't that the same chick working behind the bar with Whitty?" Buck said.

"What difference does it make?" Naji asked.

"It makes a whole lot of difference," Gamble said. "One minute, this chick is mixing drinks, and then the next, she's giving us orders? I'm not feeling that. If anything, Green should've put one of us in charge."

"Green must have his reasons," Naji said.

"And what might they be?" Gamble asked.

Naji threw back another shot. "I don't know, and I don't care. The only thing that concerns me is the numbers in my bank account. She fucks with that, then, we're going to have a problem."

"Check it out," Buck said, grabbing his crotch, "Here comes the cucumber lover."

Gamble stood up and pulled out a chair for her to sit.

"I was looking all over for you earlier," Lavita said, as she sat in the chair that just happened to be next to Buck.

"Something came up. And when I got down here, I didn't see you," Gamble lied.

"That's because I went up to The Bank looking for you."

Buck leaned toward her ever so slightly and sniffed her.

Naji shook his head; Lavita turned her head toward Buck.

"Buck, right?" she said.

"The one and only. What's good with you, Ma?"

"My name is Lavita."

"Pardon me, *Lavita*, what's good?"

"I'm living life on my terms, that's what's good."

"Nah," Buck said, leaning into her. "I mean what's really good?"

Lavita's eyes dropped to Buck's hand rubbing his crotch. "Okay... you must be drunk."

"Intoxicated is more like it. Intoxicated by your beauty."

She arched an eyebrow and then looked at Gamble. "Can we get out here?"

"Of course," Gamble said, cutting his eyes at Buck.

"Don't forget what we talked about," Buck shouted after him, referring to their earlier conversation about him getting with Lavita next. Buck bit his bottom lip as watched Ms. Lavita sway her ass from side to side. "Umm, when I get a hold of that..."

"When you get a hold of that?" Naji said. "How you know she's going to give you some?"

"You blind or something? You didn't see how she was staring at me? I could've took her out to my truck and smashed that in the backseat, but I didn't want Gamble catching feelings."

"I think you're catching delusions."

Buck waved his hand in the direction Gamble and Lavita walked off in. "Later for that broad. I got my hands full anyway."

"Full?" Naji said. "With who?"

"Don't even sit there and act like you didn't see Honey checking me out."

Naji shook his head and looked at Buck. "You are officially delusional."

"Yo, you saw how fast Trent peeled out of the meeting? You don't think he's going to do anything stupid, do you?"

"Nah. He's a lot of things, but stupid isn't one of them. I just hope Lowe comes out of that coma real soon."

"Amen," Buck said, as he downed another shot. He wiped his mouth with the back of his hand and hit Naji with the serious face. "All jokes aside, you saw how Honey was checking me out, right?"

Whitty walked into the office. She usually didn't wear makeup, but the beating Tunisha put on her had to be camouflaged. Whitty immediately noticed Dawn's outfit. "Look at you."

When she came within arm's reach, Dawn reached out and fingered the diamond necklace around Whitty's neck. "How long were you fucking him, Whitty?"

"Who?" Whitty asked, playing dumb.

"Who else? You lied to me once, don't lie to me again. That night when you were telling me about the funeral, you couldn't stop playing with this necklace. A necklace that he obviously gave you."

Whitty didn't answer.

"You and Bigger," Dawn said, getting up in her face. "How long?"

Whitty looked at Julisa and put her head down before answering. "A couple months."

"I knew it," Julisa said.

"And you know where his home away from home is, don't you?" Dawn asked, already knowing the answer.

Whitty nodded.

"Call Trent," Dawn said to Julisa.

"For what?"

"Whitty's going to give him the address of Bigger's love nest so he can give it to Tunisha."

"Why would I do that?" Whitty said.

"The last thing we need is a dead man's wife coming up in here with all kinds of drama."

"We? So it is true," Whitty said.

"What's true?" Julisa asked.

"That the boys got a new boss." Whitty winked at Dawn.

"And who ran their big mouth to you?"

Whitty looked at Dawn for help.

"Don't look at me, you opened that can of worms."

Whitty looked back at Julisa. "Cash told me."

"Cash? You fucking him too?"

"No, we're just friends."

"Friends my ass," Julisa mumbled.

"Julisa, get Trent on the phone. Whitty's going to give up that address, aren't you?"

Whitty nodded.

When Whitty left the office, Julisa walked behind her desk and sat down, "I don't want to sound like a broken record, but are you sure you want to go through with this?"

"It's a little too late to be asking me that. I'm already in."

"I could give you the money for the back taxes, the missed car payments and missed mortgage payments," Julisa offered.

"And in a few months, Dante and I will be in the same situation."

"You guys will figure something out by then."

"I've already figured something out."

"What's that?"

"No one's playing fair. I'm tired of sitting back and watching these corporate execs swindle people out of their investments, life savings, pensions, and when they get caught stealing billions, they get a few months in Club Fed and have to pay a couple million back in restitution. What's a few months in prison and a couple million in fines compared to the billions they got stashed in some off shore account collecting interest until they get out?"

"We're not Emron or AIG," Julisa said. "We get caught, we're going away for a long time."

"Well, then, we better not get caught." Dawn flipped around the laptop sitting on the desk. "Lowe's files on here?"

"He doesn't keep files on there."

"I need to see his files."

Julisa pulled a disc from the bottom drawer and slid it into the laptop's drive.

"This looks interesting," Dawn said, clicking onto a file that read *payment plan*. "There's got to be at least thirty names here. This is what Mr. Green was talking about."

"Talking about? What do you mean talking about?" Julisa positioned her chair so she could see what Dawn was looking at.

"Mr. Green said Lowe had a business of his own," Dawn said. "He's a loan shark."

"No, he's a private investor," Julisa said. "That's what Mr. Green calls him."

"Figures Mr. Green would come up with a name he could stomach: faggot."

They both looked at the screen of names; the amount they owed and their payment plans.

"That can't be right," Julisa said, pointing to a name and how much he owed.

"I don't know who this *Marv* is," Dawn said, "but he owes ninety thousand. He's paying it back at eight thousand a month. It's all starting to make sense now."

"What's that?" Julisa asked.

"What Mr. Green shared with me in his office. Lowe runs The Bank for him, and Mr. Green pays him a percentage of the monthly profits. That percentage he said now goes to you. Lowe's also the middle man between him and dealers who want to clean their money and invest their, now legitimate, money into legal ventures. Lowe receives a percentage from those dealings, as well. But this right here." Dawn pointed to the screen. "This is all Lowe's. I didn't know why Mr. Green wanted in on this until now." She scrolled down to the bottom of the screen and looked at the tally of how much Lowe collected, monthly. "One hundred and fifty thousand a month."

"My God." Julisa whipped her head toward Dawn. "You didn't agree to cut Mr. Green in on this, did you?"

"Kinda."

"Kinda? How could you? This wasn't yours to cut a deal with."

"How the hell did you think I was able to walk into his office and convince him to let me into a million dollar operation? I had to give him something."

"But you didn't know about this until he mentioned it. What did you plan on giving him before you knew about this?"

"I was going to bluff him," Dawn said.

"Bluff him with what?"

"Think about it. Why was he so fixated on *you* running The Bank? He could've gotten anybody to run this club. The truth is, he's in too deep."

"In too deep how?"

"He may have been an honest businessman, a long time ago, but once he got a taste of that *dirty* money, and saw how fast it was rolling in, he got hooked. He's not from the hood, he's too scared to try and find someone who can do what Lowe did. Now, if he could get you to take over, just until Lowe comes out of his coma then it'll be like Lowe never left."

"So, how'd you bluff him?"

"Bono told him I was your best friend and that I have a lot of influence on your decisions."

"No you don't."

"Mr. Green didn't know that. So, I gave him my word that I would convince you to stay on and run The Bank until Lowe comes to, and in the meantime, *I* would see to it that Lowe's crew takes care of the other businesses. That's when he mentioned that if I could guarantee him twenty percent of Lowe's loan sharking outfit, he would bring me on board."

"Twenty percent? What the fuck, Dawn?"

"What do you mean what the fuck? You were about to throw in the towel, remember? You weren't going to collect this money. You didn't even bother to look at Lowe's files until now."

"Still... you should've come to me first before you took it upon yourself to have a meeting with Mr. Green, and make all kinds of promises."

"I did what I felt was necessary at the time for me and you. You still get to run to club and you get eighty percent of Lowe's monthly profits."

"And what do you get?" Julisa asked suspiciously.

"I get money to pay my mortgage, back taxes, car payments, and whatever else needs paying. Then, I'm going to invest the rest in something solid, something recession proof."

"And what might that be?"

"I don't know. I'll let Dante take care of that."

"Dante? You told him what you're doing?"

"Hell fucking no."

"So, how are you going to explain all the money you're going to be bringing home?"

"We'll cross that bridge when we get to it."

Julisa studied the screen. "I really had no idea my husband was—"

"A Loan Shark?"

"A fucking genius; look." She pointed to the screen. "My baby's a businessman."

"Come again?" Dawn said, trying to see what Julisa was seeing.

"He gets paid for running the club, he gets paid for being a middle man in Mr. Green's laundering operation, and he's a private investor."

"You mean loan shark."

"I prefer private investor. So, tell me how this is going down again?" Julisa asked.

"You're going to continue running The Bank, I'm going to be Mr. Green's go-between for his laundering operation, and I'm going to make sure he gets his twenty percent of Lowe's investments."

Julisa sighed.

"What."

"You, out there collecting, and being a go-between, that can be dangerous."

"That's what I have Buck, Gamble, Naji and Trent for," Dawn said.

"I know you saw the looks on their faces when Mr. Green put you in charge. Trent was literally shaking in his seat, and to be honest with you, you can't do this without him."

"I didn't plan to. He's going to hold me down," Dawn said.

"What makes you so sure?"

"Trust me, he's going to hold me down."

Monday morning, Dawn arrived at work and completed her day as usual. The only difference between today and last Monday was the fact that she didn't need this job. Just knowing that fact, kept a smile on her face the whole day, while the other secretaries looked stressed and on the verge of having nervous breakdowns. At quitting time, she pulled out her cell and called Julisa.

"Hello?" Julisa said.

"It's me," Dawn said.

"Who's phone you calling me from?"

"I bought another phone on my lunch break. I can't use my personal phone for business."

"I hear you."

"You talk to Trent, lately?" Dawn asked.

"About an hour ago."

"What's up with him?"

"He didn't say much. He's kind of hard to read," Julisa said.

"I need to talk to him."

"You want his number?" Julisa offered.

"You know where he's at, now?"

"He's at his usual hangout spot. Naji owns a lounge in Chelsea."

"Really?" Dawn said surprised.

"Yeah." Julisa gave her the address.

"Is there anyone else on the team who owns their own business?"

"Yeah, Gamble. He owns a clothing store in Brooklyn."

"Interesting," Dawn said, as the wheels in her head started to turn.

"Interesting like you're impressed or like you're scheming?"

"Got to go. I'll call you later."

Naji did a double take at the lounge's entrance when Dawn walked in. He didn't expect her to show up at his spot and he definitely didn't expect her to show up by herself. He subtly nodded at her as she walked toward him.

"Nice place," she said, as she looked around. Naji's lounge was decked out in burgundy with silver trimming.

"Can I get you something to drink?" he said, walking behind the bar to fix it himself.

"No. I'm looking for Trent."

Naji looked over her shoulder.

She turned around and saw Trent at a pool table giving a woman pointers on how to hold her pool stick. He stood behind her as she bent at the waist and positioned the stick behind the cue ball. Trent spooned against her and whispered instructions into her ear. He grabbed the butt of the pool stick and held it steady as she struck the cue ball. They stayed in that position with Trent whispering in her ear long after the balls stopped rolling.

"Can you get his attention?" Dawn said to Naji.

"I couldn't get him off that ass if the building was on fire."

Dawn sighed and pulled out her cell phone. Trent slowly stood up and dug into his pocket for his phone. He looked at the number and turned his lip up.

"Who this?" he barked into his phone.

"We need to talk," Dawn said.

"I'm busy, right now."

"Doing what?"

"I'm giving pool lessons."

"Looks more like molestation from where I'm sitting."

Trent looked around. Dawn waved when he saw her, he folded his phone shut and looked at Naji; Naji shrugged. Trent whispered something in the woman's ear that caused her to cut her eyes at Dawn. He grabbed his bottle of beer off the pool table's edge and headed toward Dawn.

"What's up?" he said, after taking a swig of his beer.

"Like I said, we need to talk."

Trent took another swig of his beer. "Talk."

"In private."

Trent held out his hand. Naji handed him a set of keys. "Follow me." Trent led her to a door in the back marked "private." He unlocked it and allowed her to step into the polished break room. Trent grabbed a cold beer out the fridge and popped off the cap.

"Aren't you going to offer me one?" Dawn asked.

"Help yourself."

"Like you've been helping yourself?"

"What's that supposed to mean?"

"Tyrone Johnson."

"Bigger?" Trent said. "What about him?"

"I came across his name on Lowe's list."

"What list?"

"You know what list."

"Okay," Trent said with a shrug. "You came across his name."

"Lowe loaned him two hundred thousand dollars."

"Yeah."

"The funny thing is, Bigger's the only person on the list that didn't have to pay interest on his loan. Why is that?"

"Him and Lowe were tight like that."

"So why's he dead? He only had sixty-five thousand left to pay on his loan."

Trent smiled as he tapped the beer cap on the break room counter. "Shit happens."

"Shit like you helping yourself to sixty-five thousand, and then killing Bigger to cover your tracks?"

Trent stopped tapping the bottle cap. "You got a hell of an imagination."

"And it's obvious you didn't have access to Lowe's list of clients."

"And how's that obvious?"

"If you did, the police would be fishing a lot more bodies out of the Hudson."

Trent stared at her.

"Say what's on your mind," Dawn said.

"You don't want to know what's on my mind."

"Grow a pair of balls and say what you got to say."

"Fuck you! From the beginning, you were trying to convince Julisa to leave all this shit alone, I really believed you had her best interest in mind, but all the while, you were just waiting for the right moment to show your true colors."

"You finished?" Dawn said, not at all impressed with his tirade.

"I don't trust you, and if anyone is helping themselves to anything, it's you."

"Let's cut the bull. This isn't about looking out for Lowe or Julisa's best interest. You and I are seeing the same thing. Mr. Green's organization is ripe for the picking. The only difference between you and I is I'm not going to hide behind Julisa to get what I want." Dawn walked to the window and stared out at the street. Trent walked up behind her. She cut her eyes over her shoulder at him as he leaned over and looked down at her left hand.

"I don't see a ring on that finger."

"I'm still married."

"Does he know what you're doing?"

"Do you care?"

"It would be fucked up if I said I didn't."

"And you don't, so save the phony sensitivity for your pool hall floozy."

"So, you came all the way down here for…"

"You know why I'm here."

"I want to hear you say it," Trent said with a devilish smile.

Dawn turned around and tugged at the ends of his collar. "I need you."

"Do you now?" His smile got wider.

"Yeah, just like you need me."

"And how's that?"

"How long do you think that sixty-five thousand is going to last?" Dawn asked.

"You got a lot of shit with you."

"I need to know if you're going to have my back."

"What do you need me to do?"

"The carwash is yours."

"Mine? What do you mean by mine?" Trent said suspiciously.

"Mr. Green has re-opened the pipeline. A shipment of coke is coming through Friday morning."

"And he doesn't have a problem with me running the carwash."

"As long as you flip them bricks, there won't be any problems. Can I count on you to do that?"

He nodded. "What's my cut?"

"You get Lowe's cut."

"I get... what kind of game are you playing?"

"Do I look like I have time for games?"

"Do you know how much money the carwash was pulling in before Mr. Green closed it down?" Trent said.

"I'm well aware of the numbers," Dawn shot back.

"And you're just going to give me what Lowe used to get?"

"You have a problem with that?"

"Why? Why give me the profits and take none for yourself?" Trent had to ask because he couldn't believe why she would just give a chunk of money up like that.

"Simple. Mr. Green wants the carwash back in business. I don't want to deal with drugs. So, Mr. Green gets to re-open his coke business, you get to run it and get paid well, and I'll have nothing to do with it. We all get what we want."

"Why do I get the feeling you're playing me?"

"It's a straight up deal, Trent. You know who Lowe dealt with, and they know you. So, it won't be a problem for you to move weight the way Lowe did, or would it?"

Trent smiled. "I got them ringing my phone off the hook now, wanting to know when we're opening back up for business."

"So, this is a done deal?"

He nodded.

"Did you handle that situation with Bigger's wife?"

"Yeah, I went with her to the address Whitty gave me. The spare key was taped under the porch light like she said."

"So, I don't have to worry about her coming to the club and acting like a raving lunatic?"

"Hardly. The only thing she's focused on right now is cashing in that life insurance policy."

"Ahh, one of the many benefits of being married."

Trent stared into her eyes. "Who are you, really?"

"Cross me, and you'll find out the hard way."

Dawn waved at Naji as she left the lounge. He waved back and then watched Trent as he approached.

"What's the deal?" he asked Trent.

"Get Buck and Gamble on the phone, the carwash is back in business."

"You think she can run it the way Lowe did?"

"She's not running it, I am."

"Word?" Naji said, not believing Trent.

"Word, and I get all of Lowe's cut."

"How did you manage that?"

"She doesn't want any parts of it."

"She's more gullible than Julisa," Naji said.

"Not at all. She's like a female version of Lowe, only twice as cunning."

"So, what's the plan?"

"She leads, we follow. She slips, we make sure she falls hard."

"How hard?"

"Hudson River hard."

Dante was sitting on the front porch when Dawn turned into the driveway. He stood up when she got out of her car and headed toward him.

"I came to your job to have lunch with you, the front desk told me you left for the day."

"I had some things to take care of." She handed him the shopping bag she retrieved out of the trunk.

"I got a little good news," Dante said as he followed her inside.

"You found a job?"

"Yeah, but—"

Dawn hugged and kissed him. "But nothing. I knew you would be back on Wall Street in no time."

"I'm not going to be on Wall Street."

"Okay, where will you be?"

"Right here," he said spreading his arms. "I'll be working from home, right from my laptop."

"Doing what?" Dawn didn't sound too thrilled.

"I've been offered a job by an online publication called the African-American Investor. I'll be writing a weekly business column and answering questions on investing and personal finances."

"That's great, baby."

"I won't be making as much as I was on Wall Street…"

"It's a job, Dante. And it may help you get back on Wall Street."

"I was thinking the same thing."

Dawn walked into the bedroom and saw her lavender dress lying across the bed. "What's this?"

"We're going out tonight. We need to celebrate."

"Oh really?"

"Yeah, it's been a while since we went out."

She picked up the dress. "I distinctly remember you telling me that you didn't want me wearing this because it was too snug."

"I want to show you off."

"I'm not some trophy that you can just put on display whenever you want," she said playfully.

"You're not going to make me beg, are you?" He palmed her butt and pulled her to him.

Dawn looked him in the eye. "You lucky I like you."

CHAPTER 9

*D*awn smiled in her sleep when she felt Dante nibble on her ear lobe.

"I love you so much," he whispered in her ear.

"I love you, too," she whispered back. She could feel his hardness against her back. "Didn't you have enough last night?"

"I can never have enough of you." He slipped his hand around her naked thigh.

She moaned, as he played with her glistening pearl. She started to remember their all night romp fest after they came back from their dinner and movie. "You're going to make me late for work," she moaned.

"You're already late."

"What? What time is it?"

"Nine o'clock."

"Shit." She jumped up.

Dawn hustled into the bathroom and ran the shower and then grabbed her toothbrush. She peeked her head out of the bathroom. "I'm sorry, baby," she said with toothpaste dripping down the corners of her mouth.

"What am I supposed to do with this," Dante said, pointing to his erection.

Dawn held her hand up and disappeared back into the bathroom. She washed her mouth out and jumped into the shower. She hustled back into the room, grabbing a pair of panties and a bra out of her dresser. "I'll make it up to you tonight, I promise."

"What's the hurry?"

"My boss has a video conference."

"Let him set it up."

"He doesn't even know how to work his DVD player."

"Are you serious?"

"Need I explain any further?" She wiggled on a pair of Dereon jeans and pulled a red Diesel T-shirt over her head.

"Since when you started dressing like that for work?"

"Since I realized that any day could be my last. So if I'm going to get fired, I may as well dress the way I want until that dreaded day comes."

"Don't say that. They're not going to fire you."

"Whatever." She grabbed her bracelets off the dresser and slid them on her arm.

Dante looked at how her butt filled out her jeans. He got up and walked up behind her as she brushed her hair and nibbled on her ear.

"Dante—"

He spooned up against her. "I just need five minutes."

"You and I know you need way more than five minutes."

"Not if you let me do you right here, from behind."

She turned around and grabbed his throbbing shaft. She kissed him while she stroked it. "Tonight, baby," she whispered. "I promise." She bent over and pulled on her Bandolino sling-backs.

"Tonight, you bent over this dresser, with these sexy-ass jeans around your ankles," Dante whispered in her ear.

"You promise?" she said, massaging his crotch.

"Swear to God."

"It's a date, then." Dawn grabbed her purse and shot out the door. When she got into her car, she checked the messages on the alternate cell phone she kept tucked in one of the side pockets in her purse. Bono had called four times already. "Damn." She called him. He didn't answer. She pulled up to Mr. Green's office building ten minutes after ten.

Mr. Green was sitting at his desk, reading the morning paper when his secretary let Dawn in. Bono sat on the couch against the wall texting on his BlackBerry.

"Sorry I'm late," Dawn said, breathing slightly heavy.

Mr. Green closed his paper, folded it in half, and slid it into his desk drawer. "Eighty two minutes."

"Excuse me?"

Mr. Green sipped his tea and then repeated himself. "Eighty two minutes. You're eighty two minutes late."

"I over slept."

Mr. Green and Bono looked at each other and busted out laughing.

"Did I miss something?" Dawn asked.

Mr. Green folded his hands. "Yes, you did. You missed your first appointment. It was eighty two minutes ago." Mr.

Green took a deep breath before speaking. "Honey, you're not running a crack house in Charlotte."

How did he know about that? Dawn thought.

"The *only* reason why Lowe and I have stayed in business so long is because we leave nothing to chance. We have a system in place. A system with timetables. Am I making myself clear?"

"I need to be on time."

"You *always* need to be on time. One minute late could be the difference between you collecting money from one of my clients or you making a collect call from the precinct. Am I making myself clear?"

"I'll be on time."

Mr. Green cocked his head.

Dawn sucked her teeth. "I will *always* be on time."

He nodded, and then he looked over at Bono. "Everything good?"

Bono tucked his BlackBerry away and stood. "Everything's set. He's expecting us at eleven-thirty."

Mr. Green looked at his watch and then to Dawn. "I'll let you go, I don't want you to be late for your second appointment."

"Of course not," Dawn said, rolling her eyes as she followed Bono out of the office.

Dawn followed Bono to a skirted down, tinted up grey Range Rover. He pulled off before she had a chance to buckle her seat belt.

"Are you going to tell me where we're going?" she asked.

"The name of the man you're meeting with is Chance."

"And?"

"And that's all you need to know. You work for Lowe, that's all *Chance* needs to know. We arrive at eleven-thirty and we walk out at eleven forty- five."

"Y'all are serious about this whole timetable thing, huh?"

Bono didn't respond. They rode the rest of the way in silence. Bono pulled into Chance's hotel parking lot. Dawn put on her Donna Karan shades and followed him into the lobby. Bono said something to the clerk, and then headed around to the service elevator.

Chance stood outside of the elevator. "Eleven-thirty on the nose," he said to Bono, as he tapped his watch. Chance spoke with a slight accent. He looked to be West Indian, but from what Island, Dawn didn't have a clue. He was in his late forties, with a head full of bushy jet black hair. He wore his shirt loose to cover his bulging belly; his days of rocking a chiseled six-pack was definitely over. He looked at Dawn. "Honey, I presume."

She took off her shades and parked them on top of her head. "You've presumed correctly."

They stepped into the elevator. Dawn immediately noticed the camera mounted in the top corner. When they stepped out onto the top floor, it reminded her of a hospital wing. It was light bright, walls white, floors buffed to a glossy shine. She felt she could run her finger over any surface and not come away with a speck of dirt.

Chance stopped at the third door on the right and knocked. A burly man with an Uzi in hand opened the door and stepped aside.

"Please," Chance said, inviting Dawn to step in. She entered the room. A team of women was sifting through trash bags of bills while another team of women sat behind money counters, feeding bills of every denomination into them. Dawn counted seven trash bags on the floor.

"My condolences," Chance said, breaking Dawn out of her trance. "Any change in Lowe's condition?"

"No." Dawn responded. "But I wouldn't give up on him, he's a fighter."

"Yes, he is." He eyed Dawn's succulent physique and the way her hair fell across her shoulders. "Lowe never mentioned you."

"I didn't need to be mentioned."

Chance chuckled. "Riight, riight."

Bono looked at his watch.

"We almost done here?" Dawn asked.

"I know, eleven forty-five, don't worry," Chance said, all too familiar with the timetable.

One of the women disappeared into the back and returned with three more garbage bags of loose bills.

Dawn started getting butterflies in her stomach. She had never been around so much money before. At eleven forty-two the women packed two duffel bags, half a million in each. Dawn grabbed a bag in each hand.

"The turnover time's the same right?" Chance asked Dawn.

"The clean money will be in your account in three days, minus Lowe's fee, of course."

"Beautiful," Chance whispered. He led them out and back down to the lobby. Dawn slung the bags in the backseat and started to climb in next to Bono.

"Get in the back," Bono said.

Dawn hesitated for a moment and then climbed into the back. "What's up with the back of the bus shit?"

Bono started up the Range and pulled off. "Reach under the backseat on my side, you should feel a latch."

"Yeah, I feel it."

"Slide it toward you and lift up the seat."

Dawn did as instructed. She was staring at a cast iron safe. "Wow."

"Zero, one, seven, six."

She punched the numbers into the numeric keypad and tugged on the latch. She looked into the safe and saw that it ran the length on the whole seat. "You could put a body in here."

"The duffel bags will do for now."

She dropped the duffel bags in and locked it back. "You could've helped bring the bags to the truck."

"My hands need to be free to protect you."

"Me or Mr. Green's money?"

"It's the same thing when those bags are in your hands." Bono hit the phone symbol on his steering wheel and spoke. "Call Green." Mr. Green answered on the second ring.

"Tell me something good."

"Everything went smooth," Bono said.

"Did he feel comfortable with Honey?"

"Too comfortable. He was panting like a horny German Shepherd."

"Hey," Dawn said.

"Excellent," Mr. Green said. "I knew you would have that kind of effect on him."

"We're on our way to the next pickup," Bono cut in.

"You know the routine." Mr. Green hung up.

"So, where to, now?" Dawn asked from the backseat.

"The name of the man you're meeting with is Benny, that's all you need to know."

"And I work for Lowe, that's all *Benny* needs to know. I feel like I'm in an episode of Mission Impossible."

"What we're doing is far more complicated than holding down a couple crack houses while your boyfriend's doing a county bid."

Dawn leaned forward. "How'd you... Who told you about that?"

"I would say Julisa—" Bono started to say.

"And you would be lying, because she didn't know."

Bono looked at her through the rearview mirror. "You didn't think Mr. Green was going to let you into his inner sanctum on just my word, did you?"

"So, he went digging into my past?"

"No, I went digging into your past."

Dawn folded her arms and sat back in the seat.

"If it helps any, I didn't have to dig deep. We only spoke with one person."

"We?"

"Me and Eva. You remember Eva, don't you?"

"How could I forget a deranged woman putting a knife to my neck?"

"You were upsetting me, she doesn't like to see me upset."

"Whatever." Dawn wasn't mad that Bono went poking around into her past; it was her present she was more concerned about. How much did they know about Dante? Did they know about their financial difficulties? She was beginning to feel that she might have underestimated Mr. Green. She would have to regroup and rethink her game plan. Mr. Green wasn't going to be easily duped; it was going to take finesse.

"You okay back there?" Bono asked, breaking her from her thoughts.

"Yeah. Where were we?" Dawn said absent-mindedly.

"Benny—"

"Oh Yeah, Mission Impossible."

The Bank and The Vault were filled to their maximum capacities for Lowe's annual Valentine's Day Mega bash. He started the tradition a few years back. Julisa and his boys thought he was crazy when he told them that on that night, no man could get in if he didn't have on something silk and no women could get in if she didn't have on something lace. The flyers were distributed and to Julisa's amazement, men sported silk ties, bandannas, caps, and scarfs, some even let their pants hang low to show off their silk boxers. The women donned laced shirts, stockings, scarfs, and some, not to be outdone by the men, let their jeans hang just low enough to show off their lace underwear. Every year, people became more creative and more bold. Tonight, in The Bank, Julisa saw some men sporting red silk pajamas, while some women were bold enough to just have on lace teddies and high heels. In The Vault, they abided by the dress code, but the upper echelon weren't that carefree with their wardrobe.

Julisa had been walking around, mingling to get her mind off of Dawn. She'd been calling her every hour on the hour and she still hadn't returned her calls. Whitty waved her over to the bar.

"Drink up," Whitty said, sliding her a drink. "You look stressed."

Julisa took a sip. "Dawn is going to be the death of me."

"She's a big girl, she can take care of herself."

"I hate when she turns her phone off when she's out there collecting."

"She's not by herself. Trent and the rest of the crew are out there."

Whitty pointed over Julisa's shoulder. "Speak of the devil."

Julisa whipped her head around. Dawn strolled into The Vault taking in the crowd. She unzipped her pearl white mink jacket, exposing her black thigh-high Carolina Herrera dress with a lace hemline. Her toned legs tapered down into a pair of black Moschino peep-toe pumps with pearl white flecks embroidering the heels.

Julisa abandoned her drink and made a beeline to her. She grabbed her by the hand and led her up the spiral staircase to her office. She barely closed her door before she lit off into Dawn.

"You can't call me to let me know that everything's all right?"

"Why wouldn't everything be all right?" Dawn said, surprised at the interrogation.

"Don't play yourself. You know how dangerous collecting Lowe's debts can be."

"Everything's been smooth since day one," Dawn said, as she stared out the one-way mirror. "They see Trent by my side and that's good enough for them to pay up."

"It wasn't good enough for Marv."

"He came up off the dough real quick when Buck stepped up in there, though."

"No matter how smooth things may be going, you still need to stay in contact. It makes no sense for me to be sitting here worrying about you like this."

"You're right. I'll call you, okay?"

"We'll see."

"The money's secured in your office upstairs, minus Mr. Green's cut."

Julisa snorted. "I still think twenty percent is too much for doing nothing."

"It's the price we had to pay to make this work. And look," Dawn said pointing to her outfit. "It's working."

"I see. You're stepping up in here with a different mink every night. Where are you hiding all that stuff? I know you're not keeping it in your closet."

Dawn turned around with a wide grin on her face. "I want to show you something."

Dawn coasted down Bethune Street located in Manhattan's coveted West Village. Julisa lowered the window to let in the night breeze, and to get a better look at the townhouses lining both sides of the street. Dawn parked outside one of the three-story homes.

"Who lives here?" Julisa asked.

Dawn exited her car and waved at Julisa to come on. As they climbed the steps, Dawn jingled her keys until she found the one she was looking for. She unlocked the door and stepped in. Julisa stopped at the porch.

"Come in," Dawn said.

"Not until you tell me whose house this is."

"I'll tell you inside. Now, come on, you're letting the heat out."

Julisa looked around and then walked in. She followed Dawn into the living room. Her eyes got stuck on the thick Persian rug spread out in front of a stone fireplace. She blinked when the flash on Dawn's phone went off.

"I'm sorry," Dawn said laughing, "but the way your mouth was hanging open…"

"Whose house is this?"

"It's mine, silly." She took off her mink, tossed it on the couch and headed to the staircase.

"Hold up," Julisa said following behind her. "How—"

"Andre. I told him I was looking for a place."

"Place? This looks like a palace."

"He really looked out for me. A pharmaceutical company had the lease on this place for a year. They had to do some downsizing and laid off the executive who was living here. He flew back home to Texas last month. So, Andre's letting me finish out the remaining five months of the lease, rent-free,"

"But, I don't understand. Why do you need this place?"

"Why? Where else am I going to stash my things?"

"But, it's like you're living two lives."

"Ah, hello, part-time secretary by day, loan sharking, money launderer by night."

"I don't know," Julisa said, still looking around.

"You don't know about what?"

"This place, your clothes, you're spending a lot of money."

"I'm enjoying my money. I've made more money in the past three months than I've made in my entire life. I should be able to enjoy it."

"I'm not saying you can't enjoy it, I just think you should be spending more wisely."

"I wish I could just pay off the ten thousand in back taxes without Dante becoming suspicious."

"Tell him I lent you the money."

"I did that when I caught him up on his car payment."

"Well, tell him I gave you a raise."

"Used that when I caught us up on our utility. I did it all, Julisa. I told him I borrowed money from my retirement to buy a washer and dryer we so desperately needed, won the office lotto when we had to replace our hot water tank. I'm surprised he fell for all of those. I'm all tapped out of ways I can bring home large sums of money."

"How's Dante coming along with his new job?"

"Please," Dawn said, rolling her eyes. "That online magazine gig is hardly getting it."

"It pays the bills, though."

"That's all it does. After all bills are paid, he's lucky if he has a few dollars. And my miserable excuse for a check from my day job is just enough to keep food in the fridge. And the money that he thinks you're paying me for bartending is what we use for little extras, and believe me, they're *little*. If that was all the money we had to work with, I would be in panic mode, right now. You know how I get when my money gets low."

Julisa touched the paintings on the wall. "So... do you spend anytime here?"

"I come here during the day when I don't have to work."

"By yourself?"

"I know you're not accusing me of—"

"You're right, my bad."

"How could you even think some shit like that?"

"You're right. I know how much you love Dante."

"Just so that we're on the same page, don't for a second think that I've lost focus on what's important here. I'm doing all of this for me and my man. I'm also holding you down until Lowe comes back to us. Sure, I might splurge here and there and I might flirt with a few influential people at The Vault, but that's what Honey does. This," she said pointing to her clothes, "is an image; nothing more."

"All right, my bad. It's just that I *do* see how you flirt with men in the club. Sometimes... seeing you act the way you do reminds me of how you were ten years ago, when we were back in Charlotte. And it scares me, because if anything were to happen to you, it would be my fault. I dragged you into this."

"This isn't Charlotte. I'm much wiser and unfortunately, much older."

That brought a smile to Julisa's face.

"Let me show you something," Dawn said, pulling her by the hand. She led her down the hall into her home office. "Check this out." She handed her a binder.

Julisa took it from her and read the title:

WE MEAN BUSINESS

"What is this?"

"Read the first page," Dawn said enthusiastically.

Julisa read the first paragraph. "Who put this together?"

"Whitty."

"Whitty?" Julisa said, not believing it.

"That girl has a Masters degree in business administration. It makes no sense to have all that talent around me and not use it."

"So, she started this consultant service for you?"

"She drafted the necessary paperwork that I had to submit, and I took care of the rest," Dawn said, proud of herself.

"But... what do you know about business?"

"Legally, not a damn thing."

"Okay, I'm lost."

"Listen, I know this *thing* that I have with Mr. Green is over just as soon as Lowe comes out of his coma, so I secured my future."

"How? By starting a business you know nothing about?"

Dawn held her hand up. "Two months ago when Trent and I were making our rounds collecting, one of Lowe's clients, named Frank, told me that a good friend of his owns this hair and nail salon in Brooklyn and her business is booming. She went to the bank to get a loan, but as you know, banks aren't trying to give up any loans right now. He said she's desperately looking for some cash so she can renovate and expand her storefront. So, of course, I tell him I'm not interested. Only, I was, but I didn't want Trent up in my business. So I go back the next day and Frank gives me the woman's number. We hooked up for lunch, and I lent her the money."

"Okay... and what does that have to do with the consulting company?"

"Instead of me having to go and collect cash, all *my* clients have to do is write me a check every month."

"Clients?"

"I got four so far. Go ahead say it, I'm a genius."

"So, when they make a payment, they write it down as a consulting fee," Julisa said now understanding where Dawn was headed with her consulting service.

"Correct."

"You *are* a genius."

"Yes, I am," Dawn said with a grin.

Julisa put her head down.

"What's up?"

"Nothing, I was just thinking. If Lowe comes to, I know he's going to be grateful for you stepping up. I just hope he doesn't catch feelings behind you using his contacts to get yours."

"Catch feelings?" Dawn said with an attitude, but she caught herself, and smiled. "Stop saying if he comes back. He is coming back, you hear me?"

"I hope you're right. I miss him so much."

Dawn hugged her. "When was the last time you visited him?"

"Last week."

"I want to go with you to see him the next time you go."

"I thought you didn't want to see him like that."

"I don't, but I want him to know that I'm praying for him."

Julisa nodded. "Everything going well with Trent?"

"Trent is in his element, right now. Mr. Green can't believe the amount of weight he's moving out of the carwash."

"I'm glad you two were able to see eye to eye."

"Yeah, we had more in common than we realized."

CHAPTER 10

D awn checked her makeup in the rearview mirror of the milk white Range Rover she borrowed from Mr. Green's fleet of company cars. She moistened her lips with a coat of lip-gloss and then grabbed her handbag before strutting across the street to Gamble's jewelry shop, located on Fordham Road. Gamble called her earlier and told her that the shipment of watches he was waiting on finally arrived. They were slated to come out in the fall, but he was one of the few who always got a "sample" shipment months before other retailers.

The men in the shop looked toward the front door when Dawn stepped in. She'd become accustomed to the eye-raping stares that hit her from every angle whenever she walked in. She spotted a guy to the left peeking at her from behind his Valentino shades. He rubbed his hands together as he went through is mental Rolodex of pickup lines. Just as he opened his mouth, Gamble swooped in and saved the would-be slick talker from getting is feelings hurt.

"What I tell you about harassing my customers?" Gamble said to Dawn playfully, as he led her away.

"It's not my fault that they're not used to seeing a real woman with real curves."

Gamble looked at her red, spaghetti strapped dress that stopped mid-thigh. And then checked out her matching heels.

"If I didn't' have women banging down my door and blowing up my cell..."

"Please," Dawn said dismissively, "spare me. I see the type of women you deal with. You wouldn't know what to do with a real woman."

"You'd be surprised, Honey." Although Dawn knew Gamble was as doggy as they came, she was feeling his style. He was the only one on the team who started his business without Lowe's help, and if he didn't agree with her or Trent on a matter, he wouldn't hesitate to let it be known. What appealed to her most about him were his looks. He wasn't just good looking, he was the type of good looking women couldn't stop staring at. He looked like Jim Jones, but had the swagger of Tyson Bedford. Dawn stared at his butt without shame as she followed him to the back. When she first started coming to the store to buy jewelry for Dante, she barely looked at Gamble. The first time she caught herself comparing his butt to Dante's she scolded herself all the way home for having such thoughts. But she convinced herself that, that's all they were—thoughts. And what was wrong with looking at a juicy butt? Men do it all the time. She even caught Dante a couple of times sneaking a peek at another woman's rear when he thought she wasn't looking. Right now, the True Religion jeans Gamble had on was giving her a true vision of his backside.

Gamble and Dawn walked down a set of steel steps to the pair of iron doors. He removed the padlocks, pulled the doors apart, and headed to the glass counter.

"You're going to love this one," he said, as he pulled out a Rolex with a diamond encrusted band and onyx face.

"I like it," Dawn said, appraising it, "but it's too flashy, I'm looking for something you wear with a suit."

"Shit, I would wear this with a suit."

"Gamble—"

"Okay, let me see if I have something a little bit less flashy." He pulled out of tray of leather-banded watches and started reading off the brands. "Timex, Calvin Klein, Emporio Armani, Bulova—"

"There," Dawn said, pointing into the display case. "That one, right there."

"This is the new one from Robert Lighton."

Dawn admired the square-faced, diamond-framed watch. She felt the leather band and nodded. "This is the one." She looked at the price—twelve thousand. Paying for it wasn't an issue. Explaining to Dante how she paid for it would be. But the watch grabbed her. She had to see it on Dante's wrist tonight. This evening was a big event for him, and she wanted him looking his best. "I'll bring the twelve grand to the club tomorrow night," Dawn said, continuing to admire the watch.

"Why you disrespecting me like that?" Gamble said, offended.

"How am I disrespecting you?"

"When have I ever charged you full price?"

"I don't want you to think I'm taking advantage."

"Go," Gamble said, waving her off as he locked the display case. "Bring me five, and we'll call it even."

Dawn didn't move. "You got a minute?"

Gamble looked up at her. "What's up?"

"I need to ask you something, but I want it to stay between us."

"Okay."

"What's the deal with Buck? Is he stable? I mean... his whole demeanor is... creepy."

Gamble started laughing. "Yeah, he's kind of special, isn't he?"

"And the way he stares at me..." Dawn said with a shiver.

"Don't worry about Buck. He's as stable as nitroglycerin." Gamble winked.

"Thanks, that makes me feel a whole lot better."

"Seriously, he's cool. I'd trust him with my life. I wouldn't trust him with my girl, but with my life... definitely."

"I'm really feeling better now," Dawn said sarcastically. "How does he fit in with the team? I've been asking Trent for the longest and he's never given me a straight answer."

"Well... given Buck's volatile nature and his unhealthy fascination with guns, we kind of keep him in the shadows, you know?"

"You're worst than Trent. What the fuck is the shadows?" Dawn was becoming frustrated.

"He just plays the background. I don't know how else to explain it without just coming straight out with it."

"Why not just come straight out with it?"

"Can't."

"Why?"

Gamble shrugged. "Just can't, sorry."

"Sorry? I can't believe you. How are you just going to keep something from me?"

"It's for your own good."

"You dudes kill me," Dawn said with a chuckle.

"So, you and hubby going out tonight, huh?"

"Something like that. We're going to a dinner engagement at the Highline Ballroom."

Gamble smiled at her devilishly. "Be safe, and don't do anything I would do."

"Bye, Gamble."

Dante pulled up to the Highline Ballroom a little after five. The Execs at the African-American Investor were hosting a dinner honoring some of the most influential African-Americans in today's top businesses. It was nights like these that Dawn was proud of her man. Presidents, Vice Presidents, and CEOs of multi-million dollar companies approached him with reverence, complimenting him and thanking him for his insightful column. Dante introduced Dawn to his bosses and co-workers. Dawn immediately clicked with Kim Marie, the wife of an executive. Kim Marie and her husband, Allen, flew all the way from Seattle to be in attendance. Kim Marie reminded Dawn of *Good Morning America* co-anchor Robin Roberts. She was so full of energy and positivity. They sat together for dinner. Dante and Allen seemed to forget that their wives didn't speak Wall Street.

"Hedge funds is where the money's at," Dante said matter of factly.

"I don't know," Allen said skeptically. "After that multi-billion dollar Ponzi scheme Madoff pulled, I'm staying far away from anything with the word hedge in it."

"C'mon, now," Dante said. "One rotten fruit doesn't spoil the whole bunch."

Allen still wasn't convinced. "I'm a safe investor. I don't take high risks."

"There's nothing high risk in hedge funds. In fact, the objective of hedgers is to minimize risk. You invest in several companies. That gives you leverage to take advantage of the broad trends in the global economy."

"You make it sound tempting," Allen said, really giving it some thought.

"If you like, I can put together a portfolio that will yield you stable returns." Dante sensed that he was winning him over.

"What do you think, sweetheart?" Allen asked his wife.

"You lost me at hedge."

"And you lost me at Ponzi," Dawn said.

They all laughed.

"Okay, I suggest we talk about something we all find interesting," Allen suggested.

"Central Park," Kim Marie said. "I always wanted to go to Central Park."

"Girl, you never been to Central Park?" Dawn asked surprised.

"No. Every time we come to New York, Allen promises me that he would take me, but we always run out of time. Isn't that right, sweetheart?"

"We'll make it our business to visit Central Park before we fly back," Allen promised.

Dante clasped his hands together. "We can go tonight."

Dawn looked at him like was crazy.

"That's a wonderful idea," Kim Marie said.

"Ah…" Allen was at a loss for words.

"Don't you think it's kind of late," Dawn asked Dante.

"Late?" He looked at the watch. "It's only seven-fifteen."

"And the sun went down an hour ago," Dawn said trying to give him a hint.

"This event is over at eight. We'll be at Central Park by eight-thirty, and be out of there by nine." He looked at Dawn. "And we need not worry; there are plenty of police patrolling the park."

"C'mon, Allen," Kim Marie whined. "It'll be romantic."

"But we didn't plan—"

"Would you for once forget about your planning preparation and just be spontaneous." Kim Marie put him on the spot.

"Well, I guess we could—"

"Thank you, sweetie." Kim Marie hugged him.

Dante parked a short block away from Central Park West near 67th Street. As they headed in, Dante and Allen talked more about investing while Dawn and Kim Marie talked about the exec's wife who had the nerve to show up at the dinner in a spandex skirt and hooker heels.

"This is so beautiful," Kim Marie said. She wrapped her arms around her husband's arm. Dawn put her arm around Dante's waist.

"This *is* nice," Dawn said. "I forgot how beautiful it is at night."

They nodded at other couples as they passed by. Dante was right. Dawn spotted a cop like every hundred yards. Kim Marie pulled out her cell and started taking pictures. She handed her phone to Dawn and pulled her husband under a light pole. Dawn took a few pictures of them.

Dante approached a Chinese woman who was selling single-stemmed roses and bought three for Dawn. Allen followed suit.

"I must admit," Dawn said, putting her hand inside of Dante's back pocket. "This was a good idea."

"It was, wasn't it?" Dante said, looking her in the eyes.

"Yes, it was." She kissed him on the cheek.

Dante looked at his watch.

"Time to go already?" Dawn asked.

"No, I'm just admiring my time piece."

"You like it?"

"I love it."

"That makes me happy."

Dante made sure they were alone before he said his next words. "This watch looks pretty expensive."

"Why can't you just enjoy a gift without having to know how much it cost?"

"I don't want to know how much it cost, it's just that we could've used the money to pay off the back taxes we owe."

"I'm not busting my ass everyday just to give up every dime for bills," Dawn huffed.

"I know but—"

"We have to live, too."

"I know, baby, I'm just saying, in the future—"

"Forget it. I try to do something special for you, and... forget it."

"Baby." Dante tried to hug her, but she pulled away.

"Everything okay?" Kim Marie asked from the bench her and Allen were sitting on.

"We're fine," Dante said. "It's getting kind of late, maybe we should start heading out of here."

Allen and Kim Marie stood up.

"Maybe we can come back during the daytime," Kim Marie said. "That way, we can walk through the whole park."

"Sounds like a plan," Dante said.

"We'll see," Allen said, pulling his hat over his ears. The temperature was dropping. They headed back the way they came. Dawn immediately noticed that the police wasn't as plentiful as they were when they first entered the park. She cut her eyes at every tree they walked by, expecting someone to jump out. She heard a twig snap. She whipped to the left.

"You okay?" Dante asked.

"Yeah, I just thought I heard something." Dawn relaxed when she saw an officer up ahead.

When they exited the park, Dawn and Kim Marie drifted together when Allen and Dante started talking Wall Street language. As they neared the car, Allen was the first to notice the two men leaning on Dante's car. Dante followed his line of sight.

"Who the hell is that?" Dante said to Allen.

The men stood when they noticed Dante and Allen staring at them.

When Dawn noticed the dark skinned men, her heart started beating fast. The men wore jeans, heavy sweaters, and knit hats. Dante and Allen approached them slowly.

"This your car?" the chubby one asked, as he looked at Dante and then to Allen.

"It's my car. What's up?" Dante asked.

Chubby pulled his sweater up, showing the badge clipped to his jeans. His partner did the same. "This car was reported stolen."

"What?" Dante said shocked. "There has to be some mistake."

"May I see your ID?" Chubby asked.

Dante reached into his pocket. Chubby's partner kept his eyes on Allen, Dawn, and Kim Marie. Dante pulled out his driver's license and started walking toward the detectives. Chubby took it and looked at it. "How about you, sir?" he said to Allen. "You have ID?"

"Yes, of course." Allen pulled out is wallet and handed over his license. Chubby nodded as he handed Allen back his license. He held Dante's out to him.

Dante reached for it. Chubby reacted so fast that no one knew what happened til his gun was in Dante's face. Chubby's partner grabbed Allen by his suit jacket, threw him to the ground, and pressed his gun against his head. Kim Marie started screaming.

"Shut that bitch up," Chubby said to Dawn as he waved his gun in Dante's face.

Dawn grabbed Kim Marie and calmed her down. Chubby forced Dante down to his knees next to Allen. He then ran up on Dawn and Kim Marie and forced them down on their knees right behind their husbands.

The one covering Allen and Dante went through their pockets, removing their cell phones and anything he thought was valuable.

"Take all that shit off," he said to Allen and Dante, referring to their jewelry.

Dawn wanted to cry when she saw Dante removing his watch and handing it to the phony detective. She gasped when the man standing above her tugged at her loop earrings. "Come up off all that," he said, nudging her in the head with his gun. Dawn removed all her jewelry, except one.

"That ring, too," he said, pointing to her wedding band. Dawn didn't move. Chubby kicked her in the back. Dawn instinctively put her hands out in front of herself to prevent her face from hitting the sidewalk. As her hands made contact with the concrete, Chubby stepped on her right hand, pinning it to the ground while he removed her wedding band. Dawn's scream was like a knee-jerk reaction to Dante. Without thinking, he turned around while on his knees and lunged at Chubby. Chubby brought the butt of his gun crashing down against Dante's head. Dante protectively fell on top of Dawn.

"You're police officers," Kim Marie shouted.

"Didn't I tell you to shut the fuck up?" Chubby said. He walked up to her, gun raised, ready to bring it down across her face.

"Please, no," Kim Marie said, taking off her jewelry. She held it out, her hands trembling. Chubby smiled and scooped everything out of her hands.

Chubby nodded to his partner, letting him know it was time to go. "Y'all enjoy the rest of your night."

"Fuck you," Dawn said, etching their faces in her memory. She couldn't wait to get to the club.

Both men looked at her and started laughing. They looked at each other when they realized that instead of hearing two laughs, they heard three. The third was coming from behind them, and it was getting louder. They spun around and froze.

The man's laugh abruptly stopped. The men couldn't help but stare at the AR 15 he had pointed at them. The butt of the rifle was braced against his shoulder, his cheek rested on the steel as he stared down the barrel at his two targets. The man's trench whipped behind him, as the night wind seemed to haul ass so it didn't have to witness what was about to go down.

"Yo, homie," Chubby said, "We're police officers."

150

"I hate police officers." Both men dropped their guns and held up their hands when they heard the click of the safety being disengaged.

"Fuck the pooolice," the man growled. Although his face was partially hidden under the brim of his fitted cap, Dawn would recognize that voice anywhere.

Chubby tried another approach. "There's plenty here for a three-way split."

"Do I look like a motherfucker who wants a split? Up all that shit before I get an itch in my trigger finger."

Chubby and his partner sighed as they dropped everything to the ground, including the money they robbed from two tourists earlier.

"Toss them badges in the pile, as well," the gunman said.

Both men slowly unclipped their badges and threw them with the rest of the stuff.

"Now, back the fuck up." The man walked toward them as they backed up. He picked up their guns and stuffed them in his trench. "You got ten seconds. One... two..." Both men tore ass down the street.

The man lowered the AR 15 and pulled his cap down further. "Please accept my humble apologies for any inconvenience you may have suffered at the hands of those miscreants." With that said, he turned and began walking away.

"Who was that?" Kim Marie asked.

The man stopped and spoke over his shoulder. "Neighborhood watch, Ma'am." He slung his assault rifle across his back and jogged off.

Dante scrambled to his cell phone and started dialing.

"Who are you calling?" Dawn asked, as she crawled up beside him.

"I'm calling the police."

"The police?" Allen and Kim Marie said in horror, still thinking that the two phonies were really police officers.

Dawn snatched his phone from him. "Let's just grab our stuff and get the hell out of here."

"Are you crazy?" Dante said. "Two men posing as police just tried to rob us and there's a vigilante running around with a machine gun."

Dawn grabbed his hand. "Let's just go."

"What about the guy with the rifle?" Dante said, looking around like he was expecting him to reappear at any minute.

"He saved us," Kim Marie said.

"Yes, he did," Dawn said.

Dante looked to Allen for help.

"Let's just get out of here," Allen said, still shaken up.

They collected their things and walked briskly to the car. No one said a word until Dante pulled up to Allen and Kim Marie's hotel.

"I'm really sorry about what happened tonight," Dante said.

"It's not your fault," Kim Marie said. "I'm the one who brought up the whole Central Park thing."

"It's no one's fault," Allen said. "Let's just be grateful that no one was seriously hurt."

"And thank God that man showed up when he did," Kim Marie added.

Allen and Kim Marie climbed out of the backseat and said their good nights. Dante waited for them to enter the hotel lobby before pulling off. Dawn didn't break the silence until they got on the highway.

"You okay?" She rested her hand on his thigh.

"I can't believe my luck. Here I am trying to impress one of my bosses and his wife, and this happens."

"It's not your fault."

"It is my fault. I'm probably going to lose my job behind this."

"You're overreacting."

Dante shook his head. "I should've done something."

"What could you have done? They had the drop on us, they had guns."

"That fat motherfucker. I know I'm ten times quicker and stronger than his ass. I could've snatched his gun from him and pistol whipped him."

"And his partner would've shot you."

"Maybe—"

"Maybe?" Dawn said, shocked that Dante would come off so nonchalantly.

"Maybe he would've missed, maybe I could've shot him before he shot me."

"Are you listening to yourself? You're talking about being shot or shooting someone."

"Those possibilities didn't stop you or Kim Marie from praising that whacko with the machine gun as if he was some kind of... superhero."

"No one was praising him, we were just grateful that he showed up when he did. I'm sure whoever he is, he doesn't see himself as a superhero."

"Yo, I'm telling you," Buck said getting hyped. "The way I materialized out of the darkness and clowned those two goons... Man, I felt like a fucking superhero," Buck said to Gamble, Naji and Trent, as they sat at their regular table in The Vault.

"Slow down," Trent said, snatching the shot glass out of Buck's hand. "You're jumping around, only giving us bits of the story. Start from the beginning, and this time, save the drama for the TV."

"Man, how many ways do I have to tell y'all how I saved Honey's life?" Buck said with a sigh.

Trent gave him a look.

"Okay, check it. I've been following her everywhere she goes, just like you told me to. Tonight, I thought it was going to be just another boring night. At about eight o'clock, Honey, her husband, and a couple that attended that dinner drives to Central Park. Why they decided to go to Central Park at night beats the hell out of me. You know how hard it was to follow them in that park? Police was everywhere, plus I was strapped, if they would've stopped me for anything, I mean anything..."

"Back to the story," Trent said.

"Okay. So they walked around for about forty minutes, and then they headed back to their car. Two men were leaning up against it, like they were waiting for them. Automatically, I start taking deep breaths, getting into battle-mode, cause this is what I do. I don't get buck, *I am* Buck. I—"

"Buck!" Trent said.

"Yeah, so, I hung back in the shadows like you told me to. Shadows, that's what I do, I see all, but I'm not seen. So, the fat motherfucker, well they were both overweight, the chubby-fat motherfucker pulls up his sweater and flashes a badge."

"A cop badge?" Naji asked.

"Yeah," Buck responded. "So I'm like 'what the fuck do they want?' But then the chubby-fat dude hauls off and cracks Honey's husband in the mouth, that coward just dropped. I was like 'oh shit, look at this bitch-ass motherfucker on the ground holding his jaw'. Then the other dude grabs the other man and then and shoves his punk ass to the ground. I'm like 'look at this cowering motherfucker.'"

"And what the fuck were you doing the whole time this was going on?" Gamble asked, getting upset that Buck didn't intercede right away.

Buck looked at him like he was crazy. "Motherfucker, didn't you hear what I said earlier? I was playing the shadows. That's what Trent told me to do. I'm in the shadows, that's what I do."

"Finish," Trent said, starting to lose his patience.

"Like I was saying, chubby-fat and the other fat motherfucker starts robbing them for everything. That's when I know these ain't no fucking cops or they're some dirty cops, either way, I know you told me to play the shadows, Trent, 'cause that's what I do, but when that chubby-fat motherfucker kicked Honey in the back…"

Gamble, Naji, and Trent looked at each other when they saw the tears welling up in Buck's eyes.

"Something inside me snapped. I hauled ass to my car and got my AR 15."

"Your AR…" Gamble looked at Trent.

"Okay," Trent said. "Then what?"

"What do you think? I did what I do, I slid up on them fat motherfuckers with my AR ready to air 'em out."

"But you didn't," Gamble asked nervously.

Buck looked disappointed when he answered. "Nah, I let them go. I didn't want to make the situation any more unsettling for Honey. She'd already been through enough. You know, being robbed, and seeing how much of a pussy her husband is—"

"Did she recognize you?" Trent asked.

"Who do you think you talking to? This is what I do. Of course she didn't recognize me. I keep telling y'all, this is what I do."

Gamble, Naji, and Trent all looked up in shock as Dawn stood in front of their table with her arms folded. Her nostrils flared as she fixed Buck with a stare that wiped the smile right off of his face.

"You think that shit you did tonight was cute?"

Buck opened his mouth, but nothing came out.

"I want to see you in the office, right now," she said to Trent.

Trent looked up to the office. He sighed when he saw Julisa hitting him with the same stare Dawn was giving Buck.

Dawn turned to Gamble. "We kinda keep him in the shadows," she said, repeating what he told her earlier.

He shrugged.

"I'll be waiting," Dawn said to Trent as she headed to the office.

"This is what you do, huh?" Trent said to Buck.

Buck reached for his shot glass and gulped it down. Trent stood up and headed to the office.

Buck shook his head.

"Why you shaking your head?" Gamble asked.

"I should've known."

"Should've known what?"

"As many times as I caught Honey staring at me, how could she not recognize me?"

"Buck, what in the fuck are you talking about?" Gamble asked.

Buck looked at Naji. "Tell him, Naji."

"All jokes aside, Buck," Naji said. "You need help, for real."

"All jokes aside," Buck said coming to the edge of his seat. "Ya'll need to get your heads out of your asses and pay attention to what's going on around you. You didn't just see how Honey was staring at me with lust in her eyes?"

"Lust?" Naji said. "She looked like she wanted to kill you."

"What? You crazy? That's the same look women give me right after I finish putting that bedroom work in."

All Gamble and Naji could do was pour themselves another shot and toss 'em back.

When Trent walked into the office, Dawn stared at him. "Look," Trent said. "I know you didn't want a security detail following you around, especially when your husband doesn't know what you're doing, but—"

"Trent," Dawn said. "Shut up. I didn't call you in here to argue with you. I wanted to thank you." She sat down, still a little shaken up from earlier. "Everything was going so well. And then out of nowhere those men just showed up. All I kept thinking about was how helpless I was." Julisa stood by her and rested her hand on her shoulder. "And then when I saw Buck... I wanted to snatch that gun from him and murder them faggots right there on the spot."

"We can't have you killing anyone," Trent said. "That's not good for business."

Dawn stood up. "I have to get out of here, my husband's outside waiting for me."

"Honey," Trent called out to her as she opened the office door. "I know how you feel about Buck. I'll find something else for him to do."

"You know I don't want any kind of security around me. But if you're going to have someone shadowing me, I would prefer it to be his crazy ass."

Trent shrugged. "Whatever you say."

"By the way, do you think you can find out who those guys were?"

"I'll put the word out. Chances are, they do this on the regular, so someone has to know something. If I find them, what do you want me to do?"

Dawn thought about it for a moment. "Bring them to the carwash and then call me."

"Dawn," Julisa called out, but she slammed the door.

Dawn sighed as she stepped into the elevator and headed up to The Bank. She winced as she opened and closed the puffy hand that the fake cop had stepped on. It still hurt, but the pain was no comparison to the pain she was feeling mentally. She had money, she had men worth millions vying for her attention in The Vault, and she had men around her who would put that work in. If all of this was happening five years ago, she would be the happiest woman alive, but it wasn't five years ago. And what made her the happiest woman alive today was Dante. Her husband, her best friend, her true love. The man of her dreams who she'd been lying to for months. *I can't go on like this*, she thought. If he ever found out... The elevators doors opened and she stepped out into The Bank. She was making her way to the front entrance when she stopped in her tracks. Dante was sitting at the bar, Whitty was sitting on a stool next to him, listening to him. Whitty put her hand over her mouth at something Dante said. He gulped down the drink in front of him and continued talking. Whitty placed her hand on his forearm and said something. Dante nodded. Whitty crossed her legs, exposing a large amount of thigh that her miniskirt couldn't hide.

Dawn's eyelids fell to slits as she made a beeline toward them.

Whitty was the first to see her. She flashed Dawn a worried smile. "Hey, girl."

Dante turned around. Dawn stopped in front of him.

"I thought you were going to wait in the car."

"I was, but after what happened tonight, I needed a drink."

"Dante told me what happened," Whitty said in a concerned tone. She removed her hand from his forearm.

"I see you've met Whitty," Dawn said with a hint of sarcasm.

"Yes, she's the one who got me into the club."

Whitty quickly explained. "I was outside having a cigarette, when I heard him telling Cash that he was your husband. Of course Cash didn't believe him and told him to get to the back of the line."

"And how did you know he was my husband?" Dawn asked her.

"Girl, as much as you describe how fine he is... I knew it was him."

Dante blushed.

Dawn took a deep breath. *Tomorrow,* she said to herself. *I can stomp a mud hole in her ass tomorrow.* "You ready to go?" she asked Dante.

"Yes." He finished his drink. "Thanks for the drink," he said to Whitty, "and for listening."

"It was a pleasure to finally meet you." The way Whitty smiled at him almost made Dawn say to hell with tomorrow, she could stomp a mud hole in her ass right now.

"What's up with you?" Dante asked Dawn on their way home.

"I wasn't even gone for ten minutes and you were all up in Whitty's face, telling her what happened to us?"

"Like I said, I needed a drink, she got me in the club and gave me a drink. She knew something was wrong. She said she could see it in my eyes. I just planned on telling her that we had a rough night, but when I started talking, it all just came out."

"Well, Whitty or anyone else for that matter, doesn't need to be in our business."

"Look who's talking. You're the one who begged me to go out of our way to come down here to tell Julisa what happened."

"That's different. Lowe's people are pretty connected, and there's a good chance that they may know who those guys were."

"And if they do?"

Dawn didn't respond. Dante looked over at her. When he realized she wasn't going to say anything else about the subject, he focused on the road.

CHAPTER 11

*A*t five o'clock, Dawn punched out from her day job and headed to the townhouse. She waited for Buck's car to coast by. It didn't. It had been three weeks since the incident in Central Park, and for three weeks, she hadn't once been able to spot Buck tailing her, but she always knew he was there. Just like how she knew he was there, right now. She went inside, waited fifteen minutes, and then called his cell.

"Where are you?" she asked him when he picked up.

"I'm around."

"Where's around?"

"In the shadows, that's what I do."

"I need to talk to you."

"I'm listening."

"I need to talk face to face."

"Can't."

"Why not?"

"I'm not supposed to."

"Says who?"

"I'm just not supposed to."

"My bad. I'll call your master, Trent, and see if he'll let you talk to me face to face."

The doorbell rang.

Dawn smiled as she walked to the door and opened it.

Buck had on a blazer and a pair of slacks. He stood with his hands clasped behind his back. "Just so you know," he started as he took off his shades, "psychological warfare, that's what I do. So, all that calling my master... Thinking that would get me to ring your doorbell... I saw right through that."

"So why'd you come out of the shadows?"

"I just wanted to tell you *face to face* that you can't game me."

"You coming in or are you just going to stand out there?"

Buck gave the street one more glance before stepping in.

"You want something to drink?" Dawn asked, as she headed to the kitchen.

"I'm good, thanks for asking, though." Buck stood in the center of the living room.

Dawn walked out of the kitchen with a bottled water in hand. "Sit down."

"I've been sitting in my car all day."

"You can at least take off that hot ass blazer."

"I'm good."

"Is the blazer concealing something?" Dawn asked.

"Something like that."

"Is it big?"

"Very," Buck said, not missing a beat.

Dawn took a sip of her water, wetting her lips. "Can I see it?"

"What kind of guy do you think I am? I just don't go around pulling out my hardware for every woman who wants to see it."

"I'm not every woman now, am I?"

"No, you're not."

"So, show it to me."

"I don't know."

Dawn walked up to him. "Don't make me reach in and pull it out myself."

Buck took a step back and reached into his blazer. His hand came out with the biggest gun Dawn ever laid eyes on.

"It's humongous, Buck." She looked up from the gun and into his eyes. "Can I hold it?"

"It might be too much for you to handle."

Dawn put her water down. "I'll hold it with two hands." She reached for it.

Buck reluctantly handed it to her. The gun looked like a cannon in Dawn's small hands.

"What kind of gun is this?" she asked.

"Colt 45, semi-automatic. Ten in the clip, one in the head. Bullets, jacketed hollow-point. Hit a motherfucker with that, he's flying across the room and sticking to the wall."

Dawn got into a shooting stance and aimed it in different directions. She could feel the gun weighing her arms down. She lowered it and handed it back. "You're right, it's too big for me. You don't have anything smaller, on you?"

"I'm not a walking arsenal."

"I just thought that maybe—" Buck pulled a .38 snub-nose from the small of his back. "I thought you weren't a walking arsenal?" Dawn smirked.

"I'm not, but I got to have a backup."

Dawn took the gun from him. It was lighter, but felt bulky in her hands. She handed it back to him. "I guess my hands are too small for guns."

Buck stuck the gun into the back of his pants and kept his eyes on her as he bend down and pulled a .32 out of his ankle holster.

"Another backup?" Dawn asked.

"A backup for the backup." He handed her the gun.

Dawn nodded as she handled it.

"So, what did you have to talk to me about that had to be done face to face?" Buck asked, as he held his hand out for the gun.

Dawn held the gun behind her back. "I need a gun like this."

"Oh, hell no."

"Just hear me out—"

"I'm not giving you a gun, Trent will kill me."

"That night when those men tried to rob us, I felt so help-less. If I had a gun that night—"

"Having a gun, and being able to use one is two different things."

"I can shoot someone if I have to. Let me have this one."

"Honey, don't do this to me." He stuck his hand out further for the gun.

Dawn reluctantly handed it over.

"Is this all you wanted to talk to me about?" Buck asked.

"Bye," Dawn said, pointing to the door.

Buck stuck the .32 back in its holster and turned to leave. When he reached the front door, he stopped and turned around. "Can I get that bottled water you offered earlier?"

"Are you serious?"

"My throat is kind of dry."

Dawn rolled her eyes and headed to the kitchen. "Just so you know," she yelled from the fridge, "I was beginning to like you. Thanks for letting me know where your loyalty really lies." She grabbed the bottled water and headed back into the living room. "Nothing to say, huh?" She looked around. Buck was gone. She looked down on the coffee table and couldn't help but smile. The .32 lay there, in its ankle holster.

How was work?" Dante asked Dawn as she walked in.

"I still have a job."

Dante looked up from his laptop. "Stop saying that. You know they're not going to fire you."

Dawn walked up on him and kissed him. He stood up and pinned her to the wall. Dawn moaned as she felt him stiffening against her. "Slow down, sexy," she whispered. "Let me get out of these clothes and take a shower."

"Let me get you out of those clothes, and afterwards, I'll give you a shower." Dante pulled down his shorts and showed her how ready he was.

"Damn, baby. If your dick was a gun, it would be a Colt .45."

"What's that supposed to mean?"

"Private joke," Dawn whispered.

"Private joke, huh? Well this ain't no joke," he said, grabbing himself.

Dawn pulled away from him. "You know nothing's going down until I take a shower and brush my teeth."

Dante reluctantly let her go. "If you're not out in five, I'm coming in after you."

Dawn kissed him on the cheek and headed upstairs. Dante sat back down at his laptop and went back to putting the finishing touches on his article for his column. He looked toward Dawn's purse when he heard her cell phone ring. "Your phone is ringing," he yelled up to her. She didn't hear him so he got up and grabbed her bag. He reached into it and pulled her phone out. "What the hell?" He held her phone in his hand, but it wasn't the one ringing. He unzipped the inside pocket and pulled out the ringing phone. The caller ID said Andre Wilks. He started to answer it, but decided against it.

He calmed down and put the phone back. *There has to be a good explanation for this. She has two cell phones because...* *Fuck that.* He answered it. "Hello?" Andre hung up before Dante answered the call.

Feeling his blood pressure rise, Dante scrolled down the numbers on the phone. Andre, Bono, Buck, Gamble, Julisa, Naji, Trent, Whitty... The only names familiar to him was Julisa's and Whitty's. Who were the other numbers who all happen to belong to men? Dante headed upstairs to confront

Dawn, but stopped at the top of the steps. *What if I confront her and she tells me something I'm not prepared to hear?*

Dawn sat in the backseat of the Range Rover talking to Julisa on the phone when Bono pulled up to Chance's hotel. "I have to go, I'll call you when we're back on the road," Dawn said to Julisa.

"Be careful," Julisa said with concern in her voice.

"Aren't I always?"

"Just call me when you're out of there."

Dawn hung up.

"You ready?" Bono said, looking back at her.

"Yeah, I feel like a million bucks."

"Why, because you're sitting on a million?" Dawn was sitting on a million, literally. They just came from Chinatown where they picked up a million in dirty cash from Chin-li. Chinatown's biggest dealer.

"No," Dawn said. "Money isn't the only thing that can make a woman happy."

"I must be dealing with the wrong women then."

"Let's go, before I tear off in your behind for that stereotypical remark."

They got out and headed inside. Chance was at the front desk waiting for them.

"Honey," he said, extending his hand. "It's always a pleasure to see you."

"I'm sure." Dawn said.

He led them to the service elevator. Once they were inside and ascending to the top floor, Bono spoke.

"You take care of your situation?" he said to Chance.

"Situation?" Chance said.

Even though Dawn didn't know what situation Bono was referring to, she could hear the nervousness in Chance's voice.

"The situation between you and Trini," Bono said.

"It's nothing," Chance said.

"I hardly call a war, nothing."

Dawn's eyes widened.

"War?" Chance said, laughing. "I would've annihilated Trini if we were at war. He is a pestering gnat buzzing around my head."

"You can't expect to setup shop in someone else's territory and not ruffle some feathers," Bono said, keeping his eyes on the elevator numbers as they lit up one by one.

"How do you know about me and Trini's dealings?"

"Honey pays me to keep her abreast on situations that may effect her business dealings."

Dawn rolled with the story. "Lowe's business is successful because it's discreet. We're not with the unnecessary attention."

"I assure you, Honey, the last thing Trini wants is a war."

The women sitting in front of the money counters immediately started feeding money into them when Chance, Honey, and Bono walked in.

"I would offer you something to drink, but I know you will turn me down," Chance said to Dawn.

"I'm here for one thing and one thing only," Dawn said. Not taking her eyes off the money counters.

"A woman who's about her business, there's nothing more sexier," Chance said with lust in his eyes.

Dawn cracked a smile. "What I tell you about giving me compliments? You're going to make me put you over my knee."

Chance shuddered. "I pray that day comes soon."

Dawn ignored his last comment. A half hour later, the million and a half was stuffed into two duffel bags.

"Consider this a favor," Dawn said, lifting the bags. "You know I only do a mill at a time."

"Whatever you need, I will be more than happy to return the favor," Chance said.

"I bet."

He led them back down to the lobby. As they rounded the corner, Chance was saying something to Dawn, but she tuned him out when Bono put his arm around her waist. That was the danger sign. Something was wrong. Dawn had to focus on putting one foot in front of the other, so she wouldn't panic. When she looked in the direction Bono was looking in, she knew what was wrong. Three men were in the lounge area staring at them. Three men with dreadlocks.

Chance saw them and screwed up his face. "He got a lot of nerve—" he started to say, but his words were cut short when Trini reached into his jacket and drew his gun. His men followed suit. Bono had his gun drawn before Trini's cleared his side. Bono swung his gun in the dreads's direction while pushing Dawn to the ground. Bono's first bullet hit the dread on Trini's left that punched a gaping hole in his chest. The rest of his bullets hit the wall where Trini was standing milliseconds before he sought cover behind patrons unlucky enough to be in the lounge at the time.

"You're a dead man, Trini, you hear me?" Chance said, spittle flying from his mouth. He jerked forward as bullets penetrated his back. Bono spun and fired at Trini's men who crept in from the back. Dawn crawled behind the front desk where the receptionist was cowering with her hands covering her ears. Bono continued firing at the men in the rear, while taking cover behind the front desk, as well.

"Me, brother," Trini called out to him. "I have no beef with you or your lady friend. Just leave the bags them there, and you can walk out of here."

Bono looked at Dawn. She couldn't get the straps off her shoulders quick enough.

"We're walking out of here, and the bags are coming with us." Bono shouted back.

"What?" Dawn whispered. "Fuck is you talking about? These dreads don't play."

"Which is why they're not going to let us walk out of here." He ejected the spent clip in his gun and slapped in a fresh one. The men that came through the back were creeping toward them. Bono flipped his phone open and hit speed dial. Dawn looked at Chance's lifeless body. She could smell the urine and feces his body let loose upon his death. His eyes were opened, with a surprised look still plastered on his face. She jumped when Bono put his hand on her shoulder. "Get ready to bolt for the front door," he said, flipping his phone shut.

"We're pinned in from the front and the back." She nearly lost control of her bowels when she heard what sounded like a Gatling gun.

Bono grabbed her by the hand and hauled her off the ground. They ran toward the front door. Bono was firing at Trini and his man. Dawn turned her head around at the automatic cannon going off behind them. A gunman clothed in an all black leather suit, complete with a full-face helmet had crept up on Trini's men from the behind. He was firing off an AK, blowing body parts off of Trini's men.

Bono shoved Dawn through the front door. A quick scan of the street let him know the coast was clear. They ran to the Range. As soon as Dawn jumped in, bullets blew out the back window. Bono returned fire on the Benz SUV across the street. He ran over to the driver's side, while firing at Trini's men and hoped in. He peeled off just as Trini and his man exited the hotel. They fired at the Range, hitting the taillights. The Benz SUV peeled off after them, followed by Trini and the only man of his who made it out of the hotel alive.

Bono shoved his headset into his ear and hit speed dial on his phone. "Where are you? I got two on me," he said into the piece.

"I'm right behind them," Eva said into her headset. She swung the AK over the bike's windshield and fired at the SUV Trini was in. the AK's bullets tore through the truck like a wet paper bag. Four of the bullets hit Trini's driver. The truck swerved and crashed into a row of parked cars.

The shooters in the back of the Benz truck stopped firing at Bono and Dawn and directed their gunfire at Eva. She hopped the bike onto the sidewalk. Bono looked in the rearview mirror. Eve didn't have a chance against two gunmen. He handed his gun to Dawn and let down her window.

"Point and pull the trigger," he shouted, as he weaved in and out of traffic.

"What?"

"Do it! Now!"

Dawn turned around in her seat and stuck the gun out the window. She fired four shots before the gun clicked empty. The driver of the Benz truck swerved. Dawn sat back in her seat.

"It's empty!"

"I don't have any more clips." Bono looked into the rearview mirror at Eva. She was on her own.

Dawn pulled her pant leg up and pulled the .32 out of the ankle holster.

"What the f—" Bono watched her as she hung out the window and emptied the clip at the Benz truck. Most of her bullets hit the headlights and the front bumper. Smoke shot out of the grille, but the SUV didn't slow. Bono blew through the red light at the intersection with the Benz right behind him. Eva jumped the curb and was gaining on the Benz truck. A van clipped the back of the bike, sending her and the motorcycle skidding across the intersection. She got to her feet groggily and took off her helmet.

"Are you okay?" a man asked her. She grabbed the AK that was slung across her back. The man took off. Eva pointed the machine gun at the driver of a cement truck that was headed her way. The driver skidded to a halt.

"Get the fuck out," Eva said, keeping the gun on him. He hopped out and ran. She climbed in and pulled off.

"Where are you?" she said into her headset.

"Still on Fourteenth Street, and these motherfuckers are still on me," Bono answered.

"Make a left and come back up Thirteenth Street."

"You got a plan?" He listened intently and then smiled.

Dawn grabbed the door handle when Bono hung a sharp left and head up Thirteenth Street. "You're heading back the way we came."

"I know."

"What sense does that make?"

"Just sit tight."

Bono floored the Range Rover, putting a little more distance between them and the Benz truck.

"This is crazy," Dawn said.

They were coming up at the intersection fast. That's when Bono saw the cement truck. As soon as he hit the intersection, he gritted his teeth and made a hard right turn. At the same time, Eva switched lanes, putting the truck on a head-on collision with the Benz SUV. The driver of the Benz realized it too late. He hit the brakes. Eva hit the gas. The impact sounded like a box of dynamite going off. The Benz crumpled up like an accordion. The driver and passenger side airbags deployed, saving the men in the front seats. The gunman in the back, who was careless enough not to have his seat belt on, was catapulted through the sunroof and splattered against the cement truck's grille. The cement truck kept plowing forward. Grinding metal and sparks had onlookers ducking for cover. The cement truck finally came to a stop when it sandwiched the SUV against the side of a building. Eva jumped out, holding her shoulder. She ran into a nearby apartment building and stripped off the leather suit in the stairwell, revealing her short shorts and a cropped T-shirt that stopped just above her navel. She let her hair down and walked out into the crowd of dazed people, and put her headset back on.

"You okay?" She asked Bono.

"We're good, and you?"

"I'm good."

"You sure?" Bono sounded concerned.

"Positive. See you in BK." She disconnected the call. "Hey," she called out to a cab driver gawking at the accident. She walked up to him and placed a fifty-dollar bill in his hand. "I'm in a rush."

"Then, I'm your man," the cab driver said, unlocking the back door of his cab.

"You okay?" Bono asked Dawn.

"Hell no, I'm not okay." Her phone vibrated in her pocket. She screamed and swatted at it. "Dammit, shit almost gave me a fucking heart attack."

Bono cracked a smile.

"I'm glad you find this shit funny."

"Where'd you get the gun?" Bono turned serious.

"What?"

"The gun. Where'd you get it?"

"Does it matter? It's a good thing I had it." It was then that Dawn realized she was no longer holding the gun. She spotted it on the floor between her feet. She picked it up and slid it back in the ankle holster. "The woman in that cement truck, she looked like—"

"Yes, it was Eva."

"And the man on the motorcycle?"

"Wasn't a man."

"That was her, too?"

"Yes." He pulled over.

"What's up now?" Dawn asked.

"We can't drive around in a bullet-riddled car." He got out and retrieved the two duffel bags from the safe under the backseat and slung them over his shoulders. "Grab those two bags and let's go."

"Where are we going?" Dawn asked as she slung the bags over her shoulders.

Bono pointed with his chin toward the train station. Three trains later, they were in the Brownsville section of Brooklyn hailing a cab. Bono told the driver to drop them off in front of

Howard Projects. Dawn gave up on trying to get answers out of him. All he kept saying was "Keep your eyes open." He took off his suit jacket and dress shirt in back of the cab and stuffed them into one of the duffel bags. He was just wearing a white tank top and slacks.

A swarm of thugs were standing outside the building the cab stopped in front of. They all glared at the cab as it pulled up. Dawn saw a couple of them slide their hands inside their jackets. Bono grabbed her hand and exited the cab.

"Look at this nigga, here," someone in the crowd yelled out.

"Yeah," Bono replied. "Look at *this* nigga, here." Dawn's grip tightened around his hand.

As they got closer, Dawn realized why Bono had taken off his shirt. Everyone in the mob was tatted up.

"What it be?" Bono said.

"You already know," Monster-Sick replied. He looked like a cock-diesel Rick Ross.

"All day," Bono said.

"Everyday," Monster-Sick replied.

Bono walked into the midst of them and bumped fists with certain members of the group. The women in the pack were staring Dawn down daring her to get out of line.

"Who's the pretty momma that I would like to get to know better?" Monster-Sick asked Bono.

"This is my boss, Honey."

"You got a skirt pulling your strings, nigga?" Monster-Sick said laughing.

"Don't forget who pulls your strings, *nigga*."

Monster-Sick held his hands up. "I'm just fucking with you."

"I'm not in the fucking around mood."

"Neither was Eva."

"Where is she?" Bono asked.

As if she heard her name, Eva stepped out of the building. She had changed into a pair of tennis sneakers, fitted jeans, and a sky blue tank top. She was tatted up, as well. She sashayed up to Bono and kissed him passionately.

She looked at Dawn. "You okay?"

"Yeah," Dawn replied, still uneasy about the glares she was getting.

Eva caught the stares hitting Dawn from all sides. "What the fuck you bitches looking at?"

The women rolled their eyes and found some place else to look.

Bono took the duffel bags off his shoulders and handed them to Eva. "Take these and Honey upstairs. I'll be up after me and my boy handle some business."

"I love it when you come home," Monster-Sick said, rubbing his hands together. "You always make my pockets fat."

When both women entered the tiny apartment, Dawn sat the bags next to the ones Eva placed on the table.

"Thank you," Dawn said.

"For what?"

"For being there for us earlier." Eva didn't respond. "Are you okay?" Dawn asked.

"I'm fine."

Dawn could see the way she was holding her shoulder that she wasn't. "Are you sure?"

"Bitch, what the fuck did I just say? And for the record, I wasn't there for you and Bono, I was there for Bono."

Eva was five-six, an inch taller than Dawn. She had an athletic build, and the attitude of a street fighter. But with a bum shoulder, Dawn knew she could whip her ass all around the small apartment, or so she thought.

"Whatever," Dawn said with attitude.

"Yeah, whatever," Eva said with more attitude.

Bono walked in and felt the tension. He looked at Eva and then at Dawn. "Which ones are the bags from Chin-li?"

"The ones on the right," Dawn said.

Bono put them on the floor and opened the bags they collected from Chance.

"What are you doing?" Dawn asked.

"Mr. Green is expecting a million, not a million five."

"Wait—" Dawn began to protest.

"Mr. Green is going to get his mill and you and I are going to split the five hundred thou fifty, fifty; you got a problem with that?"

Dawn didn't' say another word. Bono counted off two hundred and fifty and slid it on the table in front of her. He slid the remaining two hundred and fifty toward Eva. "I want you to go out with Monster-Sick and the team tonight. I want you to put the bullets in Trini's head, personally."

Eva nodded. She scooped up the money and left the apartment.

Bono's phone rang. It was Mr. Green. Bono had been ignoring his calls all afternoon. He finally answered. "We had a problem."

"It's all over the news," Mr. Green said. "Where are you?"

"In a safe place."

"And Honey?"

"She's with me. She was able to pickup the money before the shooting started."

Mr. Green was silent for a moment. "When can you bring it in?"

"Tomorrow afternoon."

"I'll be expecting you."

Bono hung up.

"Just when I think I got you all figured out," Dawn said, looking at Bono in a whole different light.

"I was just thinking the same thing. I would've never taken you for a chick who could hang out a window of a moving vehicle, busting shots."

"I've never done that in my life. And trust me, I won't be doing that anytime soon." She stared at his tattoos. "Who are you, really, Bono? You've went from a bouncer to an enforcer to... a gang leader?"

"And who are you, really, Dawn? You've went from a drug dealer's girl to a wife of a Wall Street investor to Honey the underboss."

"Touché. So, what do we do now?"

"I'm going to get a shopping bag to put that money in and drive you to your job, so you can pick up your car and head home."

Bono dropped her at her car, but Dawn didn't head home. Instead, she made a pit stop to her townhouse to change out of her dingy and scuffed up clothing and stashed her two hundred and fifty grand and .32 that she would have to get bullets for. On her way out to the car, her cell rang. The ring tone told her it was Dante.

"I'm on my way home, babe," she said, as she answered the phone.

"I've been trying to reach you for hours."

"I got caught up." She climbed into her car and started it up.

"I'll wait up for you."

"Okay, I'll see you when I get there." She didn't get a chance to put her phone down before it went off again. "Julisa before you start—"

"I'm having a nervous breakdown," Julisa cried. "Chance's hotel is all over the news. The police are still wheeling bodies out of there. Why didn't you call me? Why didn't you answer my calls?"

"I was too busy trying to stay alive! Cut me some slack, I almost died today." Dawn shuddered at the reality of her words.

"I'm sorry," Julisa said. "I didn't know what to do. I called Mr. Green and he said he didn't hear anything from you, I called Bono's cell, and he wasn't answering, I'm a wreck, right now."

"And drunk."

"And it's your fault," Julisa slurred.

"I'm sorry for worrying you. I'm on my way home. I'll call you when I get there."

"Before I forget, Whitty's been calling you off the hook, as well."

"Yes, I know. Whatever she has to tell me can wait til tomorrow."

"Dante called her," Julisa whispered.

"What?"

"He called the club and asked to speak with her. She didn't know it was him until she got on the phone."

"What did he want?" Dawn's grip on the phone tightened.

"He thanked her for listening to him the night he came in, then he asked her for the names of the bouncers."

"Why would he want their names?"

"Whitty thought the same thing. She told him that she wasn't sure if she could give out that information. He told her to forget about it, that it wasn't that important, and then he hung up."

"I can't deal with this, right now. I'll call you tomorrow." Dawn hung up without waiting for a response. *Why would Dante want to know the names of the bouncers?*

CHAPTER 12

*D*ante was putting the finishing touches on dinner when Dawn walked in. She took the lid off a pot and took a whiff. She tried to identify the meat through the thick sauce. "Oxtails?"

"Yes, Oxtails," Dante said, wiping his hands off on his apron. "How was work?"

Between Dante calling the club wanting to know the names of the bouncers, and the tone he used to ask his question, she knew he probably called her job.

"Actually, I didn't go in today."

"But you called earlier and said—"

"Yes, I know what I said."

"So, where were you?"

"I was with Julisa."

"Julisa?"

"Yes, she's missing Lowe something terrible, so I decided to spend the day with her. We went shopping."

"Why couldn't you just tell me that?"

"Because you would've gotten on me for calling in sick just to spend the day shopping."

Dante was silent.

"What's up with you calling The Bank, wanting to know the names of the bouncers?"

"I want to know who you're working around."

"Why couldn't you just ask me."

"It doesn't matter. I want you to quit The Bank."

"What? Why?" Dawn said shocked.

"That was our agreement, remember? I find a job, start bringing in a paycheck, and you quit bartending."

"I just can't quit."

"Why not?"

"Because… that's not good work ethics."

"So now you care about work ethics?"

"I'm not quitting my job, I'm making good money. We're no longer struggling to make ends meet."

"With my job and your state job, we'll live comfortably."

"I can't believe how selfish you're being, right now."

"Selfish?" Dante said, amazed that Dawn would say that. "How do you figure that?"

"You're making me quit, because of your insecurities."

"What am I insecure about? You making more money than me?"

"No, you think someone at The Bank is going to take me from you, that's why you wanted to know the names of the bouncers."

"That's not it."

"Then what is it?"

Dante thought of bringing up the cell phone he found in her bag.

"Well?" Dawn said, putting her hands on her hips.

"Dawn, just do this for me."

"What about me and what I want?"

"Why don't you for once stop thinking about your damn self and look at what I've had to do since you took on that extra job. I'm cooking dinner almost every night, doing laundry, house chores, yard work…"

"You have the luxury of being able to work from home, so being that you're here all day anyway…"

Dante took off his apron and threw it to the floor. "I'm done. No more cooking. I don't give a damn if the hamper is overflowing with clothes. I'm not a slave." He stormed out the kitchen.

Dawn ran after him. "Dante, wait." She ran in front of him. "Look at me." He kept staring past her. "Dante, please, look at me." He dropped his eyes down to meet hers. "You know I always do what you say, right?"

He didn't answer.

"Right?"

"Yes."

"I'm making good money. Real good money. You know I am. Over four hundred dollars every weekend in tips alone." Dawn grabbed his hands and kissed them. "Baby, if you're worried about a Casanova sweeping me off my feet, that already happened. And I married him five years ago."

Dante thought about the cell phone. Maybe it wasn't hers. Maybe one of the girls left it laying around somewhere and she picked it up, planning to give back when she saw her again.

"Talk to me, Dante."

He chewed on his bottom lip for a moment. "Okay."

"Thank you, baby." She kissed him on the cheek and headed upstairs.

"Where you going? I'm about to serve dinner?"

"I'm going to change into some sweats; I'll be down in ten minutes."

Dante sighed and headed back into the kitchen. He fixed their plates and sat them at the kitchen table. On his way to the refrigerator, he spotted Dawn's bag on the counter. He looked up to the ceiling and then back to her bag. *Fuck it,* he thought. He opened her bag. His eyebrows furrowed when he found the cell phone tucked away in the same side pocket. He flipped it open and scrolled down the text messages.

Dawn where the hell are you? Call me. It was a text from Julisa at twelve o'clock.

Dawn I'm freaking out, where the hell are you? It was another text from Julisa at one thirty.

Dawn, your business with Chance should've been over an hour ago. Get your ass out of that hotel and call me, immediately!!! Julisa's last text was at two fifteen.

Dante's hands shook as he stared at the last text. All he saw was Chance and hotel.

"Hey, baby, I'm ready to eat." Dawn said, walking into the kitchen.

"I lost my appetite," he said, as he held up the phone for her to see.

"You went into my purse?"

"Who the fuck is Chance?"

Dawn's mouth dropped.

"You weren't with Julisa today. You were with this guy at a hotel."

"Dante, it's not like that."

"Julisa's messages are clear."

"It's not what you think."

"It's not what I think, It's what I know. You lied to me. First, you had me thinking you got stuck at work, come to find out, you didn't even go to work, then you tell me you were with Julisa, and I come to find out you weren't. And how did I find this out? On a cell phone that you kept hidden in your purse."

"Dante, I can explain this if you let me talk."

"You must think I'm stupid. All that extra money you've been bringing in, I knew something wasn't right. Hundreds of dollars in tip money, Julisa giving you raises, winning lotteries at your job. All this time you've been..." Dante almost retched as he said it, "fucking these niggas for money."

"Stop right there!" Dawn said, trying to shut him up.

"I saw their names. Gamble, Naji, Trent, Andre... Yeah, I called The Bank today and asked Whitty for the names of the bouncers. She covered for you though; she didn't give their names up. So I went down there myself and I asked around. It wasn't hard to find out who they were, nor was it hard to find out who you were, *Honey*."

"Dante, no, baby, please—"

"Every five minutes, all I heard was 'Honey this and Honey that'. Then when I heard 'Honey from Charlotte', I almost had a seizure. What's the chance of Honey being from the same state as my wife? Then I asked Cassidy who Honey was and she looked at me like I was one of those husbands who are always the last to know."

"Let me expl—"

"No more explanations, get out!"

"What?"

"I said, get the fuck out!" He stuffed the phone back in her purse and threw it at her.

"Dante, just please calm down."

He shoved her out of the kitchen, causing her to stumble and fall on the living room floor. He picked her up and shoved her to the front door. "Go and stay with one of the men you've been selling your ass to," Dante said, teary-eyed.

Dawn slapped, kicked and punched him as he pushed her out of the door. "Dante!"

He slammed the door in her face.

"Dante!" She banged on the door. "Dante! Listen to me." She kicked the door. "Dante!" She cried and kept calling his name for ten minutes. "Fuck you, Dante. After all I did for your sorry ass, you're going to treat me like this? I don't need you, you hear me? Fuck you!" She wiped her tears and climbed into her car. She cried all the way to the Townhouse. She let herself in and collapsed on the couch. She wrapped her arms around a pillow and tried to rock the pain away.

"You want me to take care of him?"

She spun around, shocked to see Buck standing behind her. "What?"

"I can make it look like an accident or a suicide."

"What the f… how'd you get in here?"

"You left your keys in the door," he said, holding them up.

Dawn turned back around and continued to rock.

Buck walked around and sat on the couch opposite her.

"Na, ah," Dawn said, looking up at him. "You can leave, go back into the shadows."

He didn't move.

"Where the fuck were you when all that shit happened at the hotel."

"Trent said when you're with Bono, I don't need to follow you."

"Whatever. You can go now."

"Are you going to be all right?"

"I just lost the only man I ever loved, what do you think?"

"He found out about what you do?"

"Worse, he thinks I'm… sleeping with men for money."

"Why would he think that?"

"It's a long story."

Buck stood up. "For what it's worth, when I saw him throw you out, I had made up my mind to hurt him real bad. But when I peeked into the living room window, he was sitting on the couch, like you are right now, crying his eyes out."

Dawn sniffled, as she watched him walk toward the front door.

"You sure you don't want him to have an accident?"

"Buck—"

"All right, I was just asking."

The next night when Dawn entered Julisa's office, they sat and cried together. Bono stepped in later that night and told Dawn that Trini had been taken care of, and that Mr. Green was impressed with the way she handled herself. Dawn nodded without emotion. From that night, she threw herself into work to keep from thinking about Dante.

The team saw just how much pain she had inside her when Trent finally got a lead on the phony detectives and had them brought to the carwash. Both men sat with their hands cuffed behind their backs, swearing on dead relatives that they didn't rob anyone connected to their team. They both stared at Dawn like they had seen the Devil when she stepped into the garage. The one who punched Dante to the ground, and stomped on her hand, started copping a plea, and begged for Dawn not to kill him.

"You got it twisted," she said with a sadistic smile. "I'm not going to kill you." She walked up to Buck and held out her hand. He dug into his pocket and handed her a pair of brass knuckles. Dawn slid them on and slowly walked toward the two men. "But, in about five minutes, you'll be begging me to."

Julisa looked on in horror as Dawn pummeled fat man's face. Long after he lost consciousness, Dawn was still hooking off like Mike Tyson. Fat man's partner was crying like a baby, pleading with anyone on the team who made eye contact with him. Dawn turned to him without warning and shattered his jaw with her first blow. After turning his face into mush, it took Gamble, Naji, and Trent to stop her from swinging. Julisa's screaming jolted her out of her trance. She was huffing when she commanded Trent to dump them where he found them.

Trent told Buck to drive Julisa home. He told Gamble to take Dawn home.

"C'mon, Trent," he whispered. "How come Naji can't take her home?"

"Because Naji has to stay behind and clean up all this blood. Now, grab her and call me when you drop her off."

Gamble spun on him with an attitude and approached Dawn slowly. "Hey, Trent wants me to take you home."

Dawn didn't look at him, she just walked to his car and sat in the passenger's seat. She didn't say anything the whole ride to the townhouse.

"Are you going to be all right?" he asked her, as he pulled up to the curb. Dawn got out without a word. "Hey... Honey." He got out, and followed her inside. Dawn grabbed a bottle of vodka off the kitchen counter and drank it straight.

She turned around and looked at him, surprised that he had followed her in. "See you later," she said, putting down the bottle.

"Are you going to be all right?"

"As soon as I get out of these bloody clothes and take a shower." She walked off, leaving him standing in the kitchen.

"Hold on a minute. Hey, Honey, wait." A minute later, he heard the shower. He stood there for another minute before deciding to go home. He looked at the bottle of sleeping pills next to the bottle of vodka. He snatched them both up and headed to the front door.

"What happened to my bottle of vodka?" Dawn asked.

Gamble turned around. She was looking at him the way she looked at fat boy before she turned his face into tomato soup. Gamble smiled before he answered.

"You don't need that."

"And my pills?"

"I heard those things fuck up your liver."

She came at him so aggressively that her robe came undone. Gamble couldn't believe his eyes. He wasn't shocked at seeing one of her breasts hanging out or even the fact that she was clean-shaven from the navel down. What shocked him was the dope fiend look in her eyes to get to the pills and vodka.

"Honey, you need to chill."

Dawn wrestled with him until he had no choice but to drop the pills and vodka. He grabbed her by her shoulders and shook her.

"You bugging out, yo. What the fuck's the matter with you?"

Dawn looked at him, like she just realized who he was. "It hurts." She collapsed into his arms and stained his shirt with her tears.

Gamble hesitantly put his arms around her. Dawn's arms tightened around his waist as she cried harder. Gamble's cheek was now against her hair. It was still wet from the shower. His eyes fell to her exposed shoulder, triggering pictures of her nakedness he saw just moments ago. He closed his eyes and tried his best to will himself to stop getting hard. He thought about his grandmother's funeral, the three different occasions he got shot, he was going down, but then Dawn squirmed in his arms when she tried to bury her head deeper into his chest. Shit, he said to himself as his little man inflated like a balloon. Dawn looked up at him with watery eyes. He smiled nervously.

"I can't believe you." She shoved him and pulled her robe over her naked shoulder.

"It just happened."

"You are such a dog. I'm dying inside, and in addition to all of the pain that I'm feeling, I have to feel you poking me in the stomach?"

"Honey " He reached out to her, she backed away and headed back to the living room, and plopped down onto the couch. He followed her and stood in front of her. "It's going to be okay."

"Okay? I did what I thought I had to do to keep what little Dante and I had, only to wind up losing everything."

"You still got money, this house…"

"Fuck the money, fuck the house, fuck all of this. It means nothing without Dante."

"Fuck that nigga, he's just a man."

Dawn stood up and smacked him quicker than he could blink. "He's not just a man, he's my husband, my world, my life."

Gamble didn't hear anything she said. All he could think about was the way she slapped him like he was a bitch. If it wasn't for the pain he saw in her eyes, he would've been doing a whole lot more than rubbing his cheek. He froze when she threw her arms around his neck and kissed him.

"Yo," he grabbed her hands from around his neck and stepped back. Dawn grabbed his arms and yanked him toward her, causing them both to fall back on the couch. Dawn wrapped her legs around his waist and gently sucked on his parted lips.

"Honey—" he started to say, but Dawn's hot lips latched onto his neck, short-circuiting his brain. Dawn abruptly stopped and stared at him. Gamble took a deep breath, grateful that she came to her senses. He swallowed hard when she shrugged the robe off her shoulders and began guiding his head to one of her erect nipples.

My God, was all he could say as he stared at her perfectly rounded breast, and a nipple harder than he was. He closed his eyes as his mouth made contact. He could feel the tenseness leaving her body.

She guided his head to her other nipple, as she grinded against his crotch. He could feel her gently pushing his head down. He licked between her breasts, down to her stomach. She kept pushing. When his nose dipped below her waistline, he could smell her need to have him between her legs. He licked his lips as he stared at her swollen clit. A pinch of guilt hit him when he thought of how he was going to wear her out.

"Honey, I can't."

"Shh." She rubbed the back of his head and coaxed him closer to her volcano. Gamble could feel the heat on his face.

"God," he panted. "Nah, Honey, this isn't right. What about Dante?"

"Gamble," she said, looking down at him seductively. "You're a dog, you don't give a fuck about Dante."

"I give a fuck about you, though."

"Then, give me what I need, right now."

"Honey—"

She raised her hips, bringing her juicy peach to his lips. Her nectar seeped onto his taste buds, sending them into a frenzy.

Like someone taking their first hit of crack, he was off to the races. Sweet as honey, was all he could think of as he slurped and sucked on her like a watermelon.

"Damn, you got some sweet pussy," he said, taking a breather.

"Yes," she moaned as her thighs tightened around his head. Gamble knew she was about to come, so he sped up his tongue rotation on her clit.

Dawn cried out as she released. She rode his face through two back arching orgasms. Her legs fell to the floor as she loosened her grip on his head.

Gamble crawled up her, licking her stomach and then each breast. He licked her neck.

Dawn stopped him in mid lick. "I know you're not about to try and stick your tongue in my mouth after what you just did."

He went back to nibbling on her breasts while he started pulling his pants down.

Dawn sat up and closed her robe.

"What's up?" Gamble asked.

"This was a mistake. Not only did I lie to my husband, but now I cheated on him."

"Cheated? You mean... Nah, Honey. A man eating you out isn't cheating."

"What do you call it?"

"Foreplay."

"I'm not thinking straight, you should go."

"What happened to 'give me what I need, right now?'"

"I wanted the pain of losing my husband to go away."

"Did it?"

"Yes, now the pain has been replaced by guilt."

Gamble stood up and snapped his pants shut. "The next time you speak to Cassidy, you need to apologize to her."

"For what?"

"When I get finished taking my frustration out on her, she's going to be pissing and shitting my babies for a week."

CHAPTER 13

*J*ulisa stood in her office in The Vault peering down into the den of the Elite through the one-way-mirror. Dawn was sitting in her VIP booth talking with Andre. Julisa didn't have to hear the conversation, nor be able to read their lips to know that whatever Dawn was whispering in Andre's ear had him on the verge of a mental orgasm. Dawn kept resting her hand on his thigh and would gently give it a rub before removing it. She made sure that when she laughed, she would fall against him, making sure to brush her breast against his shoulder.

Andre leaned over and brushed his lips against Dawn's. Dawn didn't back away like Julisa thought she would. Instead, she placed her hand higher up on his thigh and kissed him. Julisa wanted to turn away, but she couldn't believe that this was the same happily married woman who she introduced to The Vault six months ago. Dawn broke the kiss, but her hand was still massaging Andre's thigh and was creeping further up.

Julisa looked at the phone on her desk and thought about trying to give Dante another call. She'd called him around the clock since him and Dawn's separation. She even surprised herself and went to the house to speak to him face to face, but when he opened the door and she saw the look of hatred on his face toward her, she froze up. He cursed her out and slammed the door in her face. From that moment, she realized that in her frenzy to keep what Lowe built, she destroyed a marriage and lost two friends in the process. She picked up her BlackBerry and texted Dawn.

I need to see you in the office. Julisa looked down and saw when Dawn pulled out her phone and read the text. She put the phone back in her purse and continued talking to Andre.

Julisa texted her again. *Take your hand off his dick and get up here, now!*

Dawn seemed like she had an attitude when she dug into her purse and read the second message. She looked up at the one-way mirror with a sour look. She stuffed her phone back in her purse and whispered into Andre's ear before getting up and walking to the office.

"What the fuck is your problem?" Dawn asked, as she stepped into the office.

"You and Andre a couple, now?"

"Dre's my DWI."

"DWI?"

"Dick without intimacy."

"You lying; I know you didn't take it there with him."

"Yes, I did."

"When did this happen?"

"When we flew down to Barbados and spent the weekend in his villa."

"So, because he flew you to an Island and wooed you with his villa, you gave up the goods?"

"No," Dawn said, knowing where this conversation was going. "I gave up the goods, because I was horny as hell and I was becoming bitchy."

"Maybe I should go and find me a DUI."

"It's DWI, and yes, maybe you should. Maybe then you won't have all this free time to sit up here and watch me."

"I can't believe you just said that to me," Julisa said in a high-pitched voice.

"You know I don't' bite my tongue."

"Well, unlike you, I'm faithful to my man."

"Would he be faithful to you if you were in a coma for six months?"

"Yes!"

Dawn broke out in laughter.

"What's so funny?"

"Did you forget the lipstick on his boxers the night he was gunned down? Or about the night you called me crying, because you found used condoms in the office's trash can? Or—"

"After all I've done for you, this is how you're going to talk to me?"

"After all you've done for me? If it weren't for me, you wouldn't be sitting in this office judging me. Your ass would be home sulking, praying for Lowe to come to and save you. Wake up, Julisa. There is no happily ever after in this story. It's time for you to accept that Lowe's gone."

"Don't say that!"

"You should've pulled the plug a long time ago."

"You bitch!" Julisa yelled at Dawn.

"Are we done?" Dawn said in a bored voice.

"Fuck you Dawn! I can't believe I was feeling sorry for you."

"Get a life, Julisa." With that, Dawn left and headed back to where Andre was patiently waiting. Julisa watched with tears in her eyes as Dawn led Andre out The Vault. Julisa screamed and pounded her fists on her desk. She jumped when she heard the knock on her door. She opened it surprised to see Bono. "What are you doing down here?"

With a smile, he handed her his phone.

"Hello?"

"Hey, Jewels."

Julisa nearly fainted.

Julisa hopped out of Bono's car before it came to a full stop, and ran into the hospital, blowing by the nurse at the reception desk. "Ma'am..." That's all Julisa heard as she entered the elevator and frantically pressed the button that led to Lowe's floor. Once she arrived at his room, the police officer standing in front of Lowe's room spotted her and held his hands up.

"I'm his wife," Julisa screamed.

"Detectives are taking a statement from your husband; you can go in when they're finished."

"Are you serious? I'm his wife, I have a right to go in there, right now."

"Ma'am." Julisa tried pushing past him as she screamed Lowe's name. The doctor came to the door and immediately ushered Julisa in when he saw it was her. Two detectives stood by the bed. They both turned around when they heard Julisa call her husband's name. They moved to the side as she wrapped her arms around his neck and cried.

"Easy, baby," Lowe said just above a whisper. "Did you miss me?"

Julisa nodded as she buried her head deeper into his neck.

"If you gentlemen don't mind," the Doctor said to the two detectives. "Can you resume your interview tomorrow morning?"

"Sure," One of the detectives said. Truth be told, they had no intentions on coming back. They weren't going to waste time trying to find a carjacker who Lowe said he didn't get a look at. The detectives excused themselves and allowed the doctor to lead them out.

Julisa finally pulled away from Lowe and could see that he was crying, as well. He tried to hug her, but he was too weak to put his arms around her. She raised his hands to her mouth and kissed each finger.

"God, I missed you, Jewels."

Hearing Lowe's voice made her start to cry all over again.

He looked toward the door and smiled at Bono. "Tell me something good."

"It's business as usual."

Lowe nodded weakly. "That's what I want to hear."

Julisa rubbed his chest. "You come out of a coma, and the first thing you want to know about is business?"

"The first thing I wanted to know about was you, baby."

"Why'd you call Bono first instead of me then?"

"I didn't call Bono." Lowe paused to catch his breath. "When I came to, there was a young woman sitting in that chair over by the window reading a magazine. When she saw me blinking my eyes, trying to focus on her, she pulled out her cell and called Bono. Said she was a friend of his."

Julisa looked at Bono. He nodded.

"It's a good thing, because the hospital couldn't reach you at the house, The Bank, or on your cell."

"I was in The Vault, and I left my cell in The Bank's office. I'm so careless."

"Shhh, what's important right now is that you're here."

Julisa leaned in and kissed him. "What's important is that you came back to me. When that man pulled your truck door open and shot you—"

"You were there?"

"Yes. After our fight, I followed you."

"Thank God she didn't see you." He grabbed her hands and kissed them, and then he squeezed them as tight as he could in his weakened state.

"She? The carjacker was a woman?"

Lowe swallowed and then shook his head. "It wasn't a car-jacker, Jewels."

Julisa looked at Bono as he walked up to the bed, eager to hear the next words out of Lowe's mouth.

"That bitch tried to kill me," Lowe said.

"No," Julisa said. "The police said all evidence pointed to a random carjacking."

"It was a hit, Jewels."

"How do you know?"

"Her eyes," Lowe whispered. "There was no emotion, when she shot me, she didn't even blink."

"Baby, it happened so fast, I mean, if it was a hit, why didn't she make sure you were dead? She just hopped into your truck and drove off."

"Jewels," he barked, and then started coughing.

Julisa grabbed the pitcher of water off the table and poured him a glass of water. Lowe drank the whole cup.

"This conversation is over." He turned to Bono. "I bet Trent's been giving you a hard time."

"No, he hasn't"

"I thought he would've been power tripping."

"He would be if he was running things," Bono said.

Lowe looked at him puzzled, and then looked at Julisa. "Don't tell me you were running things."

"I tried for a minute, but I didn't have the stomach for it."

"So, who in the fuck is running my operations, Jewels?"

"Honey."

Lowe twisted up his face. "Who?"

"Lord have mercy," Andre cried out as Dawn rode him fast and hard. His eyes were focused on Dawn's perky breasts bouncing up and down in front of his face. "Jesus!" He grabbed fists-full of sheets as his body stiffened like an ironing board.

He squirted into the condom, shuddering with every spasm. Dawn climbed off of him and lay beside him.

"Damn, girl, you put that work in."

"Humph," Dawn said. The only work for her was working her way to an orgasm with his skinny seven-inch disappointment. Tonight, it wasn't worth the effort. She watched him stare at the ceiling as he caught his breath. He turned to her and tried to kiss her. She put her hand up. "I forgot, no kissing."

"You must've also forgot you got a wife at home waiting for you."

"Can a brother catch his breath?"

"You can catch your breath while getting dressed."

"You're something else." He stood up and pulled the condom off and headed to the bathroom. When he returned to the bedroom, Dawn had changed the sheets and had on her robe. He walked up to her and pulled her to him.

"C'mon, now, Dre," she said, putting her hands on his chest.

"I'm tired of you getting yours, and then kicking me out."

"You're getting yours off, too, right?"

"Not enough, obviously," he said, rubbing his fresh hard-on against her. He kissed her neck and tried working his hands inside of her robe.

"See, Dre, this is why I don't fuck with you."

"You can't blame me for wanting some more of that tight pussy, baby."

"Keep acting up, and you won't get any of this tight pussy for a while."

"Why you going to treat me like that?"

"Let's go." She led him to the front door.

"I'll see you real soon, right?"

"Good night, Dre." Dawn closed the door and headed back to her room. She lay across the bed on her stomach. A tear fell from her eye before she had a chance to blink it away. No matter how many men she slept with, no amount of sex could flush Dante out of her system. She cornered him at the grocery store, gas station, and even barged in on him at the Olive Garden when he was having dinner with his co-workers, and each time he would cut her off before she could finish a sentence. It got so heated at the Olive Garden that they were asked to leave. She was an emotional roller coaster, right now. She thought about what she said to Julisa earlier and picked up the phone. When Julisa didn't answer she left a message. "Hey, it's me. I'm just calling to say that I'm sorry for what I said earlier. You know my situation with Dante and I guess it's just making me do and say things that I wouldn't normally do and say. Anyway, call me when you get a chance."

She hung up and called Dante's cell and then the house phone. "Motherfucker." She ended the call and dialed Gamble's number. He picked up on the second ring.

"What's up, Honey?"

"Where you at?"

"Shooting pool with the fellas at Naji's."

"You want to come through tonight?"

"No doubt."

Dawn instantly started tingling between her legs. "I'll see you in a few, then." She ended the call. Gamble's tongue game

was vicious and he laid pipe like a master plumber. She got up
to take a shower and got ready for Gamble's arrival. Just before
she stepped into the bathroom, her phone rang. She ran back
and looked at the caller ID. It was Trent.

"What's up?" Dawn said.

"Guess who I just got a call from?"

"Who the fuck is Honey?" Lowe asked, trying not to get
upset.

"Dawn," Julisa said.

Lowe stared at her blankly.

"C'mon, Lowe, you know Dawn."

"The only Dawn I know is your friend Dawn."

"That's who I'm talking about."

He started to say something twice, and both times he
stopped. He grabbed the railing on the bed and tried to sit up.

"Easy, baby." Julisa used the bed's remote to raise the upper portion.

Lowe looked at Bono. "How could you let this go down?"

"Baby—" Julisa started to say.

"Shut. The. Fuck. Up!" Lowe's lips twitched with rage.

"It was Mr. Green's idea," Bono said.

"Mr. Green? How did Dawn and Mr. Green even manage
to be in the same room? Please explain *that* to me."

Bono looked at Julisa. She explained to Lowe everything
that happened from the beginning. When Julisa told him that

Mr. Green was now getting twenty percent of his loan sharking business, he closed his eyes and looked away from her.

"Baby, I didn't know what else to do." Julisa touched his cheek.

"Bono," Lowe said without opening his eyes.

"Yes."

"What's the name of that cat that does your tattoos, again?"

"Antonio."

"Yes, Antonio. I want him here first thing in the morning with a sketchpad. I want the sketch of that so-called *carjacker* on the streets no later than tomorrow afternoon, along with a fifty thousand dollar incentive for anyone who has any information on that bitch."

Julisa gently squeezed his hand. "Baby, you just came out of a coma, you almost died. Please, for me, take some time to rest and get your thoughts together."

"Rest? I rested for six months. Bono, call Trent and tell him to get his ass down here, right now, and then get Green on the phone."

Dante just checked on his roast when he heard the doorbell. It was half past six and he wasn't expecting anyone. With each step he took toward the front door, he tried to prepare himself mentally in case it was Dawn. He looked through the peephole and then opened the door.

"What do you want?"

Whitty held her hands up in surrender. In her right hand was a bottle of red wine. "I come in peace and bearing gifts." She held the bottle out to him, but he didn't reach for it nor did the scowl on his face change. "Dawn didn't send me. I'm here on my own accord."

"Why?"

"I thought maybe you might want to talk. You already know I'm a good listener."

"We could've talked over the phone."

"You wouldn't talk to me, knowing that Dawn could be listening."

"And why would I talk to you now?"

Whitty shrugged. "After the way you opened up to me that night at the club, I figured maybe..." Dante continued to stare at her expressionless. "Okay, maybe this was a bad idea." She turned to walk away.

"You hungry?" Dante asked.

"Should I be?"

"I got stuffed chicken in the oven. Figured it would go nice with that bottle of wine."

"Now that you mentioned it, I'm starving." She walked in and handed him the bottle and then her jacket.

"Dressed for work, I see," Dante said, eyeing her tight jeans and snug cotton and silk vest.

"Got to be there by nine." She followed him into the kitchen and sat at the island while he checked on the stuffed chicken breast, the wild rice, and the garlic bread. "Smells like a five star restaurant up in here."

"You mind looking in that cabinet behind you and grabbing us some plates?" Dante asked her.

"Not at all."

Dante dished out their food and started to head to the dining room with them.

"Can we eat right here? The dining room seems so... formal."

"You sure?"

"Yes, I'm sure."

He placed her plate in front of her and positioned his seat directly across from her. He poured them a glass of wine and dug into his food.

Whitty bit into a piece of the stuffed chicken and closed her eyes. "Mmm," she moaned as she savored the flavor.

Dante peeked up at her while she chewed. *Damn she got some sexy ass lips,* he thought to himself. The juice from the chicken coated her lips with that wet-glossy look that he always found stimulating. "You like?"

"I like, my taste buds are tap dancing on the roof of my mouth."

"I hope it's not too spicy."

"I like spicy, it's in my DNA, Jamaican mother, Cuban father." She took a sip of her wine and then tried the stuffed chicken with the wild rice. "Unbelievable." She closed her eyes again; this time, Dante focused on her long lashes and perfectly arched eyebrows. "I haven't had a meal like this in years."

"Don't try and gas me up."

"Humph, I can tell you every flavor that Oodles of Noodles come in and how many six inch pancakes you can get out of a box of pancake mix."

"Stop playing," Dante chuckled.

"I kid you not. Ever met someone who has all the luck?" Dante nodded. "I'm the exact opposite. Nothing ever comes easy for me."

"You seem to be doing pretty good to me."

"Don't let appearances fool you." She stood up and did a slow twirl. "My clothes are the bomb, right?"

Dante looked at her clothes, but he was staring more at her curves. "Everything is designer."

"But I didn't pay designer prices; not when my girl Bella is the best booster in the business."

"Just because you buy your clothes from a booster doesn't mean life isn't treating you fair."

"1994, Buffalo, New York. I was seventeen. I lost my virginity to Mr. Russell, our high school principal. He had me on cloud nine, talking about how he loved me and he was going to leave his wife for me when I turned eighteen. Three weeks before my eighteenth birthday, his secretary walks into his office and catches us in the act. It makes headline news and I'm portrayed as a hot-in-the-ass teen that seduced a fifty year old, upstanding pillar of the school system. And to make matters worst, I was two months pregnant."

"That's crazy," Dante said with his mouth popping open.

"What's crazier is my mother disowned me, told me to pack my shit, and said she wished she would've had that abortion like my father was trying to convince her to have. Mr. Russell's wife hated my guts, but she knew I wasn't totally at fault. She paid for the abortion and a bus ticket to New York City."

"Who'd you know down here?"

"No one. I lied and told her I was going to live with my father. Truth is, I never knew the man. I wind up getting my first job at this dive bar downtown. The owner asked me for ID. I removed my coat, showed him my figure eight body, and he never asked for ID again. I rented a room he owned above the bar. Things were going surprisingly well until I started missing underwear from my drawer."

"Get out of here."

"I thought I was bugging until one night I woke up and found my boss standing in the corner of my bedroom with his dick in his hand, watching me sleep."

Dante stopped eating. "Please don't tell me he— "

"I thank God that he just zipped up his pants and left. He was six-three, two hundred and sixty pounds. I wouldn't have had a chance."

"You must've been scared shitless."

"Scared shitless is an understatement. Try traumatized. I can never sleep in just a bra and panties again. Needless to say, I packed my suitcase the next morning and left. I moved into a one-bedroom apartment about the size of this kitchen, and that's where I've been living for the past seven years."

"No boyfriend?"

"Men take one look at my pretty face and curvy body and I become a toy they just want to play with or a trophy they want to showcase. Once they find out that I can speak in whole sentences, they quickly lose interest. Sometimes, being smart works against me."

"Don't say that."

"There are women who can't spell cat, yet are always walking up in the club with diamonds lighting up their ears, necks, and wrists; and with furs damn near touching the floor and all they have to do is keep their mouths shut, pose on their man's arm." She stood up and struck a couple poses. Dante laughed. "I can even be the Energizer Bunny in bed, but keep my mouth shut... that's why I go to bed lonely every night. God, what I wouldn't give to meet a man who would love and respect my mind and what I have to say. Wow!" Whitty caught herself rambling.

"What?"

"I came here to let you talk, and I haven't stopped running my mouth since I walked in the door."

"Can I ask you a personal question?" Dante asked.

"I guess. I mean, if it's too personal, I just won't answer it."

"Do you sleep with men for money?"

"Hell no! And neither does Dawn."

"I saw the text messages."

"Text messages?"

"Yeah, I know all about her hotel rendezvous with different men."

The shocked look on Whitty's face told him that she had no idea what Dawn was doing.

"She had you fooled, too, huh?"

"I don't know what to say." She thought back to all those nights in The Vault when Dawn would be innocently flirting with the big time ballers and industry execs. *I guess it wasn't that innocent after all,* she thought to herself. "I'm so sorry."

"Don't be," Dante mumbled.

Whitty placed her hand on top of his. "It's her loss, trust me." Dante got caught up in the sincerity of her sad facial expression. Once again, his gaze fell to her lips. Recognizing the stare all too well, Whitty dipped her head in a flush of embarrassment and removed her hand from his.

Dante cleared his throat when she broke eye contact, and drained the rest of his wine. He refilled his glass and took another sip.

"I wasn't joking, you know," Whitty said.

"About what?

"About my apartment being about as big as your kitchen."

For the first time in weeks, Dante laughed hard. "You're incredible. Co-workers and friends have been taking me out to eat and to clubs to try and lift my spirits to no avail. And now I'm sitting here with you in my kitchen and I'm feeling..."

"Feeling what?"

"That's it. I'm feeling, period. The pain of betrayal was so overwhelming that it left me emotionally drained and numb. Why would she do this to me, Whitty? To us? We had the perfect marriage. We knew each other inside and out. I can't believe I didn't see this coming." Dante knocked off his second glass of wine and poured himself another. "You don't have to give me an answer, I'm just venting. And I can't believe I'm venting to you, you're working with the enemy."

"You still think Dawn sent me?"

"Right now, I don't know what Dawn is capable of."

Whitty stood up and walked around the island and positioned herself in front of him. She gently placed her hands on the sides of his neck and stared into his eyes. She leaned forward and kissed him. "You still think she sent me?" she whispered as she pulled back.

Dante put his hands on her small waist and pulled her closer to him. This time, he initiated the kiss. The ring tone of Whitty's phone startled them apart.

"Sorry," she mouthed as she pulled her phone out of her pocket and turned it off. She placed it back in her pocked and stared Dante in the eyes, ready to do whatever he wanted to do.

Dante held her gaze for a second and then looked at their plates. "I have to clean this up and get back to work on an article that's due in the morning. So..."

"Dante, I didn't mean... I just came here to talk. Please don't think that I..."

He put his finger to her lips. "Shh," he stood up and kissed her with enough passion to stiffen her nipples. "It's seven thirty. You better get a move on. You don't want to be late for work."

Whitty ran her hand down his arm. "Fuck work."

Dante stared at her lips, once again. "Yeah, fuck work."

CHAPTER 14

*D*awn didn't know what to expect when she pulled up to the hospital. After Trent called her and told her that Lowe had regained consciousness, she almost lost consciousness. With Lowe back amongst the living, things would go back to the way they were, and by the silence on both ends of the phone, neither of them was ready for that just yet.

Dawn walked into the hospital preparing herself mentally for whatever way Lowe was going to try and come at her.

"Dawn." Julisa was on her way back from the bathroom. "I knew God was going to give him back to me."

"I'm so happy for you. You know I didn't mean all those things I said last night, right?"

Julisa hugged her. "All is forgiven."

Dawn smiled, trying not to show the anger festering in her heart. It wasn't fair that Julisa got to be happy when she didn't do a damn thing to deserve it. *I'm the one who deserves to be happy. While she sat in a corner hugging a bottle of whiskey and jumping at her own shadow, I was in the streets putting my life on the line, getting shot at, and having knives put to my neck.*

"Lowe can't wait to see you."

"I can't wait to see him, either," Dawn said half-heartedly.

They headed into the room, Julisa babbling, Dawn focusing. Lowe had been transferred to a private room and had way more visitors than the hospital normally allowed. Trent, Gamble, Buck, and Naji were all in attendance, standing around his bed. Bono stood by the window talking on his phone.

"There she is," Lowe said weakly. His boys parted and let Dawn approach. She hugged him and gave him a kiss on the cheek. "Hi, Lowe, welcome back."

"It's good to be back. Julisa and my boys have been telling me how you've been doing a hell of a job."

"I wouldn't go that far, but I couldn't sit back and watch you and Julisa lose everything."

He pointed at her and then looked at everyone in the room. "You hear that? That's a friend, that's loyalty."

"Lowe," Bono said, as he ended his call. "Mr. Green is on his way up."

"Good. Everybody get the fuck out. Me and the boss man got some business to discuss." Everyone except Bono started to leave. "You stay, Dawn," Lowe said. She stopped in her tracks.

Mr. Green entered the room with a smile and open arms. He shook Lowe's hand and gave him a bear hug. "I know you weren't ready to leave us, just yet."

"I'm here for the long haul, baby," Lowe said.

"I'm sure I don't have to tell you how much of an asset Honey has been to us."

"You mean to you. Someone tried to blow my fucking head off, and that someone isn't dead. Why is that?" Lowe said to Mr. Green.

"I had men all over this since day one. They came up with nothing. Even your own people came up empty."

"My people don't have the resources that you do, so don't take it there."

"What did you expect me to do? Start going upside people's heads until someone talked?" Mr. Green said jokingly.

"That would've been a start."

"I can't believe you. You're sounding like I was okay with what happened."

"By the way shit's been running for the past six months, it seems like a lot of people were okay with what happened."

"Hold on, Lowe—" Dawn started to say.

"And you." He glared at her. "Who the fuck gave you the right to stick your nose into my business?" Dawn was shocked into silence. "All that 'best friends for life' shit might fly with Julisa, but it isn't getting off the ground with me."

"Hold up, I don't know what you heard," Dawn said, shaking off the shock, "but—"

"I never believe what I hear, only what I see. And right now, all I see is two opportunists," Lowe seethed.

"You better watch how you talk to me," Mr. Green hissed.

"Or what?" Lowe challenged. "You ain't shit without me. Remember that."

Mr. Green hit the railing of Lowe's bed with the heel of his hand. "Fuck you, Lowe. What makes you think you're so irreplaceable?"

"The fact that you haven't replaced me yet, and the fact that you never will."

"Don't be too sure about that last fact." Mr. Green looked at Bono. "Call me when this ignorant motherfucker is talking sense." He stormed out the room.

"What?" Lowe said to Dawn who was just staring at him in disbelief.

"If we're done here, I have to go," Dawn finally said.

"We're far from done. You have some business to tend to."

"I don't work for you."

"The hell you don't. You thought you could just wiggle your ass into my operation and just walk away? You best believe, the same way you wiggled your ass in is the same way you're going to wiggle your ass out."

"Meaning?" Dawn said.

"Meaning, you're going to do what the fuck I tell you to until I don't need you anymore."

Dawn laughed. "You can't be serious."

"Bono, am I serious?"

"Very much so," Bono answered.

Dawn looked at Bono. "Do you work for Mr. Green or for him?"

"He works for himself," Lowe said. "Ain't that right, Bono?" Bono didn't respond. "Truth is, Mr. Green and I both need him, because he has what we need."

"And what's that?" Dawn asked.

"An army."

Dawn thought back to the gang in Brooklyn.

"So, you see, *Honey*, Mr. Green, Bono, and I are all on equal ground, in a sense."

"I'm out of here," Dawn said, heading to the door.

"I'm not done," Lowe tried to say with authority, but his weakened state prevented him from doing so.

"I am."

"If you walk out that door—"

Dawn slammed the door behind herself and headed for the elevator.

Julisa spotted her and caught up with her. "What's wrong?"

"Nothing."

"Give him time to adjust to what's going on." Julisa said with a weak smile.

"Lowe is always going to be Lowe. I'm done, Julisa. Your man is back, so things can go back to the way they were."

"Dawn wait—"

"Let it go."

Julisa stared at her as the elevator doors closed.

When Dawn walked outside, she was surprised to see Trent, Gamble, and Naji standing by her car. Trent waited for her to approach before giving her a hug.

"What's that for?" Dawn asked as he pulled back.

"Just wanted you to know that we got mad love for you." Gamble and Naji nodded in agreement.

"Where's Buck?" Dawn asked, looking around.

"He's not with all the mushy stuff," Trent said.

"Well, tell him I said I'm going to miss him following me around."

"I will," Trent said. "We're going to be at Naji's for the next three nights. So, if you want to stop in and say hi…"

"I just might do that." Dawn got into her car and pulled off. She fought back the tears as she headed to the townhouse. Everyone seemed to be going back to their own lives. Everyone except her. She thought about stopping by the house to try and talk to Dante, but she was emotionally drained. She headed up to her office and calculated how much money she would be pulling in a month with just her clients. For a minute, she regretted walking out of Lowe's hospital room. *Fuck it. I rather struggle than be a pawn in his sick game.* She picked up her phone and called Whitty.

"What's up?" Whitty snapped.

"What's the attitude about?"

Whitty caught herself and tried to sound normal. "You just caught me coming out of a deep sleep."

"Shit was hectic at the club last night?" Dawn asked.

"I didn't go to work last night."

"You? Miss work? You must be sick."

"No, something else came up."

"You okay?"

Whitty wanted to come clean. "Yes, no, I don't know. Last night I went to go see—"

"Before you even go into that, Lowe's out of the coma."

"Julisa called me last night and told me."

"I just came from the hospital and he's talking real reckless."

"What are you going to do?" Whitty asked.

"Right now, I have to go to work, but when I get off, I'm going to stop by your place and see if we can put our heads together and come up with something legit to invest my money in." Whitty got quiet. "Are you there?"

"Yeah, I'm just trying to think of some ways to invest."

"That's what I like about you; you're always about your business. Talk to you tonight."

Whitty hung up and rubbed her head. All morning she was gassing herself up to tell Dawn what had transpired between her and Dante last night, because she knew that if she found out any other way, she wouldn't understand. "Fuck it. I'll tell her when she stops by tonight."

Lowe sat up and took a deep breath. He could feel sharp pains where one of the bullets pierced his lung. "Bono, talk to Dawn, make her understand that she's not done until I say she's done."

"We don't need her," Bono said.

"The doctor's talking about me being cooped up in here for at least two more months for observation, tests, and physical therapy."

"Trent could run things until you get out."

"Fuck Trent. He should've stepped up when he had the chance. Instead, he allowed *Honey* to snake her way into my operation and give Green twenty percent of my business. And let's not forget how he so graciously accepted all the profits from the carwash and didn't give my wife a fucking dime. Nah, fuck that. I need Honey. I need for her to work off all the money she's cost me."

Dawn stood up from Whitty's kitchen table and stretched. "This shit is crazy." She picked up the pad she scribbled their ideas on and read it. "Okay, so now we narrowed it down to two possibilities. Opening a club or purchasing an apartment complex that's going into foreclosure."

"With Andre's connects, he could weave his way through all the red tape and get you a great deal on a building, whether it be for a club or for renting," Whitty said.

Dawn sighed. "I don't' know. I just want to invest in something that would double or triple my money without having to get licenses, permits, or hiring employees."

"The only two things that come to my mind is the stock market and the drug game, and neither is doing too well, right now."

"There has to be something," Dawn said.

"Why don't you keep doing what you're doing right now?" Whitty asked.

"I want something legit. This loan sharking thing is only going to last but so long. There may come a time when somebody's not going to want to pay, then what? I'm not trying to hire people to beat people up for my money. C'mon, Whitty, you're the one with the Masters, think." Dawn bumped into the table for the third time. "Why is your damn apartment so small? It feels like the walls are closing in on me. You need to—"

"Enough about my apartment, already!" Whitty stood up so fast that the back of her knees shot the chair against the wall.

"What's wrong with you?" Dawn sensed Whitty was on edge.

Whitty grabbed her head. "I'm trying to help you out, but all you keep doing is shooting down my ideas and complaining about how small my fucking apartment is. You're stressing me the hell out."

"You looked stressed out when I first got here."

"I've got something to tell you. It's about last night. I didn't go to work, because I stopped to see—"

"Hold up," Dawn said, as she felt her phone vibrating on her hip. It was one of her clients. "Hello? Wait, slow down... he said what? Listen, I don't give a fuck what Lowe told you. You owe me, you don't owe him. You hear me? Hello? Hello? Shit."

"What was that about?" Whitty asked.

"This motherfucker Lowe. I don't know how, but he found out who my clients are and he's contacting them and telling them that they owe him, and he expects them to start paying him directly, in cash." Dawn grabbed her coat and bolted for the door.

"Where are you—"

Dawn was out the door before Whitty could finish her sentence.

Dawn's phone rang off the hook as she headed to Naji's. Her clients were calling to inform her that they were ordered to pay Lowe or they would lose their businesses to arson or vandals. Dawn tried to assure them that the issue would be resolved in the morning, but the shakiness in her voice told them otherwise. She pulled up to Naji's and calmed herself before walking in.

Buck was the first one to spot her when she walked in. He tapped Gamble and Naji. She walked right up to them.

"Where's Trent?"

Naji saw the hurricane brewing in her eyes and grabbed his keys. "Follow me."

"I'm not following you anywhere until you tell me where he is."

"He's not here," Gamble said. Dawn cut him a stare that made him blink.

"Honey, please," Naji said, as he started walking to the break room. She reluctantly followed him with Buck and Gamble trailing. Once inside she couldn't contain her anger any longer.

"How could you?" Was all she kept saying as she looked at them one by one.

Naji sighed. "You know how this go."

"No, Naji, I don't know how this go. I didn't know that Buck was trailing me just to tell Lowe who all my clients were."

"Hold on," Buck said. "Lowe didn't ask me anything about your clients and I didn't tell him anything about your clients."

"So how else would he know, Buck?"

"He didn't find out from me."

"What did you expect was going to happen when Lowe came out of the coma?" Naji asked.

"I wasn't thinking about that, because I was too busy making sure all of you got yours off the top, because y'all are his boys," Dawn said on the verge of tears.

"Honey," Gamble tried to interject.

"And you. I'm too through with you; after all we've been through. I just got one question for you. Did you speak up for me when Lowe was deciding to fuck me out of my business?" Gamble didn't respond. "Exactly what I thought."

"Honey—" Naji said, but Dawn shot out of the break room and headed back to her car. She felt her phone vibrating on her hip. It was Julisa.

"What?" Dawn answered with an attitude.

"Dawn, I need for you to come down to the hospital."

"Hell no."

"Please, Dawn, I've been talking to Lowe and he wants to work something out with you."

Dawn let her head fall back against the headrest and sighed. Too much was going on. She needed to buy herself some time to figure things out.

"Dawn are you there?"

"Yes, I'm here. I'll be there in an hour."

Lowe was talking to Trent when Dawn walked in. She wanted to run right up on Trent and smack the smile right off his face. Julisa was on the other side of the bed holding Lowe's hand.

"Honey," Lowe said, acting like he was glad to see her.

"Cut the bullshit." Dawn cut to the chase. "Julisa said you wanted to work something out, I'm listening."

Lowe turned toward Julisa. "Give us some privacy, will you, Jewels?"

"I'm staying."

"This doesn't concern you," Lowe said.

"She's my friend, so it concerns me."

Lowe shook his head while looking at Trent. "Women. Okay here's the deal," Lowe said to Dawn. "From here on in, Trent is running everything until I get out of here. Everything except what me and Mr. Green got going on. It seems as if he'd rather close down his laundering operation than to put it in Trent's hands. So, until I'm at a hundred percent, you'll continue working with Mr. Green and Bono, while still receiving your cut from that side of the operation."

"What's the catch?" Dawn asked.

"That's the only cut you're getting."

"Meaning?"

"Meaning, that's the only money you're going to see."

"That's bullshit. I built my own lending company—"

"Off my clients. Without them, you wouldn't have shit," Lowe wheezed.

"And without me, you would've woken up broke."

"She has a point," Julisa interjected. "She had my back when shit got hectic."

"Trent had your back," Lowe said.

"Trent?" Julisa responded in disbelief.

"I tried to have your back, but you wouldn't let me step up and do what needed to be done," Trent said.

"You're so full of it. All you were concerned about was your own damn self," Julisa said to Trent.

"Enough!" Lowe said. "This is what I'm offering. Take it or leave it." Dawn turned to walk away. "You walk away this time, there will be no more talking."

"Dawn," Julisa called after her.

Dawn stopped. "I'll play your game, for now."

Lowe clapped. "Beautiful."

Bono knocked on the door and walked in, nearly bumping into Dawn. "A manager at the Hyatt recognized the woman in the sketch."

Lowe's eyes widened. "Who is she?"

"Don't know. Every time she comes in from out of town, she uses a different name to register under and she pays cash."

"How does he know she's from out of town?"

"He said she has a strong southern accent."

Lowe went through his mind, trying to pinpoint any down south cats he may have crossed in the past.

"What female are you all talking about?" Dawn asked.

"The bitch that posed as a carjacker to fucking kill me," Lowe said.

Dawn started to say something, but Julisa's facial expression told her that she would explain everything later.

"Okay," Lowe said. "The manager says she rents a room from time to time. So, chances are she'll be showing up there again."

"I already told him that he'll get his 50Gs after he notifies us of her arrival," Bono said.

"Excellent. Okay, I need for everyone to leave. My wife and I have more private matters to discuss."

Dawn looked at Julisa, who couldn't even look her in the eye. She just shook her head and left.

When everyone left, Julisa punched Lowe in the arm.

"Ouch."

"Ouch, my ass. You lied to me," Julisa said.

"Lied to you?"

"When I gave you the list of her clients, you told me you were only going to use it for leverage."

"And I am. If I allow her to collect that money, why would she want to work for me?"

"But you don't need her, she's done enough, sacrificed too much as it is."

"Green's not going to deal with anybody but her. So, in a sense, I do need her. I've come too far to let this fish slip away. You know the deal that I've been working on with Green from day one, and you know how much money's involved. Your friend was a Godsend. This whole deal would've fallen through if it wasn't for her."

"But Lowe—"

"A bank, Jewels. Do you hear me? And I'm not talking about a club. I'm talking a bona fide commercial bank that will lace our pockets with millions. You've seen the plans, sat in on the meetings. We're going to create over ten thousand jobs and we're going to fund small business and community development projects that are going to breathe life back into our communities and economy. This is my time to finally go legit and I can't afford to lose Mr. Green now. If he wants her to continue running the laundering operation until I get on my feet, then that's what's going to happen."

"I just don't like the fact that you're using her."

"Yes, I am using her, but I've been also considering giving her a very lucrative position with our bank when it opens up next year."

"You serious?" Julisa said, perking up. She no longer felt bad for betraying Dawn.

"She's a go-getter. I need people like her around. I'm going to take real good care of your friend, you'll see."

"I know you're mad at me, but you know how this go," Trent said, as he caught up to Dawn in the hospital parking lot.

"Humph, you sound like somebody I just not too long ago spoke to. Well, you got what you wanted; you're the man now."

"I can see that we're never going to get along."

"And it only took you six months to figure that out." Dawn got into her car and started it up. She met his gaze and then rolled her eyes at him before pulling off. She reached for her cell phone and called Whitty. She sucked her teeth when Whitty's phone went right into voice mail. Opening a club was out of the question. The last thing she needed was for Lowe to see her as competition. She was going to pitch her idea about buying an apartment building to Andre. But first, she wanted to run it by Whitty. "Whitty, where the fuck are you?"

Dante took his glasses off and rubbed his eyes. He'd been working since six this morning and it was now eleven o'clock. He didn't mind the extra hours that came with the promotion. He was now the Editorial Assistant right under Mr. Allen. After the Central Park nightmare, he didn't expect to ever hear from him again, which was why he was surprised that he had called him and offered him the job personally.

"Breakfast is served," Whitty said, as she walked out of the kitchen with a plate of pancakes.

Dante closed his laptop when she put them in front of him. "You know you didn't have to do this, right?"

"It's the least I could do. Besides, the way I acted the other night was way out of line."

"Kissing me wasn't way out of line, especially, when I was kissing you back."

"I figured if I kissed you, you would believe that Dawn didn't send me, but when I tasted your lips... I needed to taste *everything* else."

"Believe me, I wanted you to taste *everything* else, but I'm not ready to move on."

"You're going to take Dawn back after knowing that she slept with men for money?"

"I didn't' say I was going to take her back. I'm just not ready to give my heart to someone right now."

"I wasn't after your heart last night," Whitty said, looking down at his crotch with a smile.

"Well, with me, you get the whole package or nothing at all."

"Stop talking and start eating, because you're turning me on, right now."

"So these are your famous pancakes, huh? They are all the exact size." Dante examined them.

"Six inches in diameter, golden brown, with crunchy edges. They don't call me the Pancake Master for nothing." She sat across from him and watched him as he bit into one.

"Damn," Dante mumbled, as he tore into them.

"I told you."

Dante dug back into the plate of pancakes. As he gobbled down the last one, he peeped the way Whitty was staring at him starry-eyed, but he acted like he didn't notice. He pushed the plate forward and rubbed his stomach. "Those were the best pancakes I've ever had."

"Stop lying," Whitty said blushing.

"I'm serious."

"I'm glad you like them." She grabbed the plate and headed to the kitchen.

Dante followed her.

"I got this," she said. "Go back to work."

"Yeah, right, work."

"You don't sound too enthused."

"I appreciate my job and the doors it's opening up for me, but I miss being in the thick of things."

"You said Wall Street was filled with cut throats and back stabbers."

"But they all weren't cut throats and back stabbers."

"And with this recession, investing isn't profitable anyway," Whitty sighed.

"Who told you that?"

"Everybody knows that."

"Everybody's wrong," Dante said with authority.

"But the Stock Market—"

"Stop right there."

"What?"

"You said investing isn't profitable."

"Yeah," Whitty said.

"Investing, the Stock Market, and the recession are three different things. There are people, as we speak, who are making millions in this recession."

"In the Stock Market?" Whitty said surprised, because the newspapers painted a different picture.

"Not in the Stock Market; in investing."

"Okay, I'm officially lost."

"Check this out." Dante got back on his laptop and pulled up an article on President Obama's stance on stem cell research.

"Okay," Whitty said. "He's all for it."

"Now look at this." He pulled up an article in the Medical Journal written by Dr. Richard Acobi, Head Research Scientist of Nu-Life Corp. "Before I was scapegoated, my firm had set up a luncheon with Dr. Acobi and me to discuss the possibility of investing into his ground breaking research if Obama should've won the presidential election. I did a shit load of research, at the time, and I knew that if Obama won the presidency, he was going to give the green light for stem cell research and Nu-life was going to blow up."

"Did they?"

"They are currently the leaders in stem cell research, and their initial investors are now millionaires."

"Millionaires? Sign me up, I want to be a millionaire."

"You and me both."

"If you had all this information, why didn't you invest?"

"I had the information, but I didn't have the money."

"How much you talking?"

"Three hundred thousand is the minimum."

"So, if you would've invested three hundred thousand, like six months ago, you would be a millionaire by now?"

"Pretty much," Dante said.

"What if you invested three hundred thousand today?"

"Nu-life is still in its infancy. Anyone who's climbing aboard within the next year is guaranteed to be millionaires."

"If I were to give you three hundred thousand—"

"Yeah, right. What are you going to do, rob a bank?"

"I'm serious," Whitty said.

Dante shook his head.

"What?"

"Even if you were to miraculously get your hands on three hundred thousand, it would do you no good."

"Why not?"

"Because Nu-life has strict guidelines for their investors, and they are very selective with whom they let onboard. Basically, you need to know someone."

"I know you."

"No, Whitty, I'm done with that line of work."

"What do you mean 'no, Whitty'? You just said you miss being in the thick of things."

"I was just talking."

"No you weren't. You're a stockbroker. Investing is what you do."

"I can be the best investor in the world, but without a way in—"

"You have a way in. Dr. Acobi. I'm quite sure he wouldn't have a problem meeting you for lunch and discussing the possibility of bringing on another investor."

"Why am I even having this conversation with you? You don't have three hundred thousand dollars."

"But a friend of mine does."

"And who's this friend?"

"They're legit, if that's what you really want to know."

"Well, it's none of my business." He pulled up his column for next week's publication. "This is my business."

"Business? Please. That's nothing but a pastime."

"A pastime?" Dante furrowed his eyebrows

"Yes, you need something to keep you busy while you shake off what your firm did to you. Once you recover, they're going to wish they never let you go."

"And how do you know this?"

"A good man only stays down for so long, and then he gets back up. I've only known you for a short time, but I know a fighter when I see one."

Dante smiled. "You're something else."

"So, you'll do it?" Before he got his words out of his mouth, Whitty clasped her hands together. "Please don't make me beg, you know I will."

"How do you even know this friend of yours would even give you the money?" Dante asked.

"Let me worry about that. You just worry about getting us in the front door. If you can pull this off, I know my friend is going to spread the word, and you're going to have investors lining up at your door. Shit, I don't know why you didn't start your own business."

"It's funny that you should say that, because Dawn was trying to talk me into starting my own investment company." He smiled, but he couldn't conceal the pain in his eyes.

Whitty touched his cheek. She quickly pulled her hand away. "I'm sorry. I didn't mean to touch you in that way."

"What way is that?"

"The way that would force me to have to go home and take a cold shower."

"You're too much," Dante chuckled.

"You never answered the question."

Dante stared at her for a moment. "And this friend of yours is legit?"

"One hundred percent."

"If I decide to do this, you're friend will become rich and I'm going to get a hell of a commission. How are you going to profit from this?"

"Don't worry about me, I'm going to get mine."

"Okay, I'll look into it."

Whitty hugged him, "Thank you. When are you going to meet with Dr. Acobi?"

"Right after I meet with your friend."

"Huh?"

"Huh? Your friend. I'm not going to just take their money and not explain what it is I'm actually doing with it. So, when can you set up the meeting with your friend?"

"In a couple days," Whitty said, watching her dream crumble.

"Okay, you do that."

"I have to go. I have some running around to do before I head to work. I'll give you a call tomorrow."

"Talk to you then."

A cab pulled up to Mr. Green's office building. A woman wearing a form-fitting Fendi pantsuit paid the cabbie and stepped out onto the curb. At first glance, a passerby would take her to be mulatto, with her straight hair and fair skin. When she entered the building and removed her shades, her slanted eyes coupled with her straight hair and fair skin made her out to be of Spanish or Asian descent. When she approached Mr. Green's secretary, her name and accent told another story.

"Good afternoon. My name's Helen Dubber. I have an appointment with Mr. Green for one o'clock." Her British accent was crisp and sharp.

"You can go right in; he's been expecting you."

"Thank you."

When she entered Mr. Green's office, he immediately hung up his phone and stood up from his desk. He walked toward her and kissed her on the cheek. "I apologize."

The woman who he knew by many names spun on him and fixed herself a drink. She gulped it down and then removed the jacket to her pantsuit. Mr. Green eyed the compact automatic pistol tucked into the left side of her shoulder holster. He opened his mouth to say something, but she held her hand up.

"Before you say anything, Poppi," Her Spanish accent was strong. "Let me remind you that I was in Cancun, on a beach sunbathing buck naked with a man named Junito, who was also

239

buck naked, and his chulu was down to here," she said striking the inside of her lower thigh.

"Again, I apologize. I should've called you from the beginning, but Stella owed me a favor and the job was simple enough. Nothing could go wrong."

"Obviously, something went wrong, otherwise, I wouldn't be here."

Mr. Green sighed and sat back down behind his desk. "Lowe is an arrogant son of a bitch. He thinks he's untouchable. All I needed Stella to do was let him know that he could get got. She was supposed to shoot him up a couple times, nothing fatal, just a couple flesh wounds. She winds up putting him in a coma for six months."

"Other than you dropping two hundred and fifty thousand in my account, why am I here?" the woman known as Molina said.

"I need you to remove Lowe from the equation."

"You didn't want him dead before; what's changed in you *equation?*"

"Before this incident, I didn't think I could move forward on the project me and him were partners on."

"You're talking about the commercial bank you two are supposed to be opening together?"

"Yes. But when Lowe was in a coma, a woman stepped up to run his operation, and she did a hell of a job."

"So your partner goes from irreplaceable to expendable."

"Yes."

"He won't be a problem," Molina said.

"He's not the only problem," Mr. Green said, locking eyes with her.

Molina folded her arms across her chest. "I'm listening."

"He got a look at Stella the night she hit him up. When he came out of his coma, he had a sketch drawn up of her and a hotel manager at the Hyatt recognized her. He's supposed to notify Lowe if she ever returns. I can't afford to have her linked back to me in anyway."

Molina dug into her purse and pulled out her compact and checked her makeup in the mirror.

"Can you handle this situation?" Mr. Green asked, knowing it was going to cost him an arm and a leg.

"Yes, just as soon as you deposit an additional two hundred and fifty thousand into my account."

"Two fifty, plus two fifty? You want half a million dollars for two hits?"

"No, I want half a million dollars for having to clean up your mess, and for dragging me away from Junito." Molina shook her head. "Down to here," she said striking the inside of her thigh again.

"Molina—"

"That's my price. Take it or I'm going back to Cancun." Mr. Green agreed. "Good. Now, get Stella on the phone and tell her you have another job for her."

CHAPTER 15

W hitty finally caught a break from serving drinks. She spotted Dawn as soon as she waltzed into The Vault. She thought about what she was going to do. Could she pull it off? Could she convince her to invest in Nu-life without knowing that Dante was going to be her broker? Of course she could. She had to if she wanted to see any part of that million Dante talked about. Dawn made her rounds, stopping at select tables to chitchat. Her curve-clinching Donna Karen dress kept the eyes of onlookers glued to her ass until she sauntered out of their line of sight. When Andre spotted her, he dismissed Lavita and waited for her to approach his table. She finally worked her way to him and pecked him on the cheek as she sat down. She whispered something in his ear and then they headed up to the office.

Whitty twirled the ring on her index finger. The meeting was going down and she didn't have a chance to tell Dawn about the surefire investment. Whitty flipped her phone open and called Cassidy who was working in The Bank.

"What's up?" Cassidy answered sounding bored.

"You busy up there?"

"Do I sound busy?"

"I need you to cover for me."

"How am I supposed to get down there?"

"Take the elevator to the garage, Cash will get you down here."

"You sure?"

"What I say?"

"Okay."

Whitty called Cash and told him what she needed him to do. Cassidy showed up five minutes later.

"What's so important that you got Cash breaking the rules to get me in here?"

"I got to take a shit."

"Nah, ah," Cassidy said, crunching up her nose. "I did not need to hear that."

"Just cover for me until I get back." Whitty dipped into the bathroom to check her makeup before heading up to the office. When she got to the office door, she knocked.

"Yes!" She heard Dawn say.

She walked in. Her jaw locked in shock as she saw Dawn leaning back on the couch with her legs cocked open. Andre was sucking on her swollen clit.

"Yes," Dawn said again, oblivious to Whitty's intrusion.

Whitty realized that Dawn's yes, was a yes of ecstasy, not a yes of permission to come in. Dawn grabbed the back of Andre's head and held him in place as she filled his mouth with her honey. She opened her eyes, surprised to see Whitty standing in the doorway with the door wide open, but the intensity of her orgasm kept her locked in place until it was over.

"I'm sorry—" Whitty started to apologize.

"Don't just stand there. Come in and close the fucking door!" Dawn said, as she shoved Andre's face from between her legs and started pulling her dress down.

Andre turned around, also surprised to see Whitty. He licked the remains of Dawn's juices from his lips and winked at Whitty. "You want to join the party?"

"Wait for me downstairs," Dawn said, popping him in the back of the head.

Andre cleared his throat and headed for the door. "If you change your mind," he said while brushing past Whitty, "Dawn has my number."

Whitty cringed as she slammed the door behind him.

"How the fuck are you just going to walk up in here like that?" Dawn said to Whitty.

"I knocked. When you said yes, I thought that meant come in."

It was obvious that Dawn was embarrassed by the way she avoided eye contact. "Don't judge me."

"Excuse me?" Whitty said, not understanding what Dawn meant.

"You heard what I said. Don't judge me. I have to do what's right for me, at the moment. I can't keep living in the past, hoping Dante will beg me to come back home."

"Honey—"

"It's his fault why Andre's between my legs, anyway. He wouldn't even let me explain. I mean... how much could he have really loved me if it was so easy for him to believe that I would sleep with men for money?" Tears started to form in the corners of her eyes.

"What?" Whitty acted liked she had no idea what she was talking about.

"That's why he cut me off. He found the cell phone I used for business and he saw Buck, Gamble, Naji, and Trent's numbers on it. That's why he called you that night wanting to know the names of the male employees. Then he read the text that Julisa sent me when she found out about the shoot out in Chance's hotel. He finds a phone with men's numbers, then he read Julisa's text about Chance and a hotel and he assumes I was... was... hoing around."

Whitty looked more shocked than when she saw Andre between Dawn's legs. Dante had misunderstood everything and now his five years of marriage was on the verge of officially being over.

"Why are you up here, anyway? And where the hell have you been? I've been trying to reach you since this morning. I wanted to tell you that I was going to run our plan down to Andre. That's why I brought him up here, but then one thing led to another and..."

Whitty just stared at her, not knowing what to say. Should she go forward with the million-dollar plan? Or should she come clean about her and Dante and help Dawn get her man back?

"Whitty!" Dawn snapped her out of her thoughts. "What are you thinking about?"

"Nothing. I came up here because... because I've got the perfect plan."

"The perfect plan for what?"

"In six months, we're going to be millionaires."

Dawn sat in the passenger side of the Range Rover lost in thought. Her and Bono just came from their monthly China-town pickup. As usual, Mr. Chin-Li was all smiles and bows. And as usual, Bono was all business. They were in and out before the Range's motor stopped clicking.

"You okay," Bono asked her, as he alternated between keeping his eyes on the road and in the rearview mirror.

"I'm fine," Dawn said, trying to accompany her words with a reassuring smile. The truth was, she'd been on edge for the past couple weeks. She didn't like the way Lowe was sitting his bony ass up in the hospital throwing orders around like he was some Don. Mr. Green had stopped by to see him three times in the past two weeks. Lowe's doctor was pleased with his speedy recovery and the progress he was making with his physical therapy. He assured Lowe that he would be leaving the hospital in two weeks. Dawn could feel the tension between Lowe, Mr. Green, and Trent. She tried getting Bono to talk about it, but he remained tight-lipped. She even talked to Julisa about it to see if Lowe shared anything with her, but he hadn't. As far as Julisa was concerned everything was good between the three men, but Dawn knew better. But she had her own pressing matters to worry about.

Whitty was still sweating her about investing into Nu-Life. Dawn wasn't feeling the whole setup, because Whitty wouldn't tell her whom her source was. She only referred to them as a well-connected friend, who wanted to remain anonymous for the time being. Dawn was on the verge of caving in until Whitty told her how much she needed to invest.

"Three hundred thousand?" she remembered saying to Whitty. "You want me to give three hundred thousand to a person I don't know?"

"Just think of it as you're giving it to me."

"Bitch, I don't even know *you* like that to be giving you that amount of money."

Whitty finally relented when she realized that Dawn wasn't giving up any money without knowing whom she was dealing with. So she agreed to set up a meeting.

Bono's cell rang. Dawn's phone rang a second after his. It was Julisa.

"What's up Julisa?"

"Where are you?"

"We just left Chinatown. What's up?"

Julisa started whispering into the phone. "That's what I'm trying to find out. Lowe got a call and he just started bugging out. He wouldn't tell me what it was about, he just kicked me out of the room, said he had some calls to make."

Dawn looked over at Bono who was still listening to whoever was on the other end of his phone. "If I find anything out, I'll give you a call."

"Okay."

Dawn hung up. A minute later, Bono hung up and hit speed dial on his phone.

"What's up?" Dawn asked.

He held a finger up as he waited for the person on the other end to pick up. "Yeah, Eva, it's me. I need you and the wolves clipped up and ready to roll." Bono hung up.

"What's going on?" Dawn asked.

"Lowe just got a call from the manager at the Hyatt. Our southern friend just checked in."

Whitty sat in her car parked across from Dante's house. She ran her hand over her golden-dyed brush cut and sighed. This was it. If she couldn't pull this off she could kiss the millions good-bye. She got out of her car and headed to the house. She rang the doorbell and said a silent prayer.

Dante opened the front door, standing before her in a pair of black knee-length shorts, a white tank top, and a black do-rag. He motioned for her to come in as he spun and continued talking on his cell.

Whitty's eyebrows shot up as she brazenly eyeballed his toned calves, wide back, and rounded shoulders. She placed her hand on her belly to stop it from jumping.

"Yes, I read the e-mail," Dante said to the person on the other end of the phone. "That's a big leap for me. Writing a column is one thing, but a book? I'm going to need a couple more days to think about it." Dante turned around and winked at Whitty. Her body temperature shot up five degrees. "I'm going to have to let you go. I'll call you in a few days." He ended the call.

"Did I hear that right? A book deal?" Whitty said.

"Yeah, can you believe it? The Marketing team convinced the big wigs that I'm very profitable, right now. Their survey concluded that seventy five percent of our subscribers see my column as the absolute authority on investment advice and tactics."

"You're really building a reputation for yourself, Mr. Wall Street. Speaking of which, I wonder what your following would think of you if they saw you dressed like that."

"I don't think they would expect me to play ball in a suit."

"I didn't know you played basketball."

"I go to my old neighborhood and hook up with my boys from back in the day, and we play a few games, politic, and bullshit. You know, guy things."

"Just when I thought I got a handle on you, I come to find out that you're not all business."

Dante snapped his fingers. "That reminds me. I spoke with Dr. Acobi. He said he could get us in the door."

Whitty was jumping for joy on the inside, but she had a part to play.

Dante noticed that she didn't seem too interested in the good news. "Everything okay? I thought you would be doing cartwheels."

"Nah, I'm good. It's just that…" She didn't continue.

"That what? Don't tell me your friend backed out. Do you know what I had to go through just to get a meeting with the doctor?"

"It's not about my friend, it's about me."

"What's wrong?"

"I haven't been totally honest with you."

"Whitty… don't do this to me. I trusted you."

"I know. That's why I want to come clean with you." Whitty could see Dante's jaw muscles twitching. "This is hard for me, so I'm just going to say it. My friend loved the idea, and they're all for it, but when I mentioned your name—"

Dante stopped her. "Don't even say it."

"They want to move forward with the deal; they just don't want… they don't want you to have any parts of it."

"Really? Well, tell your friend I said good luck in trying to get in without me. I have to go, I'm running late for my game."

"Dante, wait. I know you got a raw deal with your previous employer, and because of them your reputation is still suffering, but you're still fortunate enough to have a following that treats your column like the gospel. Your people are even offering you a book deal. I guess what I'm trying to say is, no matter what happens to you, you will always seem to come out on top. Me, on the other hand… shit never works out for me. I finally thought my luck was beginning to change. I was going to use the money that I got from this deal to open up my own business."

"Your own business? And what would that be?"

Whitty shook her head. "You'll laugh if I tell you. Besides, it's not going to happen now, anyway."

"I promise I won't laugh."

Whitty folded her arms and spoke real low. "I was going to open a waffle house." Dante smiled. Whitty punched him in the arm. "You said you weren't going to laugh."

"I'm not laughing, I'm smiling."

"Well, I have to go. You have to politic with your boys over a game of basketball." Whitty turned to leave. It took every fiber in her being not to run back inside. *I can't believe he's just going to let me leave.* She got to her car and reached for the door handle. She jumped when she felt Dante's hand come down on top of hers.

"For the record," Dante said, "If your friend was drowning and begged me for a life jacket, I would throw him an anchor. But I'm not going to let my dislike for your friend stop you from opening your waffle house."

"What are you saying?" Whitty said, trying to contain herself.

"I'm going to talk to Dr. Acobi in the morning and arrange a meeting between him and your friend."

"Yes!" Whitty pumped her fist in the air. She jumped in Dante's embrace, wrapping her arms around his neck and her legs around his waist. She kissed him on the cheek. "You're the man."

He let her down. "Say it again."

"You are the motherfucking man."

Dante stared down at her five-four frame and the way it filled and stretched the fabric of her clothes.

"What?" Whitty said, looking down at her clothes.

"You play ball?" Dante asked.

"Are you serious?"

"Yeah."

"I can play a little, but I'm not getting on the court with your friends. All they're going to do is feel up on my ass."

"I was thinking more like a game of one-on-one, and I would be the only one feeling your ass." Dante's stare had Whitty paralyzed like a deer caught in headlights.

"Dante—"

He leaned down and kissed her. Whitty stood on her tiptoes and kissed him back. She sucked on his bottom lip. Dante pulled back and waited for her reply.

Whitty thought of what Dawn shared with her a couple weeks back. If Dante found out that he had misunderstood what was going on, there was a good chance of them getting back together. Where would that leave her? She shook her head. She couldn't sleep with her friend's husband, which would be low, even for her. She stared at his lips. Damn he had some sexy, thick lips. Thick lips meant he was swinging a big stick. Just the thought of having her walls stretched and pounded had all of her openings throbbing.

"You game or what?" Dante whispered in her ear.

Whitty palmed his butt. "My ball first."

Dawn felt her stomach bubble as Bono weaved in between cars and run three yellow lights. "Where are we headed?"

"To drop this money off."

"And then?"

"And then that's it."

"What about the carjacker?"

"Eva will take care of that. She knows what to do."

Buck sat parked across the street from the Hyatt in a Chrysler 300C. The only time he left his car was to give the hotel manager his fifty Gs. He drummed his thumbs against the steering wheel as he kept his eyes glued to the front entrance. He looked at his watch. It had been forty minutes since he called Lowe and told him about Miss Southern Belle. Lowe told him to sit tight and let Bono's people bring her in.

This is bullshit. I could've had this chick in my trunk, heading to the carwash. He formed a mental image of her according to the description the manger gave him. She's dark-skinned, about five feet, five inches tall, the manager said, approximately a hundred and twenty pounds. She has a baby face, but her breasts and ass... plenty to hold on to, you know what I'm saying?

Buck sucked his teeth. Five-five, a hundred and twenty pounds. She definitely didn't fit the bill of a contract killer. He looked at his watch again. If Bono wasn't there in fifteen minutes, he was going in.

Dante arched his back as he finally came. Whitty came with him. She came so hard that she had to bury her head in Dante's chest to muffle her moans. Minutes later, she took her legs off his shoulders and let him slip out of her. Dante tried looking at her, but Whitty refused to look him in the eye.

"What's wrong?" he asked.

"I'm so ashamed."

"What is there to be ashamed of?"

"How can I look Dawn in the eyes when I see her?"

"You don't have anything to be ashamed about. You hear me?"

Whitty nodded. "Do you think you two will ever get back together again?"

"I don't know. And I'm not giving it too much thought. I have other things to think about."

"Like your book deal?"

"No, like you and me." He kissed her long and hard. "Am I going to see you again, or was this just the spur of the moment thing?"

Whitty sat up on one elbow. "Let's put it this way. After the way you just put it on me, I'm yours to do whatever, whenever."

"Don't say whatever, I might take that literally."

Whitty looked him in the eyes. "Whatever and whenever."

CHAPTER 16

*B*uck looked at his watch; twenty minutes had passed. He sucked his teeth. *Fuck this.* He got out of his car and headed into the hotel. He hit the elevator call button and stuck his hands in his coat pocket as he waited. When the elevator arrived, he stepped in and hit the button for the fifth floor. His plan was simple. Use the key that the manager gave him to gain access to the room. If she tried anything funny, put a bullet in her leg, knock her unconscious, and wait for Bono to finally show up. He reached into his coat and unsnapped the leather strap holding the .22 silencer in place. He looked up at the numbers lighting up one by one. The fourth floor light just lit up. He reached into his pocket and pulled out the key. The chime for the fifth floor sounded and the door opened. His eyes widened as Stella stepped onto the elevator.

"Hi," she said, as she gave him a little wave. Her southern accent was thick.

Buck smiled, hoping that his shock of seeing her didn't give him away. She hit the lobby button and then stood directly in front of him. *No fucking way,* Buck thought. *A contract killer?* The manager was right. Even though she was wearing a loose-fitting tracksuit, he could see that she had a nice body.

"I was just on my way down to see you," she said, bringing Buck out of his thoughts.

"Excuse me?"

"I said... I was just on my way down to see you. I figured I'd bring it to you, seeing how you is too afraid to bring it to me." Stella was still facing forward.

Buck reached inside his jacket. Stella caught his movement in the mirror mounted in the corner of the elevator's ceiling and spun around. Her right hand shot out like a coiled snake. Her fingers felt like claws as they dug into his neck and squeezed his larynx shut.

Buck instinctively dropped his gun and reached for her hand. Stella pulled back, leaving him to grab nothing but air. At the same time, she kicked his gun to the front corner of the elevator. Her right hand shot out again. This time, she poked her fingers in between Buck's ribs, causing him to yell out. He swatted her hand, only to feel the excruciating pain of her fingers digging back into his throat. He threw a wild punch, which Stella easily slipped. The momentum of Buck's punch pitched him forward, allowing her to slither behind him and poke him in the kidney. He fell to his knees, not knowing where he was anymore. Stella's fingers felt like blunted ice picks. She kneed him in the face and had her knee on his neck when his back hit the ground.

"Who sent you?" Stella whispered. Buck was barely conscious. She dug her fingers under his ribcage and was literally touching his lung. Buck's eyes popped open. "Who sent you?" she asked again. Buck blacked out.

Stella got off of him and retrieved his gun and stuck it in her pocket. As the doors opened into the lobby, she bumped into a business woman who was on her way into the elevator.

Stella saw the cell phone glued to the woman's ear and pointed to Buck. "My boyfriend. He had a seizure, he's not moving, please call the police."

"Your boyfriend just moved," the woman said, pointing to Buck.

Stella looked at Buck. An explosion went off in her head as the woman cracked her upside the head with her cell phone. Stella stumbled back into the elevator. Molina brought the cell phone down on Stella's skull again. The cell phone look-alike was a five pound piece of steel that turned Molina's arm into a virtual sledgehammer.

Molina stepped into the elevator and pressed the button for the sixth floor. As the doors closed, Stella rushed her. Molina swung the piece of steel. Stella ducked under the swing and stabbed into the flesh of Molina's groin with her fingers. Molina howled in pain as she raised the steel over her head with both hands and brought it crashing down. Stella back peddled, avoiding the fatal blow. But just as fast as she was out, she was back in delivering a poke intended to dig in between Molina's ribs.

Molina used the block of steel to shield herself from the stab. It was Stella's turn to howl in pain as her fingers crumpled against the block of steel. Molina slipped behind her and cracked the back of her skull open. Stella fell face first and didn't move. Molina bent down and felt for a pulse. There was none. The elevator doors opened and Molina stepped out and made sure the coast was clear before heading to the stairwell.

Buck groaned as the pain of Stella's pokes brought him back to consciousness. He reached for the handrail and pulled himself up as he tried to regain his equilibrium. He looked down at saw Stella sprawled out with blood seeping out of her ears. He blinked realizing he was in an moving elevator. He looked up at the numbers; the elevator was descending. He jumped back when the doors opened up into the lobby and he saw people standing in front of him.

Eva looked at him and then down at Stella. "What the fuck happened?"

Buck stumbled out of the elevator. Monster-Sick caught him before he hit the ground. Eva sighed and pulled out her cell phone.

Bono and Dawn walked into Mr. Green's office with the duffel bags of money. Dawn tossed them in front of the couch and then started heading back out.

"Hold on," Mr. Green said. "Why are you in such a hurry?"

"There's no reason for me to stick around."

Bono's phone rang. Mr. Green and Dawn stared at him as his face knotted in disbelief.

"We'll meet up later," Bono said, then ended the call. "That was Eva. The carjacker's dead."

"That's good news," Mr. Green said.

"No, it's not," Bono countered.

"Why not?" Dawn asked.

"She was dead when Eva got there. She was face down in an elevator. Buck came stumbling out mumbling and then fell out."

"So Buck killed her," Dawn said.

"No," Bono responded. "When Eva revived Buck in the van, he said the chick beat him the fuck up and knocked him out. He said when he came to, she was dead."

"Okay," Dawn said. "How do you explain that?"

Bono shook his head. "Somebody got on the elevator, killed her, and then got off."

"And no one saw a thing?" Dawn said. "It's a hotel. I'm sure people are getting on and off those elevators all the time."

Bono shrugged. "The only person who could've answered that was Buck, and he was unconscious. I never saw anything like it."

Mr. Green placed his hands in front of his mouth to hide his grin.

"I'm out of here," Bono said.

"Where are you going?" Mr. Green asked.

"Eva's taking Buck to the hospital so he can tell Lowe what happened. I want to be there when he does. He has to know something."

"Keep me informed," Mr. Green said, but Bono was already out the door. He turned his attention to Dawn. "Honey, please sit down."

"I have places to be."

"I only want a little bit of your time, please."

Dawn sat on the couch. She leaned back and crossed her legs. "I'm listening."

"Lowe's being discharged from the hospital in two weeks."

"I can't wait," Dawn said sarcastically.

"What are you going to do once he's back conducting business?"

"I'm going back to my old life."

"By old life, you mean going back to being a secretary for the state?"

"Actually, I never stopped working my state job."

"All this money you're making and you still worked that 9 to 5? Why?"

"Don't know."

"When Lowe no longer has any use for you, maybe you want to consider working for me."

"No."

"I'm sure I'll pay way more than that state job."

Dawn stood up and walked to the window. "When I walked into your office that day and you agreed to put me on, I thought I was going to be seeing a shit load of money, and all of my problems were going to be solved."

"You've seen a shit load of money," Mr. Green said.

"And I have a shit load of problems to go with it."

"If you agree to work for me, you'll have enough money to pay your problems to go away. Money can buy anything."

"Can it buy back time? Can it buy back what I've lost?" Dawn said, becoming emotional.

"May I offer you a little advice?"

"On?"

"Your husband?"

Dawn's eyelids dropped to deadly slits. "I'm listening."

"Men are emotionally fragile, sometimes more so than women. But we mask it so well that you would never know. You say that you've lost your husband. When was the last time you saw him?"

"What does that have to do with anything?" Mr. Green awaited a response. "A month ago, at the Olive Garden."

"Was he still wearing his ring?"

Dawn thought before answering the question. "Yes, but what does that have to do with anything?"

"If you lost your husband like you say, he would've taken it off. He can't help but think of you whenever he looks at it. Don't you think of him every time you look at yours?"

Dawn looked down at her ring and closed her eyes.

"Don't be so quick to give up on him. And don't be so quick to decline my offer."

Dawn's phone vibrated. It was Whitty. "What's up?" Dawn answered.

"The meeting with Dr. Acobi is a go for tomorrow afternoon. We're meeting him for lunch at twelve-thirty at the Steakhouse on Madison and Fifth."

"Twelve-thirty, got it." Dawn ended the call. She looked at her watch. "Mr. Green, I have to go."

"Think about what I said."

"About my husband?"

"Yeah, that too."

Whitty walked into the steakhouse at five minutes to twelve. At twelve o'clock on the dot, Dr. Acobi walked in and was shown to the table. Whitty stood and shook his hand.

"It's a pleasure to meet you, Doctor."

"Same here," Dr. Acobi was a white, thin man in his early forties with a headful of gray hair. He wore an off-the-rack-suit with a pair of Payless shoes. It was obvious that he was too into his work to care about fashion.

"Dante has told me so much about you," Whitty said, as they sat.

"Dante's a good man. We only met a few times, but he has a good head on his shoulders."

"Yes, he does."

Dr. Acobi looked at his watch.

"Dawn should be along shortly. I swear, that girl's going to be late for her own funeral." Whitty said with a chuckle. "We can order if you like."

"No, I'll wait."

"Well, while we're waiting, did Dante explain why he didn't want his name mentioned?" Whitty asked nervously.

Dr. Acobi shook his head. "What his firm did to him was cruel and wicked. In business, a person's reputation is what defines them."

"Well, Dante is hard at work redefining himself. And when he's done, his firm is going to wish they never hung him out to dry."

"Yes. I agree."

"So, for now, Dante doesn't get mentioned," Whitty said.

"I won't mention him. But the Board is going to require that your friend has legal and financial representation."

"Not a problem."

Dr. Acobi picked up the wine menu. "I think I will have a glass of wine while we wait for your friend."

"So will I."

Dawn walked in at twelve twenty-five, surprised to see Whitty and the Doc conversing.

Dr. Acobi stood up as Dawn approached. He introduced himself and pulled out her seat for her to sit.

"Here I am trying to be early, and you two are already here." Dawn said, as she sat.

Whitty looked confused. "Early?"

"You told me the meeting was for twelve-thirty."

"No, I said twelve."

"Twelve? I could've swore… never mind." She turned her attention to Dr. Acobi. "So talk to me, Doc."

An hour later, Dr. Acobi was shaking Dawn and Whitty's hands and heading out the restaurant.

"So?" Whitty asked.

Dawn couldn't hide her smile. "We're going to be millionaires."

Lowe was in his hospital room shadowboxing wearing nothing but a pair of boxers when his doctor knocked on the door and walked in.

"Hey, Doc," Lowe said, as he threw a few more punches and danced around an imaginary opponent.

"You wanted to see me," his doctor asked.

Lowe pulled on a tank top and slid his feet into his slippers. "Yeah, Doc, check it. I know I'm supposed to be out of here next week, but I need to be out of here tomorrow."

"Tomorrow? Hospital policy states that—"

"Fuck hospital policy. I've been cooped up in here for so long that I'm starting to feel like I'm in prison, you feel me? Plus, I got a business to run."

"I would've assumed that you would put your health before your business."

"Right now, my health is dependent on my business."

"I don't know what that means, but I still can't—"

"There's no such thing as can't, Doc."

"If I do this, there would be forms you'll have to sign absolving the hospital, and me from any future malpractice suits in the event that you may suffer any medical complications due to us releasing you before your scheduled time."

"Yeah, whatever. Just get the paperwork together." Lowe sat on the edge of the bed, staring at his cell phone. He gripped it as he thought about the crazy story Buck related to him.

Buck was a street soldier, and he was one of the best. Lowe wasn't accustomed to seeing him on the bad side of a beating. But what really had Lowe on edge was the way Buck told the story. Lowe could hear the awe, fear, and respect in his voice at certain parts of the story. For Buck to say with conviction that he got his ass thoroughly whipped by a girl said a lot. That, and the fact that he couldn't take a deep breath without wincing and holding his side.

Lowe knew that she wasn't a run-in-the-mill gun for hire. Not the way she broke Buck down with just two fingers. What really had Lowe's mind reeling was the fact that *someone* had killed her. Bono theorized that Buck may have killed her and then blacked out, Buck quickly shot that theory down. The last thing he remembered was her knee crushing his neck as she had her finger jabbed into his lung. Buck was positive that he didn't kill her. Someone entered that elevator when he was unconscious, and took out the Southern Belle.

Bono and Lowe looked at each other. Both knew whom the other suspected was behind this, but neither spoke it aloud. Lowe kicked everybody out of his room and called Mr. Green. As he dialed his number, he remembered their first conversation when he had come out of a coma. The part when Mr. Green struck the bedrail and said, "What makes you think you're so irreplaceable?"

"The fact that you haven't replaced me yet, and the fact that you never will."

"Don't be too sure about that last fact."

Don't' be too sure of that last fact, huh? Lowe said to himself as he waited for Mr. Green to answer.

"Hey, Green, it's me."

"Is this important? If not, I'm going to have to call you back. I'm running late for a meeting," Mr. Green said.

"Listen, I just want to apologize."

"For what?" Mr. Green asked, taken aback by Lowe's sudden change in attitude.

"For the brash way I've been acting. I was just so fucked up about almost being taken out by a bitch. Now that she's dead, I'm focusing on what matters most."

"And what's that?"

"Me showing my appreciation for the opportunity you're giving me."

"A very lucrative opportunity," Mr. Green added.

"Yes, it is, and I just want to let you know that I'm just ready to play my position."

"Glad to hear that. I'll call you back when I can." Mr. Green hung up. He stared at the ceiling, wondering if he'd been like Lowe and had been brash in his decision to sic Molina on him. He picked up his phone and dialed her cell. She wasn't answering. He looked at his watch. He was running late for his meeting. *Fuck it,* he thought. *I'll call her later.*

Lowe looked up when he heard a knock at his door. He took a double take at the Latina standing by his door with fresh linen in her hands.

"I'm sorry," she said, as she noticed Lowe only had on a pair of boxers and a tank top. "I'll come back."

"No," Lowe said, hopping off the bed. "Come in and handle your business."

She walked in with a shy smile and started to strip his bed.

"So, where have they been hiding you?" Lowe asked, as he focused on the roundness of her butt. The thin material of her scrubs outlined it perfectly. She didn't look to be no more than twenty-two, twenty-three.

"I work in the children's ward, but I'm covering for a friend today."

Lowe licked his lips. A tent was forming in his boxers and he positioned himself where she could see it.

She saw the protrusion and blushed. "Maybe you should put some clothes on."

"I was thinking about taking some clothes off. As fine as you are, you got to know that this is the normal reaction of a man who lays eyes on you."

"I think the only thing you're laying on me is game."

"Is it working?"

"No comment." She took a long stare at the front of his boxers, and then continued changing his sheets. That look brought Lowe to full erection.

"So, what else do you do besides change sheets?"

"I help patients to the bathroom, and I help them into bed." She slid his pillow into the pillowcase, and gave it a fluff before stepping back. "All done."

"How about helping me into bed?" Lowe said with a wink.

"I think you can manage that on your own."

"I can manage it much better with your help."

She smiled and folded the top sheet down. "Come on, I'll tuck you in."

Lowe got into the bed and stared at her as she covered him with the sheet.

"Now, get some rest," she said, as she turned to leave.

Lowe grabbed her by the hand. "How am I supposed to get some rest with this," he said, looking down at his erection.

She looked down on his bedside table and saw a bottle of baby oil. Lowe knew she was up to something when she kept looking back at the door.

"Maybe I can do something about that," she whispered. She pulled out a latex glove.

Baby oil, glove; Lowe understood what was about to go down. He smiled as she reached into her pocket and withdrew another glove. She cleverly concealed the syringe she pulled out with it in the palm of her hand and behind her first three fingers. Lowe clasped his hands behind his head and awaited his genital massage.

The girl's cell phone chirped. She unclipped it and read the message. "I'm so sorry, I have to go."

"No!" Lowe grabbed her by the arm. "This won't take but a minute."

"I'm really sorry," she said, removing his hand from her arm. Molina walked out of his room, sticking the gloves and syringe back in her pocket. She called Mr. Green as soon as she climbed into her car. "Talk to me."

"I changed my mind," Mr. Green said.

"I don't give refunds."

"I don't care about the money."

"I should've asked for a mil, then. So, what changed in your equation?"

"Lowe decided to play nice."

"Good bye, Green."

"What's the hurry?"

"Junito is waiting for me in Cancun."

"You mean the one with—"

"The chulu down to here."

Mr. Green couldn't see her, but he knew what she meant. He closed his phone when she ended the call. He thought about Lowe. *I hope allowing you to live doesn't come back to bite me in the ass.*

CHAPTER 17

D awn sat back in her office chair and stifled a yawn as her computer did a spell check on the three-page memo she just typed up for her supervisor. She corrected her errors, and then clicked the print icon on her screen, then rolled her chair back from her desk. She looked at the secretaries who were left. Their numbers had diminished to a skeleton crew. Even though Dawn was part-time, she was still doing the same amount of work as if she was full-time. She thought of Mr. Green's question. *Why am I still working here?*

Dawn stared at the other secretaries with scorn and pity. She despised them because the only thing that was keeping them employed was the color of their skin. Of the six black secretaries that worked in their department, she was the only one left, and if it wasn't for Mr. Morgan making her part-time, she would've been out of there, as well. But Dawn pitied them because day in and day out, they would complain about the recession and how they were barely making ends meet. Most of them brought bag lunches from home, and washed their dry ass bologna and cheese sandwiches down with water from the water cooler. One of the highlights of Dawn's day was ordering lunch from the various upscale restaurants in the area, and having it delivered to her desk.

The third page of the memo dropped onto the printer tray. Dawn gathered up the document and headed to Mr. Morgan's office to drop it off. On her way, Susan waved her into the photocopy room. When she entered, Susan was standing in front of the photocopier staring at the screen with a blank look.

"Is there a problem?" Dawn asked.

"I'm about to pull my hair out. I'm trying to copy these forms."

"And?"

"They're double-sided, and I'm trying to figure out how to get this thing to make double-sided copies."

Dawn walked up to the machine and pressed a button. "Try it now."

Susan hit start and waited. "Oh my God. How did you do that?"

"I pressed the double-sided button."

Susan looked at the button and shook her head. "Unbelievable, I can't believe I didn't see that button."

Dawn hit her with a fake smile. Straight dingbat. *I wonder who she had to fuck to keep her job?*

"I love your boots," Susan said, looking down at Dawn's Chanel platform booties. "You won't find those at Payless." Susan said laughing.

"You won't find me there either," Dawn said laughing right along with her.

Susan's copies were done. "Okay, I better get these forms to the boss before he chews my butt off."

Dawn looked down at Susan's flat behind and shook her head. *He won't have much to chew off.* When Dawn returned to her desk, she saw that Julisa had texted her.

U had lunch already?

She texted her back, *no.*

Want 2?

U paying?

Don't I always?

Meet u in pk at 1.

Dawn entered Battery Park at one. Julisa was sitting at their regular table in the Ritz Carlton lounge.

Dawn hugged her and sat down. She looked around.

"Who you looking for?" Julisa said.

"Your bodyguards."

Julisa smacked her hand. "You got jokes, *Honey?*"

"There's no more Honey."

"And there's no more bodyguards. It's just us, like it used to be."

"Yeah, like it used to be," Dawn mumbled.

Julisa heard the sadness in her voice, and placed her hand on top of hers.

"So, what's your husband been up to?" Dawn asked, trying to liven the mood.

"He's still celebrating. He's only been out of the hospital for three weeks, and he's already done everything that his doctor told him not to do."

"That's the Lowe I know."

"Forget about Lowe, what's up with you? What can I do for you?"

"I'm good, Julisa."

"I'm not trying to hear that. Lowe and I wouldn't have shit if it wasn't for you."

"Julisa, I'm good."

"What about the townhouse?"

"I got that covered. The last thing Dre wants is for me to cut him off. He can't go two days without begging me for a piece."

Julisa dug into her purse and pulled out an envelope. She slid it to Dawn.

"What's this?" Dawn asked.

"Open it."

Dawn looked inside and pulled out the check. It was for ten thousand dollars. She put it back in the envelope and slid it back. "Julisa, you know I love you like a sister, and I would never do anything to hurt your feelings, but you know I don't bite my tongue."

"And that's what I love most about you."

"After the way Lowe treated me, I don't want a dime from him."

"This is my money."

"You got a job now?" Dawn asked.

"Lowe's money is my money."

Dawn shook her head. "I'm good. That investment that I made with Nu-Life was a sound one. My financial adviser is projecting a hundred percent return on my initial investment within six months. Whitty really came through for me when I needed her."

"So, what are your plans for tonight?"

"I don't have any."

"No plans for a Friday night?"

"It's just another night for me." Dawn looked around, not believing what her life had become.

"Unacceptable. Tonight, me, you, and Whitty are hanging out."

"You paying?"

"I don't know. You have a problem with me using Lowe's money?"

"Not when it comes to you footing the bill." Dawn winked. They both started laughing.

"We'll meet up at the townhouse," Dawn said.

"Sounds like a plan. Now, let's spend some of Lowe's money on a couple of steak burgers, and whatever else I can think of."

Friday nights at The Bank was usually crowded, but tonight it was filled to its capacity, and there was a line that stretched half way down the block of partygoers who were determined to get in. Lowe had three of the hottest R&B groups slated to come through and perform their hit songs. It was shows like these that nearly doubled The Bank's profits in the short time that Lowe had been out of the hospital.

Him and Julisa were on the dance floor shaking it up, something he refused to do before getting shot. After an hour straight on the dance floor, they walked off and headed to their booth in the VIP section. A fifteen second walk turned into a half hour journey as people stopped Lowe to welcome him back, and to praise him on having the hottest club in the Metro area. Julisa nearly came out of character a few times when females blatantly flirted with Lowe as if she wasn't by his side. But she kept her cool when she saw how quick Lowe was shutting them down.

Buck, Gamble, Naji, and Trent were all sitting at the booth next to Lowe's watching the ladies on the dance floor drop and shake their butts for the DJ.

"Why don't y'all go down there and get with a few women instead of sitting up here gawking," Julisa said, as she sat at her booth.

"We don't go to women," Trent said, "they come to us." Buck, Gamble, and Naji gave him dap.

"Yeah, whatever," Julisa said.

Lowe poured them both a drink and held his glass up. His boys held up glasses, as well.

"To the New York City Boss Playas," Lowe shouted. "We're playas—"

"But we don't play nooo games," Trent said, finishing off their slogan.

"Y'all need to grow up," Julisa said, not touching her drink.

"Drink up," Lowe said to her.

"I already had more than I should have. Plus I'm going to be drinking later on tonight."

"I forgot, you and the girls are going out. You know you owe me, right?"

"For what?" Julisa glared at him.

"I gave Whitty the night off so she can hangout with you. It's Friday night; you know how packed it's going to be in The Vault tonight."

"She deserves to have a little fun once in a while, on a Friday night, too."

"Yeah, yeah."

"Yeah, yeah," Julisa said, mimicking him. She looked at her watch. "It's that time." She kissed him on the cheek. "Don't wait up for me."

Lowe grabbed her by the arm. "Don't play yourself. I want you home before the sun comes up."

"Or what? You're going to ground me for a month?"

"Let that sun come up and you ain't home."

"Bye, Daddy." Julisa grabbed her coat and bag out of the office and headed down to the garage.

"You have a nice night," Lou said, as she walked to her car.

"Give Whitty my love," Cash said.

"Give it to her yourself," Julisa shot back at him.

"She won't let me."

I'm surprised, Julisa said to herself. "See y'all tomorrow." She got into her car and exited the garage.

Cash pulled out his cell and called Lowe. "She just left."

"Good look, Cash." Lowe closed his phone, and downed his drink.

By the time Julisa drove to the corner, her leg was shaking. She thought of how far Dawn's place was and how bad she had to pee. *Shit.* Julisa made a U-turn and headed back to The Bank. She parked across the street, and headed to the front of the line. The bouncer immediately removed the velvet rope when he saw her coming. Julisa ran into The Bank's private office and into its bathroom. She barely had her pants down before her urine hit the water. She moaned as her bladder shrank. Julisa was pulling her pants and panties up when she heard voices filling the office.

"We run this shit," Lowe shouted.

Buck, Gamble, Naji, and Trent followed him into the office. He plopped into his chair and kicked his feet up on the desk.

Julisa turned the knob, getting ready to walk out of the bathroom.

"You decided what you're going to do about Honey?" Trent asked.

Julisa froze.

"Why'd you have to bring that shit up?" Gamble asked.

"Because I want to know what's up. You didn't catch feelings for that bitch, did you?"

"Picture that," Gamble mumbled.

"I'm picturing it real good," Trent said.

"Fuck you."

"Enough!" Lowe said. "Look at y'all, arguing about a bitch."

"That's why I treat bitches how I do," Buck said. "Fuck 'em and then move on to the next ho. I could've fucked Honey."

"Here we go," Naji said.

"You saw the way she used to be staring at me."

"How come you didn't fuck her then?" Trent asked.

"I was fucking with six bitches at the time. I had my plate full, you know?"

"Well, you should've hit that when you had the chance, cause she got some of the tightest pussy I ever sunk my dick into," Gamble said.

"Her shit's like that?" Lowe said.

"Man listen, I had to look down a few times to make sure I wasn't in the wrong hole, you dig?"

"Damn," Lowe said, rubbing his crotch. "You got me wanting to hit that."

Julisa couldn't believe her ears.

"So, what's up with her?" Trent asked again.

"I have to spell it out for you? She knows my whole operation and she's not part of my team."

"What do you think Mr. Green will say when she comes up missing?" Trent asked.

Julisa felt like she had to pee again.

"Fuck Green," Lowe shouted. "I'm two seconds from putting a bullet in his fucking head. I know he was behind that whole carjacking shit. And then he called someone else in to kill that bitch, because he knew if I would've gotten my hands on her, she would've given him up."

"Are you going to let Bono take care of it?" Naji asked.

"Fuck Bono. I don't trust his ass, either. The only motherfuckers I trust are the ones in this room. Bono may have to come up missing, as well."

Everybody looked at Buck.

"That's not too much for you to handle is it?" Lowe asked Buck.

"Nah. Just tell me when."

There was a knock at the door.

"Come in," Lowe said.

Cassidy walked in with a chilled bottle of champagne and a glass. "Sorry I couldn't bring it in earlier, I got tied up at the bar."

"Y'all break out," Lowe said to his crew. "We'll continue this discussion at a later time."

Everybody left except Cassidy. She stood there with the bottle and glass in her hand.

"Fuck is you just standing there for?" Lowe asked.

She walked across the room, and placed the champagne and glass on the desk.

"You can at least open it and pour me a glass."

Cassidy opened it and filled the glass.

Lowe took it from her and guzzled it down. "Come here," he said, patting his lap. Cassidy didn't move. "Bitch, I said come here?"

Julisa turned the knob and cracked the door. She saw Lowe grab Cassidy by the elbow, and pull her down on his lap.

"What's up with you acting all brand new on me?" Lowe asked.

"It's been a while," Cassidy said real low.

"And?" Lowe stuck his hand under her shirt and groped her breasts. Julisa's eyes damn near popped out her head.

"I didn't know if you still felt the same about me," Cassidy said timidly.

"C'mon, girl, you know you my white chocolate, stop playing." He sucked on her neck, and stuck his hand down the front of her pants.

Julisa's teeth were so clenched her jaw started trembling.

"I'm so fucking stressed right now." Lowe slid her off his lap. He unbuckled his jeans and pulled out his semi-hard erection. "You know what to do."

Cassidy got on her knees, and got in between his legs. She grabbed his shaft and was about to put it in her mouth when he stopped her.

"Hold up." Lowe grabbed some tissue off his desk and wiped off her lipstick. "Last time you left lipstick all over my fucking boxers, and I had to hear Julisa's fucking mouth." He hit the power button on the CD player. He sang along with *The Dream* as Cassidy bobbed up and down his shaft.

Tears were running down Julisa's cheeks as she watched the scene through the crack of the door.

"Stand up," Lowe commanded. He stood up with Cassidy, and bent her over the desk. He impaled her with one thrust, and hammered for about thirty seconds. And just when Julisa thought it couldn't get any worse, he pulled out of her and penetrated her anally with no mercy.

Julisa was crying audibly now, but the stereo's surround sound masked her sobs. She put up with a lot of Lowe's shit throughout the years, but this? Running up in a female's ass without protection?

Cassidy tried pulling away, but Lowe had a death grip on her waist. She was forced to take his pounding until he squirted deep in her bowels. He waited until he went soft in her and then pulled out. He flopped down into his chair and poured himself another glass of champagne.

"That's what I'm talking about," he said, wiping the sweat from his brow. "Pull your pants up and go get a washcloth from the bathroom."

Julisa stopped breathing as she watched Cassidy pull up her pants and head to the bathroom. Julisa looked around the tiny area. There was no place for her to hide. She yanked the strap off her purse and wrapped it around her fist. *Fuck it. I'm going to jail tonight. I'm going to punch this bitch's face in, and then try like hell to strangle this no good motherfucker.* She stood behind the door and readied herself.

Cassidy stepped into the bathroom. When she hit the light switch, Julisa slammed the door. Cassidy spun around and almost shitted on herself. Julisa looked like a rabid dog. Her nostrils flared as drool and tears slid down her chin.

"I'm so sorry, I'm so sorry," Cassidy said over and over. She yelped and fell to her knees when Julisa raised her fist. Cassidy covered her face. "Please, I'm so sorry. Please."

Julisa's adrenaline was pumping, her fist tightened, and her heart demanded retribution, but the way Cassidy's body shook with fear paralyzed her.

"What the fuck is taking you so long in there?" Lowe shouted over the music.

Julisa snatched a washcloth off the rack and ran it under the water. She threw it at Cassidy. "You give him that and then meet me in front of the club, you hear me?"

Cassidy's head jerked up and down. She got off her knees and walked out of the bathroom. Julisa watched her as she tossed the washcloth to Lowe and ran out the office.

"Yo, where the fuck you going?" Lowe called after her. "Crazy bitch."

Dawn looked out the front window of the townhouse, expecting to see Julisa pulling up any minute. "Call her again," she said to Whitty.

"I just did, and she's not answering."

"Did you text her?"

"Yes, and so did you."

"This doesn't make sense. She got us sitting here all dressed up for nothing." Dawn started undoing the straps off her shoes.

"Let's give her five more minutes," Whitty said, hoping like hell that Julisa wasn't going to stand them up.

"She should've been here an hour ago."

"Damn." Whitty stomped her foot. "This is the first Friday night I ever got off and I can't even enjoy it."

"It's only ten o'clock. You can still hang out."

"Not by myself."

The doorbell rang.

"That's her," Whitty said.

Dawn walked to the front door and swung it open. "Bitch, where the fuck..." She stopped when she saw Julisa's red and puffy eyes, and her hand clamped around Cassidy's forearm.

Whitty ran up to the door and stopped short. "Oh my, God. What happened?"

Julisa flung Cassidy through the door, and then she cried in Dawn's arms. Dawn hugged her for a minute as Whitty tried getting something out of Cassidy, but she wouldn't say a word. Dawn led Julisa to the couch and they both sat. Cassidy and Whitty sat on the opposite couch. Cassidy hugged herself and stared at the floor.

"Somebody needs to say something," Whitty said. "This shit is freaking me out."

Dawn looked at Julisa. "Talk to me."

"I went back to the club to use the bathroom in the office. As I was coming out, Lowe and his boys came in. They were talking and then they left. Then she comes in and..."

Julisa and Cassidy started crying.

"I hate you," Julisa said, as she lunged for her. Whitty pulled Cassidy out the way just as Julisa's nails came swiping down for her face. Dawn grabbed Julisa around the waist and held her back.

"Kill her," Julisa said, as she turned to Dawn with a crazed look on her face. "I want her dead."

Cassidy started to cry even louder.

"Take Cassidy into the kitchen and calm her down," Dawn said to Whitty. When they disappeared into the kitchen, Dawn focused back on Julisa. "You want her dead; what about Lowe, he's just as guilty."

"I want him dead, too."

"We're not killing anybody, you hear me?"

"He's going to kill you."

"What?" Dawn stopped breathing.

Julisa related to her everything she heard while in the bathroom.

Dawn was stuck between anger and fright. "Okay, let's just calm down, maybe you didn't hear him right."

"Didn't you hear what I just said? He's going to have Buck kill you. He said you know too much about his operation. He was also talking about killing Bono, as well."

"Mr. Green would never allow that."

"Lowe also said he knows that Mr. Green was behind the phony carjacking scheme."

"So, he's going to kill Mr. Green, too?"

"He needs Mr. Green."

"Why is that?"

Julisa told her everything. Everything from the bank they were opening up to telling Dawn that she was the one who gave Lowe the list of her clients. All Dawn could do was drop her head.

"I'm so sorry," Julisa said crying. "He swore to me that he was going to hook you up with a cushiony exec spot at the bank when it opened. I didn't mean for this to happen."

Dawn hugged her. "This isn't your fault, you hear me?"

Julisa nodded.

"And it's not Cassidy's fault either."

"What?"

"Lowe's a dog. He's been cheating on you from day one. I won't be surprised if he threatened to fire her if she didn't do what he said. You know I'm telling the truth."

"Fuck him. I don't even care anymore. It's over between us. After what I saw him do tonight, he can never make love to me again. For six months I prayed for God to bring him back to me, now, I wish that he'd died that night."

"You don't mean that," Dawn said.

"That nasty motherfucker stuck his dick in that bitch's ass. I want him bound to a chair with his hands cuffed behind his back, so I can beat him an inch away from death like you did to those faggots pretending to be cops. Then I want to pull his dick out and cut it off and watch what little life he has left drain out onto the ground."

Dawn looked into her friend's eyes and knew something inside her had snapped. She hugged her again. Only this time,

Julisa didn't fold into her embrace. She was hard as a statue. Dawn pulled back and noticed that she wasn't crying anymore.

"Julisa—"

"Are you going to help me kill him or not?"

"Julisa—"

"I'm not going to allow him to hurt you or anyone else anymore. I came here so you could help me get away with it, but if you're not going to help me, then... I'll just do what I have to do, and if I get caught, then so be it."

Dawn took a deep breath and exhaled. This was the very thing she was trying to avoid. She just wanted to get in, get some money, and get out.

"Dawn, are you going to help me or not?" Julisa whispered.

"*If* I agree to help you, this has to be done my way, understand?"

"I'll do whatever it takes to get him in that chair."

"You're going to have to go back to him, play the perfect wife."

Julisa looked like she wanted to throw up. "Fine."

"And he can't know that you know about Cassidy."

"Fine."

Dawn looked toward the kitchen. "Whitty! Come out here and bring Cass with you."

Whitty walked out with Cassidy trailing behind her hesitantly. Whitty sat down, Cassidy stood behind the couch.

"Sit your skinny ass down," Dawn said to her.

Cassidy sat beside Whitty, shifting her eyes between her and Julisa.

"Cass, you got a decision to make, and you've got to make it now. You can do exactly what I tell you to do and all will be forgiven, or all four of us are going for a ride and only three of us are coming back."

"Whatever you want me to do, I'll do." She looked at Julisa. "Please forgive me. I'm Canadian. I'm here illegally; I told Lowe that the day he hired me. One night he called me into his office and told me that he needed me to, to... help him relieve some stress. I refused, and then he threatened to fire me and spread the word to the other clubs that I was here illegally and that he fired me because I was stealing and coming to work high. I did what I felt I had to do."

Dawn looked at Julisa.

Julisa smiled and stood up. Cassidy was on the verge of tears when Julisa grabbed her hand and pulled her to her feet. She hugged her tight. "I forgive you, Cass, I know my husband is a piece of shit. He's going to pay for what he did you."

Cassidy broke down in Julisa's arms, thanking her for understanding.

Whitty looked at Dawn and mouthed. *What the fuck is going on?*

"Okay, y'all," Dawn said. "Enough of the mushy shit, we got work to do."

CHAPTER 18

*J*ulisa tapped her finger on the desk as she waited for the download to be complete. For the past half hour, she'd been copying all of Lowe's files from his computer and laptop onto a flash drive.

Whitty pulled into the garage and parked a few cars away from Julisa's Caddy. She got out of her car and stared at Julisa's. Cash and Lou craned their necks to see what she was staring at. She approached Julisa's car and picked up Julisa's car keys off the ground.

"I swear that woman would leave her head somewhere if it wasn't attached to her head," Whitty said to Cash and Lou, as she approached them. She tossed the keys to Cash. "Can you have Bono give these to her?"

"No Problem."

"Thanks, hon."

"Anything for you," Cash said smiling.

Julisa jumped when her phone rang. "What?"

"Lowe just left the bar, I think he's on his way to the office," Cassidy whispered into her phone.

"Okay." Julisa ended the call. The last download was almost complete.

She jumped again when she heard a soft knock at the door. "Come in."

Bono stepped in, dangling her car keys. "You must've been in a hurry. You dropped these."

"Shit. I've got a lot on my mind, right now." She held her hands up for him to toss them.

Bono cut his eyes at the laptop before leaving the office. When the last of the files had finished downloading, Julisa grabbed her purse, and started heading out the door before Lowe got there. "Shit!" She turned around, realizing that she had left the flash drive plugged into the side port of Lowe's laptop. She rushed to the desk and yanked it out. When Lowe's office door opened, she dropped the flash drive into the chair.

"What's up?" Lowe asked, surprised to see her.

"Nothing," Julisa said nervously.

"Nothing, huh?" He walked up to her and started kissing her.

Julisa took her mind someplace else as he slid his hands up her shirt and groped her breasts.

"You like that?" he said with a smirk.

"Yes, baby." Julisa said between clinched teeth.

He slid his hand down the back of her skirt and ran it down the crack of her butt. "You've been avoiding me for the past couple days. I got needs you know."

"I haven't been avoiding—" Her breath got caught in her throat as he shoved her into the chair.

"Damn, baby, you look stressed," Lowe said. "What's been going on? Talk to me."

She gave him the sexiest smile she could muster and rolled the chair away from the desk. "Now that you mention it, I am kind of stressed." She hiked her skirt up and moved her panties to the side. Lowe swallowed as she parted her lips and showed him her wet clit. "You wanna help relieve some of this stress?"

Lowe fell to his knees like he was about to pray to God and stared at her twitching clit.

"Handle your business," she cooed.

Lowe unbuckled his pants and freed his nine-inch lead pipe. "I'm going to need to relieve some stress, as well."

Julisa looked down at him and licked her lips. "I got chu, Boo. Do me and then I'll do you."

Lowe dove between her legs, tongue first. Julisa looked down at him in disgust. Lowe was so focused on how good it was going to feel sticking his dick down her throat that he didn't notice that her body wasn't responding to his touch.

She grabbed the back of his head with one hand while reaching into the chair for the flash drive with the other. Once she got her hand wrapped around it, she stuffed it into her purse and sighed. She looked down at Lowe's head rotating and moving from side to side. *Fucking bastard, I can't wait to cuff you to that chair. Until then, hold this down.* Her butt cheeks jiggled as she farted in his face.

"Aye, yo, what the fuck?" Lowe backed up, falling on his butt.

"I'm so sorry, Boo, it slipped out."

"That shit caught me right in the mouth, Jewels, damn."

"I'm sorry, baby, let me make it up to you."

"Nah." Lowe got to his feet and pulled his pants up. "You know that shit turns me the fuck off. Fuck!" He stormed into the bathroom and slammed the door.

Julisa pulled her skirt down and tiptoed to the bathroom door. "I'm so sorry, baby."

Lowe opened the door. "Yo, just get the fuck out of here. Go shopping or something," he said around the toothpaste in his mouth.

Julisa tried kissing him on the cheek. He pulled away, and went back to brushing his teeth. Julisa grabbed her purse and left. She busted out laughing when she got out into the corridor. She reduced her laughter to a smile as she approached the elevator. Bono pulled out his key and opened the elevator for her.

"Thank you, Bono."

"Not a problem."

Julisa waved at Cash and Lou as she exited the elevator.

"Enjoy the rest of your night," Lou said.

"You too; see y'all tomorrow." Julisa fumbled in her bag for her keys as she headed towards her car. A shadow separated itself from the column next to Julisa's car and headed straight for her. Julisa didn't see the figure until it was too late. One second, she was staring at the whites of someone's eyes whose face was hidden behind a ski mask, and the next, she was being head butted. She stumbled onto the car beside her and slid down to the pavement.

She felt the shadow snatch her purse. She tried to focus her eyes on the assailant, but there was no one to focus on, they were gone.

"Help!" She cried out.

Cash was the first one to arrive. "Mrs. Jones, what happened?"

"Someone just robbed me."

"Don't move." Cash pulled out his phone and called Lowe.

Dawn rushed to The Bank when Whitty called her and told her what happened. Bono met her at the front of the club and escorted her in.

"How is she?" Dawn asked.

"She's fine. Lowe's the one who's flipping out."

When they got to the office, Julisa was laying on the couch with an ice pack on her head. Lowe was on his knees next to her, holding her hand.

When he saw Dawn, he stood up. "I need to talk to you, outside."

"Lowe—" Julisa said, but he had already grabbed Dawn's hand and was standing out in the corridor.

"What's up?" Dawn asked.

"Listen to me very carefully," he whispered to her. "Talk to her. I know she had to see something that can help me find out who did this to her. I want this person, you hear me?" His eyes narrowed.

"I'll talk to her."

He nodded and headed back to The Bank.

Dawn entered the office. "You okay?" She asked Julisa.

"Is he gone?"

"Yeah."

Julisa sat up and threw the ice pack in the wastebasket. "Girl, if I would've known shit was going to go down like that…"

Dawn sat next to her. "And you're sure it wasn't just a mugging?" she whispered.

"No one has ever been mugged in our garage." She held her hands up. "They didn't take any jewelry, just my purse, and Lou found it outside the garage minus the cash—"

"And the flash drive."

"Bingo."

Dawn looked toward the door. "He's good." She was referring to Bono.

"I dropped my keys by my car door for Whitty to pick up, as planned," Julisa said.

Dawn nodded. "Whitty called me when she got down into The Vault, and told me she gave your keys to Cash, and that he was on his way to give them to Bono."

"He stepped into the office and tossed me my keys. On his way out, he cut his eyes at the laptop. He saw the flash drive."

"You sure he saw it?"

"Positive."

"He must've headed straight down to the garage as soon as he left you."

"No. He was standing right here at the elevator when I was leaving."

"Did you get a look at the person?" Dawn asked.

"No, but whoever it was he was tall and wide as hell."

"Monster-Sick," Dawn said.

"Who?"

"Now, I know for a fact Bono's got the flash drive." She looked at the bump on Julisa's head. "Girl, I'm so sorry. I just knew he was going to confront you on the elevator or in the garage and ask you what you downloaded. I never thought he would—"

Julisa waved her hand at her. "It was worth it. You saw how that conniving bastard, Lowe, was on his knees holding my hand?"

"He looked like he wanted to cry in the hallway a few seconds ago." Dawn replied.

"Fuck him."

"Now, now, Miss-have-to-play-the-perfect-housewife." Dawn said.

"I tried to… but—"

"But? Julisa what did you do?"

"He walked into the office as I was leaving."

"And?"

"He wanted to get busy."

"And?"

"And I opened my legs like the perfect wife, and allowed him to lick the kitty."

"And?"

"And I grabbed the back of his head and farted in his face."

Dawn tried to keep a serious face, but she pictured the scene and busted out laughing. "You's a nasty bitch."

"Girl, you had to be there. I got that motherfucker good. You know how gassy I get after eating broccoli and cheese. And that sucker was hot and stiiink."

Dawn had tears in her eyes now. "Shut up," she said trying to catch her breath.

"You should've seen how fast he pulled his head back, and ran to the bathroom to brush his teeth."

"You're supposed to be a lady, Julisa," Dawn said, wiping tears from her eyes, and still trying to catch her breath.

"Humph. That motherfucker's lucky I didn't have to shit."

They were both holding their stomachs as they balled over in laughter.

Dawn finally calmed down. "All jokes aside, there's no turning back."

"I can't wait for Bono to see those files, along with the ones we forged. I just hope it's enough for him to act," Julisa said.

"Believe me, it's more than enough."

Bono waited for everything to calm down before pulling out his cell phone and making a call.

"I got it, and I'm looking at the files now," Eva said, when she answered her phone.

"Anything we need to worry about?" Bono asked.

"Hold on." He could hear her typing in the background. She was e-mailing a document to his phone. "This is just the tip of the iceberg."

Bono checked the document she sent to his phone. He ended his call with her, and called Mr. Green. "It's me. We have a problem."

Mr. Green took his glasses off and rubbed his eyes. "And you know for a fact she got this off his laptop?"

"I saw the flash drive in the laptop myself."

Mr. Green slammed his fist on his desk. "I can't believe this motherfucker's been playing me all these years." According to Lowe's files, he wasn't truthful with the club's financial statements. Mr. Green also found out from the files that Lowe was selling the keys of coke from the carwash for twenty-five thousand a piece. Five thousand over the price they had agreed upon. Then there was the file listing the names of the future board members of Mr. Green's bank. Dawn was surprised that all of the board members were the individuals who were laundering their money through Mr. Green. The document that sealed Lowe's fate was the one Dawn had made up. It was a letter to a Daily News reporter to go along with the files. Everything was supposed to be sent to this reporter if anything was to happen to Lowe.

"What do you think his wife was going to do with these files?" Mr. Green asked.

"Best-case scenario. She's tired of his bullshit, and she's going to blackmail him for a divorce," Bono replied.

"Worst-case scenario?"

"She's working for the cops," Bono suggested.

Mr. Green sighed. "What do you suggest?"

"You have a weak link in your chain."

"I can't afford any weak links. Talk to Julisa, find out what her intentions were."

"And Lowe?"

"Let's not worry about him right now."

Dawn parked in the alleyway of Chen-li's ice cream parlor, and cut off her engine.

"Now what?" Julisa whispered.

"Why are you whispering?"

"I don't know. It's dark, quiet, I've never been this deep into Chinatown... this whole set-up is spooky."

"You sure this is safe?" Whitty asked from the backseat. "I mean what's stopping these guys from just taking the money, shooting us in the head, and dumping our bodies into one of these dumpsters?"

"Or into their beef fried rice," Cassidy said from the backseat.

They all looked at her.

"What?" Cassidy said. "They eat cat and dog."

Dawn shook her head. "I should've came by myself, like I started to."

A pair of headlights suddenly appeared behind them. A mid-sized mover's truck drove past them, and parked on the opposite side of the alleyway. A young version of Chen-li hopped out of the truck and walked toward the car.

"That's Zen, Chen-li's son," Dawn said.

Zen had his shoulder-length hair pulled back in a ponytail and was wearing a pair of Red Monkey jeans and a tank top. Even with the dim lighting, the women could see that Zen's arms and chest were chiseled like Bruce Lee's.

"Umph, I wonder if he likes dark meat?" Julisa said.

"Damn, that china man's fine," Whitty chimed in.

Dawn looked at Cassidy through her rearview mirror. "What? You ain't got nothing slick to say?"

"Nope, I'm too busy drooling."

"We're here to do business, that's it," Dawn said. She opened her car door and stepped out.

Zen bowed his head slightly. Dawn did the same. He approached her and gave her a hug. A hug that made Julisa, Whitty, and Cassidy look at each other and wonder. Zen stooped down and looked into the car. "Hi, ladies."

"Hi," Julisa waved.

He grabbed Dawn by the hand, and led her to the truck. He opened the back, and hit a switch. The overhead light came on.

"Holy shit," Whitty said.

Julisa got out the car.

"She said to stay in the car," Whitty said.

"That don't apply to me." Julisa headed to the truck.

Dawn and Zen were already in the back when Julisa approached.

"Didn't I tell you to wait in the car?"

"I want to pick out my own gun."

"It's okay," Zen said. He held his hand out to help Julisa up into the rear of the truck.

Julisa looked at the racks of guns that lined both sides of the truck's rear interior. She reached out and grabbed the barrel of a Mack 11.

Dawn swatted her hand. "Don't touch anything."

Zen took them farther into the truck's interior.

Dawn saw an assortment of handguns. "This is more like it. What's this one?" She asked Zen.

".380. It's compact, but very powerful." He picked it up and laid it in her hand. Dawn studied it, and then passed it to Julisa.

She looked at it and then looked back at the Mack 11.

Zen walked back to the rack and pulled it out. He held it out with both hands toward her as if he was handing her a sacred artifact.

Julisa took the submachine gun from him and inspected it. "This is it," she whispered.

"I'll take six .380's with holsters and ammo." Dawn stared at Julisa cuddling the Mack 11 as if it was a baby. "And I'll take what she has in her hand."

Zen grabbed a duffel bag, and put everything into it. Dawn gave the bag to Julisa and told her to take it to the car. A few moments later, her and Zen hopped down from the back of the truck. He pulled the door down, and walked Dawn back to her car.

"Good night, ladies," he said, as he bent down to look into the car.

"Good night," Cassidy, Julisa, and Whitty responded at the same time. They watched as he put his arm around Dawn's waist and pulled her close. He kissed her on her neck and whispered something in her ear. Dawn smiled and pulled away from him. She opened the trunk, put what she owed him in a bag, and handed it to him. He waved to everyone one last time before heading back to the truck.

"You slut," Julisa said, as Dawn got into the car.

"Fuck you, it's not what you think."

"Yeah, right. We saw the way he was eyeing you and hugging all up on you," Whitty said.

"Zen ain't hitting that?" Julisa asked.

"Nope."

"Not once?"

"Not once. He licked it a couple times, though."

They all started laughing.

They returned to the townhouse just before midnight. Cassidy, Julisa, and Whitty sat around the dining room table and paid close attention to Dawn as she gave them a crash course in loading, firing, and how to carry their .380s. Everyone picked up quick except Whitty. Dawn had to go through the loading procedure three times with her.

"C'mon, Whitty, this is simple." Dawn grabbed a clip off the table. "Shove the clip in, pull the slide back, that's it." Dawn pulled the clip out and ejected the bullet in the chamber. "You try." She held the gun and clip out to her.

Whitty grabbed the gun with her thumb and forefinger and then reached for the clip. She fumbled with the clip as if she was trying to fit a square block into a round hole.

"Damn, this isn't rocket science," Julisa said.

"Just shush, you're making me more nervous." Whitty finally shoved the clip in. "Okay," she said with a huff.

"And?" Dawn said.

"Oh yeah." Whitty bit down on her lip as she pulled the slide back and let it go.

"Okay, now unload it," Dawn said.

Whitty turned the gun upside down and squinted at the catch. "I pull this, right?"

"Are you asking me or telling me?" Dawn said.

Julisa sighed.

Whitty sucked her teeth and pulled the catch. She pulled the clip out and placed it on the table. "Ta-da," she said, impressed with herself.

"What about the one in the chamber?" Dawn asked.

"Shit."

"Damn, girl," Cassidy said.

"You bitches act like I'm supposed to know this shit just because I got a degree. I graduated from college, not an Al-

Qaedah training camp." She tossed the gun on the table. "I don't see why I need this anyway."

"It's for protection," Cassidy said.

"This shit isn't going to protect me. I can barely load the damn thing, and I sure as hell ain't shooting anybody with it."

"Shit is about to get hectic," Dawn said. "Hopefully, you won't need it, but I rather you have it and not need it than need it and not have it."

Whitty shook her head. "I don't know."

"Just carry it in your purse for the next few days," Dawn said.

Whitty reluctantly grabbed the gun. She slammed the clip in and pulled back the slide, and then stuffed it in her purse.

Dawn sat down at the table. "This is it. I know Bono showed those files to Mr. Green, and if I know Mr. Green like I think I do, he's figuring out the best way to confront Lowe."

"And we can't allow that," Julisa said.

"No, we can't. Which is why we're dealing with Lowe Thursday night."

"Thursday night? Why so soon?" Whitty asked.

"Thursday is perfect. Every Thursday, Lowe is at the club by himself, because Buck, Gamble, Naji, and Trent, hangout at Naji's place, shooting pool and bullshitting. They won't notice Lowe's missing until Friday night."

Julisa nodded. "I agree Thursday's the best time. We make it look like a professional hit; Trent and them will automatically point the finger at Mr. Green. And if they try and get at him—"

"Bono will annihilate them," Dawn said.

"So when all this is over, what happens to us?" Cassidy asked.

"Once this is over, we're going to put our heads together and we're going to become the wealthiest women in Manhattan," Dawn said. "We don't need Mr. Green, The Bank, Bono, or anyone else. We can open and operate our own shit."

"That's what I'm talking about," Whitty said.

Dawn looked at her. "Thank you."

"For what?"

"For having my back. You came through for me when I needed you most. I didn't know what I was going to do for money, but then you came up with that Nu-Life investment. I can never repay you for that." Dawn got up and hugged her.

Whitty felt like shit. She watched as Dawn hugged Julisa and then Cassidy. She thought about Dante. She didn't know when it happened, but she was in love with him. She shook her head as her eyes welled with tears. *I love Dawn, and I'm in love with her husband. How do I find myself in these fucked up situations? It's only going to be a matter of time before Dawn finds out about me and Dante, and it's only a matter of time before they both find out that I used both of them in order to pull off the Nu-life investment. Dante loves me, I know he does. If I explain everything to him, he'll understand. I know he will.*

"Whitty, you okay?" Dawn asked.

"Me? I'm just peachy."

Lowe entered the reception area of Mr. Green's office with Buck and Trent in tow. When they approached the receptionist's desk, she could tell from their hardball faces, and violent strides that today may be the first time she would have to call security.

"I need to see him immediately," Lowe said to her, as he stood directly in front of her.

She was about to ask him if he had an appointment, but the twitch in his right eye snapped her mouth shut. She picked up the phone. "Mr. Green, Mr. Jones is here to see you... Yes, sir." She hung up. "You can go—"

Lowe and Trent flashed past her. Buck now stood in front of her with a smile.

"Can I help you?" she asked him.

"It's break time," Buck said, leaning over her counter.

"Excuse me?"

Buck disconnected the line from her phone.

She stood up. "Excuse me, you can't—"

"Sit. Down." His face turned hard, hers turned red.

She slowly sat back down, never taking her eyes off him.

"That's it, just relax, and kick those pretty toes of yours up. You know you got some sexy-ass toes for a white girl, right?"

Her face turned redder.

Mr. Green was on the phone when Lowe and Trent walked in. He held his finger up. "Yes, I will have the contracts faxed to you this afternoon. Something's just come up; I'm going to have to call you back." He ended the call. He looked at Lowe like he was crazy. "What's up?"

"What's up? That's what I'm here to find out. You shut down the carwash and the laundering operation. Now, I find out from Bono that you postponed the board meeting. What the fuck is going on, Green?"

"I already told you what's going on."

"Fuck what you told me, what aren't you telling me?"

"First of all, you need to calm down and remember who you're talking to."

"You see," Lowe said, pointing at him. "Therein lies the problem. It seems like you've forgotten who you're talking to."

"Lowe—"

"Fuck you! Motherfuck you! You think you can pull this off without me? We'll see about that."

"Are you threatening me?"

"I don't make threats. I make things happen." Lowe turned. Trent opened the door.

"Lowe!" Mr. Green stood up.

Lowe walked out, Trent slammed the door behind them.

Lowe cocked his head as he approached the receptionist's desk. She had one foot propped up on her desk, and from the look on her face, it was against her will. Buck was caressing her toes. "What the fuck are you doing?"

"Just making sure she was comfortable."

The receptionist jerked her foot down. Buck winked at her before turning to leave with Lowe and Trent.

"You really need help," Lowe said to Buck, as they rode the elevator down to the lobby.

"Help? You talking about… Man, listen. I was two seconds from getting some head in the employees' bathroom. You saw the way she was enjoying that foot massage."

"Buck," Lowe said. "Shut the fuck up. Just… just shut the fuck up. I want Dawn dead before the week's out. Can you do that?"

"No problem."

"You think Green's trying to get her to take your place?" Trent asked.

Lowe punched the wall. "Fucking Green. That's exactly what he's trying to do. Well, when I get done, he's going to see just how much he needs me." He turned to Buck. "You know what? Fuck Dawn. Don't kill her. I got a better idea."

Dawn grabbed her things and headed to the time clock.

"Good night," Susan called after her.

"Good night." Dawn took her state ID from around her neck and stuck it into her purse. As she stepped outside her office building, she spotted Monster-Sick on the sidewalk staring at her. Her gun was in her glove compartment. She turned around to walk back into the building and bumped into Bono.

"We need to talk."

"You scared the shit out of me." She saw Eva standing a couple feet away, her eyes on everyone within thirty feet of them. "What's up with the wolf pack?"

"It's Buck."

"What about him?"

"He's gone."

"So."

"When Buck disappears, people die."

Dawn eyes widened.

Bono pointed to the van. "Now, let's go have that talk."

They pulled up to the carwash. Monster-Sick remained in the van while Bono, Dawn, and Eva headed to the office.

Dawn blinked when they entered the office and she saw Gamble.

Bono looked at him. "Speak."

"Honey. Lowe's my man and all, and there are times when I don't agree with certain decisions that he makes, but I roll with him anyway. But this is one that I can't roll with."

"Which one is that?" Dawn asked.

"A couple weeks ago, he talked about doing something to you."

"Something?"

"Killing you."

"Really?" The blood drained from her face.

"I thought he was just talking shit, cause that's what he does. But then yesterday, Lowe is telling me and Naji about his meeting with Mr. Green yesterday and how it was time to teach Mr. Green just how far he's willing to go to prove that he's not to be fucked with. I asked him where Buck was, and Trent told me not to worry where he was at, and that I should keep my distance from you."

Dawn's belly jumped.

"The only person I could tell was Bono. And here I am."

"You did the right thing," Bono said. "You better head on out of here."

Gamble looked at Dawn, and then exited the office.

Bono picked the flash drive off the desk and tossed it to Dawn. "This is what I want to talk about."

"What about it?"

"Why was Julisa downloading Lowe's files?"

"Why don't you ask her?"

"I'm asking you because I know she wouldn't do this on her own, I'm asking you because if you don't give me a straight answer, I can hurt you til you do. What were you planning on doing with these files?"

Bono took off his jacket and rolled up his sleeves. "Okay, if this is how you want to play it."

"What are you going to do, hit me?"

"No, she is."

Dawn turned to look at Eva. She turned right into a fist to the temple. Dawn stumbled and fell over a chair. Eva was on her. She grabbed her by the neck and punched her two more times in the face and let her go. The back of Dawn's head hit the floor with a loud thud.

Bono sat on top of the desk and looked down at her. "What were you going to do with the files?"

Dawn looked up at him with tears in her eyes. Her lips trembled, but she wasn't going to talk.

Bono looked at Eva. "Break her arm."

Dawn drew her legs to her chest and kicked at Eva each time she approached. Eva feinted left. Dawn kicked out, but Eva was on the right and then on top of her. She punched Dawn in the face, dazing her and then put her arm in an arm bar.

Dawn screamed as Eva applied just enough pressure to cause the maximum amount of pain without breaking the limb. Eva looked at Bono.

"Do it," he said.

"Wait!" Dawn cried.

"I'm listening."

"Julisa caught Lowe fucking Cassidy."

"Lowe's been fucking Cassidy, everybody knows that," Bono said.

"Julisa didn't."

"The wife's always the last to find out. So, anyway…"

"So, she wanted to get back at Lowe."

"How was she planning on doing that?"

Dawn didn't answer. Eva applied pressure. "She wanted to empty his accounts. All of them."

Bono shook his head. "Women. Why is money the first thing you go for?" He looked up at Eva. "Why do you do that?"

"The only thing better than getting even is getting paid," Eva said.

"Can't argue with that." He nodded at Eva. She let Dawn's arm go.

Dawn brought her arm to her chest and massaged it. Eva extended her hand to help her off the floor. Dawn swatted it away.

Eva made a fist. Bono held his hand up. She took a deep breath and backed up.

"Sneaking me is the only way you can beat me, bitch," Dawn spat, as she got to her feet.

Eva snorted. "Next time, I'll let you see it coming, bitch."

"All right," Bono said. "You two can talk on your own time, right now, you're on mine." He looked at Dawn. "It seems like you're going to need my help."

"I don't need anything from you."

"So you're going to go gun-to-gun with Buck?"

"Like I said, I don't need your help." She stormed out the office.

"Put two men on her," Bono said to Eva.

"She said she didn't need your help."

Bono looked at her.

"Fine, I'll put two on her. You believe her about the files?"

"I believe that she's too dangerous for her own good. Whatever she had planned may have very well destroyed Mr. Green and Lowe."

"You think it's over?"

"Not by a long shot."

CHAPTER 19

As soon as Dawn got home, she called Julisa and told her about her *talk* with Bono.

"Are you sure you're all right?" Julisa asked her for the umpteenth time.

"I'm fine. I don't know if Bono believed me or not so we're going to have to do this tonight."

"It's Wednesday, Dawn. Gamble, Naji, and Trent are going to be here all night."

"That's okay. We're just going to have to lure Lowe away from them and do what we have to do."

"How are we going to do that?"

"I'll tell you when I get there. I'm going to get dressed. Call Cassidy and Whitty and tell them to be ready."

Dante walked up behind Whitty as she filled the dishwasher with their dinner plates from earlier and wrapped his arms around her waist. He kissed her on her neck just below her ear. She smiled and closed her eyes. She turned around in his arms and looked up at him.

"I should've never showed you my weak spot," she whispered. "You know what happens to me when you kiss me there."

"And you know what you do to me when you walk around here with nothing on but my T-shirt."

She gently sucked on his bottom lip as he slid his hands under the T-shirt and teased her nipples. She pulled out of his embrace.

"What's up?" Dante asked.

"Nothing." She looked at the floor.

"You've been in another world the whole night. Something's bothering you." He caught her looking at his ring. "You and Dawn got into something?"

She walked away from him.

"Hold on." He caught up with her in the living room. "Talk to me, Whitty."

She turned into his arms and hugged him. Dante could feel the warmth of her tears on his chest.

She finally pulled back, and looked him in the eyes. "I've never been in love before, but I know what I'm feeling isn't lust. Just the thought of us not being together brings tears to my eyes."

"I... I don't know what to say."

"You don't have to say anything. I just want you to know that no matter how this ends, my feelings for you are real."

"End?"

"How could you just stop loving Dawn? I can't think of anything that you can do to me right now that would make me just stop loving you."

"I never stopped loving her."

"Then why am I the one standing here, and not her?"

Dante shook his head. "Why did she hurt me? She hurt me deep." His voice cracked, as he tried to hold back his tears.

Whitty hugged him. Dante put his head on her shoulder and hugged her back. His tight grip on her let her know that he wished that he was hugging his wife.

"I do love her, Whitty," he sobbed. "And there's not a day that goes by that I don't' want to call her or go to her job and beg her to come home, but I know that I can't be with her after what she did."

"She didn't do anything."

"I saw the text messages."

Whitty looked up at him. "Dawn is guilty of a lot of things, but prostitution isn't one of them."

"No," Dante said shaking his head. He tried to pull out of her arms but she wouldn't let him go.

"Look at me, Dante. Look at me. I've never been so happy in my life. You've done things to me that I know I will never experience with another man, cause that's just how fucked up my luck is. But for once in my life, I have to stop thinking about myself. Dawn has shown me nothing but love, and all I've done was shit on her." She caressed his cheek. "Give her a chance to explain what she's been doing. I swear to you, it's not what you think."

"Why don't you explain it to me, then?"

"You need to hear it from her. Hearing it from me will only make things more confusing."

"Everything is confusing to me, right now. The only thing I'm not confused about is how you've made me feel for these past couple months." He leaned in to kiss her, but she stopped him. "Don't do this. I'm not the one you want."

"You're the one I want right now."

Whitty tried to pull away from him. He kissed her weak spot and then teased it with his tongue.

"Dante, please don't do this to me," she moaned.

He reached under the T-shirt again and ran his hand down the crack of her butt and slid a finger into her.

"Umm." She pushed back on his finger, allowing it to slid all the way in. "I need you inside me."

He lifted her off the ground and wrapped her legs around his waist. He walked with her to the living room wall, and pressed her back against it, and started sucking on her neck.

"Damn you, Dante."

Dawn walked into The Bank wearing a black and white Coogi sweater dress that fell just below her butt. Tonight, she wasn't dressing flashy, but she wanted to be noticed. Julisa waved at her from the bar. She had on a red cocktail dress with a pair of patent-leather platform shoes.

"You good?" Dawn said, as she approached the bar.

"How are we going to do this? Lowe's been with his boys all night. They're in the VIP section popping bottles and acting a fool."

"We can do this."

"I hope *we* doesn't include Whitty."

"What happened to Whitty?"

"She's off Wednesday nights, I've been calling her all night; she's not answering her phone."

Dawn spotted Cassidy at the other end of the bar. "You told Cassidy?"

"Yeah, but maybe we should wait."

"We can't wait, Julisa. What if Mr. Green confronts Lowe about those files? This has to be done tonight. You have our change of clothes?"

"In the storage room."

"Storage room? Hmm."

"Hmm, what?"

Dawn waved Cassidy over. She watched her as she sashayed over. Dawn pulled her close and whispered in her ear. Cassidy's face turned beet red, but she nodded and walked away.

"What did you tell her?" Julisa asked.

"No time. Let's go."

Julisa stepped into the storage room with Dawn right behind her. She walked to a rack and used a chair to reach the wine box on the top shelf. She laid it down on the ground and opened it. She pulled out the black sweat suits and sneakers. They took off their dresses and shoes and put on the sweats and sneakers.

"Guns?" Dawn asked.

Julisa reached into the box and pulled out the .380 and handed it to her. She reached back into the box and pulled out the Mack 11. Dawn shook her head.

"What?" Julisa said.

"You and that big ass gun."

"Don't worry about the size of my gun; worry about how we're going to pull this shit off."

"You talk a lot of shit. You better not choke."

"Choke?" The only choking I'm going to be doing is sticking the muzzle of my *big ass* gun down Lowe's throat. So, what's the plan?"

Dante traced the rim of Whitty's navel with his finger. She swatted his hand away and pulled the T-shirt down over her stomach.

"You know I'm ticklish." He nibbled on her neck. "Stop, Dante. You know how you got me."

"Tell me how I got you."

"You breathe on me too hard my legs automatically part." He breathed on her. She covered herself with the bed sheets and rolled away from him. He climbed on top of her and tried to unwrap her. "No, Dante."

"I just want to talk."

"I can hear you."

"I want to see your face."

"You don't have to see my face to talk."

"I was thinking about what you said earlier. That feeling that you said you had for me, well, I feel the same way about you." Whitty stuck her head from under the covers. "Don't' play with me, Dante."

He looked her in the eyes. "Do I look like I'm playing?"

Whitty closed her eyes. When she opened them, she couldn't look him in the eye. She squirmed from under him and sat on the edge of the bed.

"Didn't expect to hear that, huh?" Dante said.

"I didn't' expect any of this. I didn't mean for any of this to happen. I just wanted to… oh God." She covered her face.

He put his arm around her. "You have to stop beating yourself up. What happened between us just happened."

"No, Dante, it didn't' just happen. I made it happen. The night when I first came here, I had every intention on sleeping with you."

Dante laughed. "What are you talking about?"

"Dante, Dawn's not the ho, I am."

"What?"

"I don't sleep with men for money, but I sleep with them to gain access to their money."

Dante stood up.

Whitty stood up with him. "Like I said, I had every intention on sleeping with you, getting what I could from you, and then splitting."

"Get what you can from me? I don't have any money. You can't get anything from me."

"I got Nu-life from you."

"Nu-life?"

"The friend that I told you about, it was Dawn."

"What?"

"She invested the three hundred thousand."

"Where in the hell did she get three hundred thousand dollars from? Don't answer that, just get dressed and get the fuck out of my house."

"It's not about the money for me, anymore, Dante. All I care about is being with you."

"Being with me? You think I would want to be with you after the shit you just shared with me?"

"I didn't want to lie to you anymore. I thought you would understand."

"Understand? I allowed you into my home, into my life, into my heart. Not only did you play me, you played me *and* my wife with the Nu-life investment. You're worse than a ho. Get the fuck out of my house before I kill you."

Whitty dropped to her knees and cried. Dante tossed her clothes to her. When she didn't move to get dressed, he ripped his T-shirt off her.

"Either you get dressed or I'm going to put your clothes under one arm, you under the other, and I'm going to throw you out on the sidewalk."

Whitty got dressed. She cried all the way down the stairs, all the way to the front door. "Dante—"

"Just get the fuck out." He swung the door open. The last thing Dante remembered was his face hitting the floor and hearing Whitty scream.

Cassidy looked up from the bar and saw when Lowe stood up to mingle with the folks who came to The Bank tonight.

She pulled out her iphone and called Dawn.

"What's up?" Dawn answered on the second ring.

"He's politicking, right now."

"You know what to do." Dawn hung up.

Cassidy put her phone away and told the woman working the bar with her that she'd be right back. She dashed into the bathroom, removed her panties, and headed for Lowe.

"I need to see you." She grabbed him by the hand.

"What's up?"

"I need to talk to you."

"Later."

"It's important."

Lowe screwed his face up at her. He excused himself from the women he was talking to and followed her to the storage room.

"What's up?" he asked, as she closed the door.

"Over here." She headed toward the back of the room.

Lowe followed her, realizing that she was headed to the tiny bathroom in the back. "I don't have time to be playing games with you, Cass."

She stopped at the bathroom door and turned to face him. She grabbed his hand and placed it up her skirt. His manhood twitched when she rested his hand on her naked peach.

"Bitch, you walking around here with no panties on?"

"I feel slutty tonight." She inserted one of his fingers into her wet opening.

"You know what I do to sluts, right?"

"Show me." She reached into his pants and massaged his shaft. She saw Dawn creeping out of the shadows. Lowe spun Cassidy around and shoved her against the wall.

"Keep your hands on the wall," he said, as he pulled himself out and raised her skirt. "This is how I treat sluts."

Cassidy's eyes widened as he spread her butt cheeks and lined himself up on her tiny opening.

Just as she was going to pull away from him, she heard a sickening clunk of steel hitting bone. She jerked around in time to see Lowe drop to his knees. He tried to shake off the blow while getting to his feet. Dawn brought the butt of her gun down on his head again. This time, he fell on his back and didn't move.

"You okay?" Dawn said.

Cassidy just realized that she was shaking. "Yeah, I'm good."

Julisa stepped out of the shadows and looked down at her husband. "Piece of shit." She bent down and snatched the chain she bought for him from around his neck.

"Open the bathroom door," Dawn said to Cassidy.

She opened it and stood to the side while Dawn and Julisa dragged Lowe into the storage room's bathroom. They sat him on the toilet and cuffed his feet. Then they cuffed his hands behind his back.

"You ready?" Dawn asked Julisa.

"Yeah," Julisa said in a jittery voice.

"Julisa," Dawn said, checking to make sure Julisa wasn't having any last minute regrets.

"I said I'm ready, let's do this."

"You can leave, Cassidy," Dawn said.

"No, we're in this together."

"Fine," Dawn stood in front of Lowe and smacked him. When he didn't respond, she smacked him again. He mumbled and his eyes fluttered. The third time she smacked him his head snapped up at her. She jerked back.

"Fuck is going on?" he yelled. He twisted against the cuffs. He stopped when he saw Julisa. "Jewels? What the fuck are you doing"

She raised the butt of the Mack 11 up and smashed him in the mouth.

"Are you fucking out of your mind?" he stuttered in shock.

She smashed him in the mouth again. "You don't get to ask any questions, you hear me you piece of shit?" He glared at her and then he looked at Dawn and then at Cassidy. He looked back at Julisa.

"Jewels, you need to come to your senses, and you better do it quick. I don't know what these bitches have been filling your head with, but—"

"How long have you been cheating on me?" Julisa cried.

Lowe screwed his face up. "What? This is what this is about?"

"Answer the question."

"Jewels get these cuffs off me or else—"

"Or else what?" She brought her gun up to hit him again. Lowe braced himself for the hit. "I asked you a question. How long?"

"I don't know, three years maybe."

"All this time, I've been faithful to you, I never once thought about sleeping with someone else."

"That's because you're a woman. Men fuck other women. That's what we do. So, you're going to kill me for being a man? You're going to shoot me, right here in the club with all these witnesses?"

Julisa raised her gun. "Yes, I am going to shoot you, right here in the club, but there won't be any witnesses. No one can hear anything over the loud music. Good bye, Lowe."

"Wait!" His eyes were bulging out the sockets. "Please, Jewels, just wait. I fucked up, okay? All these years that we've been together, I always made sure you didn't want for anything. I always put you before everyone including myself, right or wrong?"

Julisa put her head down.

"You know I'm telling the truth. I love *you*, Jewels. I fucked those other women, but you know I don't love them, you know you're the only love of my life. You are my life."

"You're lying."

"I'm about to close on the biggest deal of my life with Mr. Green. All this, the club, the streets, the women, I'm putting all this shit behind me. We're supposed to be starting a family, remember? So, let's just put all of this behind us. Dawn and I can work out our differences, Cassidy and I can do the same."

"Lowe, no matter how much money you have, no matter what new life you may make for yourself, you will always be the same shitty motherfucker who doesn't give a fuck about anyone but himself."

"Jewels—"

"See ya." She pulled the trigger. Lowe's head snapped back. When it fell forward, his blank stare landed on Julisa. Her eyes filled with tears.

Dawn handed her gun to Cassidy.

Cassidy didn't hesitate. She shot Lowe twice in the chest and nonchalantly handed the gun back to Dawn as if she was passing her a cigarette. Dawn was now certain of two things. First, Cassidy just made herself an accessory to murder, so she definitely wasn't going to the cops. Second, the way she pulled the trigger with no hesitation, led her to believe that she wasn't a stranger to violence. Dawn made a mental note to ask her what was the real reason for leaving Canada.

"We have to go," Dawn said. She looked down at Lowe one more time and saw his cell phone. She snatched it off his belt and closed the bathroom door.

Dawn and Julisa took off their sweat suits and put their dresses back on. They tossed everything back in the wine box.

"I did it," Julisa said. "I killed his fucking ass."

"Yes, you did," Dawn said. They hugged each other.

"Get over here, girl," Julisa said to Cassidy. They all hugged each other.

"I need you to go back to work and act like nothing happened," Dawn said to Cassidy.

"No problem."

Dawn picked up the wine box. Julisa led them out of the club through the backdoor. Dawn put the box in the trunk of her car and exhaled. "I need a drink."

"Amen to that," Julisa said.

CHAPTER 20

*T*rent looked at his watch again. "Where the fuck did he go?" he said loud enough for Gamble and Naji to hear. "We're supposed to be on our way to the carwash to complete this deal."

"He's probably in the office sticking his dick down Cassidy's throat," Naji said.

"Cassidy's right there at the bar," Trent said.

"I saw her leading Lowe by the hand somewhere ten minutes go."

"Leading him where?"

"How the fuck should I know? I'm sitting here with you."

Trent stood up.

"Where you going?" Gamble asked.

"To find Lowe." He headed to the bar and grabbed Cassidy by the arm. "Where's Lowe?"

Cassidy snatched her arm from him. "I don't know, don't be grabbing on me like that."

"What do you mean you don't know? You were just with him."

"I wasn't with him. I'm working so if you don't mind…"

Trent looked around one time and walked back to the table. "You sure you saw Cassidy with Lowe?" he asked Naji.

"That's what I said, right? She was leading him by the hand."

"She said she wasn't with him."

"Who you going to believe?"

Trent called Lowe's cell phone.

Dawn jumped when Lowe's phone started vibrating in her hand.

"What?" Julisa asked.

"This phone scared the shit out of me," she said, looking down at the phone. "It's Trent. He's probably calling Lowe to find out where he's at."

"Should we go back inside or go home?" Julisa asked with a scared look on her face.

"Let's go back inside. It won't look cool if we disappear the same time Lowe does. We'll hangout in the office."

"Yeah, and we can have that drink."

Trent redialed Lowe's number. "He's not picking up." He looked toward the bar and peeped when Cassidy quickly turned her head.

"He'll be back in a few, just chill," Gamble said.

"What direction did you see them going in?" Trent asked Naji.

"What?"

"I said what direction did you see them go in?"

"I don't know; toward the bathrooms, I think."

"Why would she lie?" Trent said out loud, but he didn't wait for Gamble or Naji to answer. He walked to the bar. "I need to see you."

Cassidy looked him up and down. "For what?"

"Bitch don't get smart with me. You know I'll make a scene up in here."

Cassidy rolled her eyes and walked from around the bar. "What is it?"

"Why'd you lie to me?"

"Lie to you?"

"Naji said he saw you leading Lowe by the hand toward the bathrooms."

"Naji is drunk out of his mind."

Trent grabbed her by the hand and started walking toward the bathrooms.

"Trent what the hell are you doing?"

Trent busted into the men's bathroom with Cassidy in tow.

"You're crazy," Cassidy said, trying to pull away from him.

Trent then barged into the women's bathroom. He could hear someone getting their groove on in the last stall. He pushed the door in.

The man stopped in mid-stroke. "What the fuck?" He had a pretty little red-bone bent over the toilet. She was so high out of her mind that she was still grinding on the big man.

"You're hurting my wrist," Cassidy said.

Trent was heading back toward the bar when he caught the door in his peripheral vision. He knew he was on to something by the way Cassidy stopped beefing and started sweating. "What's in here?"

"Can't you read the sign on the door?" she said nervously.

"The next time you get fly on me, I'm going to smash your head against this wall. Open the door."

"I can't. The only ones with a key to the storage room is Lowe and Julisa."

Trent was on the move again.

"Where are you going now?" Cassidy asked.

"To Lowe's office, you better pray he's there."

Julisa poured her and Dawn a glass of Jack Daniels. She handed Dawn her glass and then raised hers. "To my Boo. May he rest in peace while I cash in on this life insurance policy and act a fool."

"You don't have to act," Dawn said, holding up her glass.

Julisa flipped Dawn the finger as she downed her drink. There was a soft tap at the door.

"Yes," Julisa said.

Bono stepped in. "Trent said he needs to speak with you, it's important.

Julisa looked at Dawn.

"Fuck is you looking at me for? He wants to talk to you."

"Let him in," Julisa said to Bono.

Julisa was surprised to see Trent dragging Cassidy in with him. "What's up?" she asked him.

"You seen Lowe?"

"Last I saw him, he was with you, popping bottles."

"We got this deal that's supposed to be going down as we speak and he's nowhere to be found."

Julisa shrugged. "I haven't seen him."

Trent looked at Cassidy. "Naji said he saw Cass with him earlier."

"That's a damn lie," Cassidy blurted out.

"Why are you holding on to her like that?" Dawn asked.

Trent realized that he was still holding Cassidy by the arm. He let her go. "Lowe's not here, he's not answering his phone, he's late for this meet, something's wrong."

"Lowe disappears and automatically you think something's wrong?" Julisa asked. "He's probably doing something that married men aren't supposed to be doing."

"Let me see your keys," Trent said to Julisa.

"What?"

"Your keys," he repeated.

"For what?"

"I want to check something out."

"He wants to look in the storage room," Cassidy said.

Dawn's face didn't change, but all of the color left Julisa's, and Trent peeped it immediately.

He stuck his hand out. "Keys."

"I'm not giving you my keys. You're bugging, you need to stop drinking whatever it is that you're drinking and sleep that shit off."

"Either you give me the keys or I'm going to kick that door in."

"Motherfucker—"

Dawn cut Julisa off. "Give me the keys."

"No—"

"Julisa. Give me the keys," Dawn said.

Julisa looked at her for a second and then fished her keys out of her bag and handed them to her.

"You know how motherfuckers are with their conspiracy theories; always making a big thing out of nothing." Dawn tossed Trent the keys.

He caught them and left the office.

"Are you out of your mind?" Julisa whispered.

Dawn swiped the letter opener off the desk and slid it down her bra. "Both of you stay here."

"You can't be serious," Cassidy whispered.

"This is getting out of control," Julisa said.

"Just stay in here. I'll be back." Dawn downed the rest of her drink.

"And if you don't come back?" Julisa asked.

"Let's cross that bridge when we get to it," Dawn said with a wink.

"Hold up," Dawn said, catching up to Trent.

He spun around. "What?"

"I'm coming with you."

"I don't need you coming with me."

"Julisa ragged my ass for giving you her keys, so, I told her I would make sure you're not in the storage room making copies of them."

"I don't know who's crazier, you or her."

They stopped at the storage room.

"Where's Buck? I haven't seen him all night," Dawn asked casually.

Trent unlocked the door. "You'll be seeing him soon enough." he said, as he stepped into the storage room.

"What did you expect to find? Lowe tied up in a corner with a gag in his mouth?"

He turned toward her. "If that was the case, guess who would be the number one suspect?"

She stuck her middle finger up at him. She caught him looking over her shoulder. "What?"

"There's a light on in that room."

"You solved the mystery," Dawn whispered. "Your boy is probably in there gutting some nasty hood rat. While my girl is playing the perfect wife."

Trent started to head toward the door. Dawn put her hand on his chest.

"You sure you want to disturb him?"

"He may not even be in there. Yo, Lowe!" He called out.

"No answer," Dawn said. Trent pushed past her and headed for the door. Dawn pulled out the letter opener and held it with a death grip. Her throat dried up and she felt like she was hyperventilating. She took a deep breath, said a prayer, and crept up on him.

When Trent got to the door, he knocked. "Yo, Lowe." He opened it and stumbled back. "Oh shit!" He reached for the 9mm tucked at the small of his back while spinning around. The crazed look on Dawn's face froze him in place. Her eyelids were slits, her teeth bared like a vampire's, and there was a gleaming object headed toward his face. The last part didn't register til the letter opener punctured the left side of his neck and came out on the other side. He jerked back so hard that the handle snapped.

Dawn looked at the handle in her hand and then back to him. He was clawing at the blade with one hand while trying to get at his gun with the other. Panic overtook him and he used both hands to grope at the blade. He screamed for help, but the only sounds that left his lips were gurgling noises. He fell to his knees and stared at Dawn. She still had that crazed look. She watched as he tried to stop the blood from gushing out of his neck, but the faster his heart pounded, the harder the blood shot out. He finally stopped struggling and fell face first. Dawn walked up to him and grabbed the keys out of his pants pocket. Then she reached into the back of his pants and pulled out his gun. She found an old cigar box and put the gun inside of it and slung the box under her arm. She locked the storage room door and headed back to the office.

Gamble and Naji looked at each other when they saw Dawn coming back from the storage room alone.

"Lowe heads off with Cassidy toward the bathrooms and doesn't come back. Now we just sat here and watched Trent go with Dawn toward the bathrooms and he doesn't come back. What the fuck is going on?" Naji said.

Gamble emptied his glass. "I don't know," he said nervously.

"Well, we're about to find out." Naji stood up.

Dawn peeped when Gamble and Naji stood up and started heading toward her.

"Honey, wait up," Naji said.

"What's up?" she said nonchalantly.

"What happened to Trent?"

"Trent? How should I know?"

"I just saw you and him walking toward the bathrooms."

"Well, there's your answer. He must be in the bathroom."

Gamble looked around nervously. He knew just like Naji knew that something wasn't right.

Naji stared at Dawn for a second.

"What?" Dawn said.

Nothing." He looked down and squinted at Dawn's feet.

Dawn looked down and saw specks of blood on her shoes. When she looked back up, Naji was glaring at her. She backed up real slow. Naji never took his eyes off her as he started reaching for his gun.

Dawn took off running toward the office. When she got through the soundproof doors, she opened the cigar box and pulled out Trent's gun.

Bono saw her running with a gun in her hand with Gamble and Naji right behind her. He drew his Glock.

Dawn stopped in her tracks; so did Gamble and Naji.

"What the fuck is going on?" Bono asked, keeping everybody in the sights of his gun.

"Ask her," Naji said. "She's the one with blood on her shoes."

Bono glanced down at Dawn's feet and saw the blood. "I'm going to need you to drop your gun, Naji."

"What about her?"

Bono looked at Dawn. "I'm going to need you to drop yours, too, Honey."

"I'm not dropping shit until he drops his."

"I'm not dropping mind until she drops hers," Naji said.

Bono kept his gun trained on them. "I'm not going to ask y'all again."

"Drop the gun, Naji," Gamble said. "This is crazy."

"Nah, my nig. Ain't happening. I never trusted this bitch. She's got blood on her fucking shoes, man. She probably bodied Lowe and Trent."

"Naji—" Bono said.

"Fuck you! I'm not dropping shit. I'm not the one with blood on my shoes."

Dawn kept her gun leveled at Naji. She didn't say a word.

"Honey," Bono said. "Don't make me shoot you."

"Do what you got to. I'm not dropping my gun."

The elevator light caught Bono's eye. When the doors opened, his eyes widened. He turned his gun on Buck and fired. Buck didn't have a chance. Both bullets struck him in the chest. He fell back against the elevator wall. That's when all hell broke loose.

Dawn let off two shots. One hit Gamble in the chest the other just missed Naji. He returned fire. Dawn ducked into the conference room. The bullets intended for her kept their course, finding their way into the wall just above Bono's head. He fired at Naji, all three bullets hit him in the center of his chest.

"Dawn!" Julisa ran out of the office.

"Go back inside!" Bono told her.

Julisa saw Gamble and Naji laid out and covered her mouth.

"I said go back into the office!" Bono repeated. She retreated and slammed the door.

"Honey, it's over," Bono called out. "You need to come out so we can get our stories straight. You know I have to call the police for this one."

Dawn stuck her head out and looked both ways. She saw Gamble and Naji sprawled out on the floor. She backed up toward them, while keeping her gun trained on Bono.

"They're gone, Honey."

She got on one knee and touched the side of Gamble's neck and then Naji's. "Got to make sure; don't want any surprises."

"You need to give me that gun." When she didn't move, he put his gun away. "Give me the gun."

"And then what?"

"Buck, Gamble, and Naji got into a heated argument. Buck came back here to cool off, Gamble and Naji followed him. Words were exchanged, Naji pulled out on Buck, Buck pulled out a Glock and a 9mm. Shot Gamble with the nine, shot Naji with the Glock."

"It's that simple?" Dawn asked sarcastically.

"It is when you have four witnesses. You, me, Julisa, and Cassidy."

Julisa came out into the hallway, followed by Cassidy.

"We don't have time to waste," Bono said.

Dawn lowered the gun and started walking toward him.

Julisa screamed when she saw Buck run out of the elevator with gun in hand. Dawn raised her gun, Bono turned. Buck shot Bono in the stomach. He tried to get a shot off at Dawn, but she was already firing in his direction. He spun and ran toward Julisa and Cassidy. Dawn stopped firing. He grabbed Julisa by the neck and pulled her in front of him.

"Move and I'll shoot you in the head," Buck said to Julisa.

Dawn took a step forward. Buck pressed his gun to Julisa's head.

"Bono shot you," Dawn said.

"You didn't know?" Buck said. "I'm bullet proof." He tapped the vest he was wearing under his trench coat. "This is what I do. Where's Lowe?" he asked Julisa.

"He's dead," Dawn answered. Buck looked at her. She pointed behind her. "They're all dead. You'll be joining them real soon."

Buck laughed. "If Lowe was dead, Julisa would be having a nervous breakdown, right now."

"I'm the one who killed him," Julisa said through clenched teeth.

Buck stopped laughing and spun her around. The look in her eyes told him she was telling the truth. He spun her back around. "Y'all are some crazy bitches."

"I tell you what," Dawn said. "Why don't you just take a walk? I promise not to shoot you in the back. You can just disappear. There's no need to kill me now, Lowe's dead."

"Kill you? You think Lowe wanted me to kill you?"

"That's the word," Dawn said.

"If I wanted to kill you, you'd be dead. You got it twisted, Honey. Lowe didn't want me to kill you. He wanted me to kill someone else." The gleam in his eye brought tears to Dawn's eyes. She felt her knees shaking.

Buck smiled when he saw Dawn's reaction. "Something wrong?"

Julisa finally caught on to what was going on. "My God, Dante?"

Dawn started walking toward Buck and Julisa. Buck put his gun back to Julisa's head, but all Dawn cared about was emptying the rest of her bullets into him.

Buck realized he lost his leverage and tried something else. "He's still alive, for now." Dawn stopped in her tracks "I caught him just as he was opening the front door. Wham! Right in the mouth. He dropped like the bitch that he is. Then I stood over him with my gun, this gun. Whitty saved his life."

"Whitty?" Dawn whispered.

"You should've seen her. She dropped to her knees and begged me not to kill him."

"Whitty?" Dawn said.

"She crawled over to him and..." he started laughing. "She puts herself between him and my gun and begs me not to kill him."

"Whitty?" Dawn said again.

"Oh, you didn't know?"

Dawn's finger tightened around the trigger.

"You pull that trigger, you kill Dante."

"Why... Why didn't you kill him?" Dawn asked. Tears were streaming down her face.

"Like I said. Whitty saved his life. She knows that the only thing I like more than killing is, money. And that's why I'm here. I've been trying to get a hold of Lowe for the longest to tell him of the new development. When I couldn't reach him by phone. I decided to come here and talk to him face-to-face. But he's dead and so is the rest of my crew. Being that it's just me now, I guess I'm going to have to broker this deal myself. Dante and Whitty are locked in a dark room, handcuffed to a radiator, with no food or water. And I'm the only one who knows where they are."

"What do you want?"

"Two million."

Dawn's knees buckled. She shook her head. "You're out of your mind. You know I don't have that kind of money."

"That's not what Whitty told me."

"I don't give a fuck what Whitty told you."

"That's the deal. Take it or leave it."

Buck and Dawn tensed up when the elevator doors opened. Cash and Lou stepped out with their guns drawn. Buck fired on them, hitting Lou in the arm and thigh. He pushed Julisa to the floor and took off toward the soundproof doors. Cash and Dawn took off after him.

When the people saw the gun in Buck's hand, they panicked and started stampeding to the nearest exits. Cash and Dawn lost him in the sea of people running for their lives.

"No," Dawn screamed. "God, this can't be happening."

CHAPTER 21

*D*awn ran out into the street, hoping to spot Buck. After searching through the crowd as best she could, she ran back inside toward the office. She saw Cash knelling beside Bono.

"He's still alive," Cash said. "I called the cops and the paramedics. Are you okay?"

She ignored his question and ran into the office. Julisa and Cassidy were pacing the floor.

"Dawn," Julisa cried out. She ran to her and hugged her. "This shit is crazy."

Dawn broke away from her and snatched up Lowe's cell phone. She scrolled down the names and thanked God when she saw Buck's.

"This can't be Lowe," Buck said, answering his phone. "He's supposed to be dead."

"Where's Whitty and my husband?"

"Wouldn't you like to know?"

"How do I know they're even still alive?"

Buck ended the call.

"Hello? Hello?" Dawn kept calling back, but Buck refused to pick up.

She collapsed on the couch and started crying. Julisa and Cassidy sat on either side of her. Julisa gently pulled the gun from her hand and stashed it behind the bookshelf.

"I killed him," Dawn said, referring to Dante.

"Don't say that," Cassidy said.

"I should've never gotten involved with all of this. God, please don't let my husband be dead."

"We're going to find them," Julisa said.

"How?" Dawn waited for her response. Julisa didn't have one. Lowe's phone rang. Dawn fumbled with it. "Hello!"

"Dawn?"

"Dante! Where are you?" Dawn could hear the phone being snatched from him.

"Two million," Buck said. "Or I do him right now."

"I don't have two million, Buck."

"I'm sure if you dig deep enough you'll find it."

"Where am I supposed to be digging?"

"Nu-life is a start. Whitty told me all about it."

"That's worth a half a mil, maybe, and if I liquidate it, I will only get about two-thirds of that."

"What about the safe at the townhouse? Whitty said there has to be at least a hundred thou in it."

"A hundred and fifty," Dawn corrected him.

"So between Nu-life and the money in the safe we're talking close to a half a mil."

"You can have it, Buck, all of it."

"It's not enough."

"What do you want from me?"

"I want two million, cash, in three days."

"Buck—"

"That's it. No more talking. I'll call you in three days."

"Hello? Buck?"

"What did he say?" Julisa asked.

"He wants two million in three days. I don't have two million. He's going to kill them."

Dawn, Cassidy, Julisa, and Cash sat in the hospital waiting room while the doctors operated on Bono. One of the doctors came out earlier and told them that Lou was going to be fine. He was going to be released tomorrow morning. The police had an A.P.B. out on Buck. Dawn told them the story that Bono ran down to her just before he got shot.

Dawn turned her head toward the nurse's station where there was some kind of commotion going on. It was Monster-Sick. He was turning out.

"Eva!" Cash said waving her over. She saw Cash and put her arm on Monster-Sick's shoulder. He immediately calmed down.

"Where is he?" Eva said to Cash, not even acknowledging Dawn, Julisa, or Cassidy.

"They're operating now," Cash said.

The head surgeon came out into the waiting room.

"How is he?" Eva asked.

"All in all, he's going to be fine. Lucky for him, we were able to remove all of the bullet fragments."

"I want to see him," Eva said.

"Are you immediate family?"

"I'm his wife."

"Of course you can," the doctor said.

When Eva walked in, Bono was trying to sit up. She mushed him.

"Baby—"

She smacked him. Bono's jaw twitched, but he just stared at her. Eva finally let her dam of tears fall.

"Eva—"

She held her hand up. "All I want is a name and location."

"It's not that simple."

"It is that simple. Just tell me who did it, and where I can find him."

"It was Buck and I don't know where he is."

"I'll find him."

She spun to leave.

"Wait!" Bono called out.

She kept walking.

"I may know where he is."

She stopped and turned around.

"Is Dawn out there?" Bono asked.

"Yeah."

"Get her in here."

"For what?"

"Just bring her in."

Eva came back with her, and then stared at Bono.

He looked at Dawn, "You okay?"

"No. He's going to kill Dante and Whitty if I don't give him two million in three days."

"How much of it do you have?"

"I can get five, Julisa has two fifty in The Bank and she has about two fifty worth of jewelry she's willing to pawn."

"You're a mil short."

"It's all I have," Dawn said defeated.

"Don't worry about the rest. I got you," Bono said.

Eva took her shades off and looked at him.

"Wait outside," he said to Dawn. She nodded and left.

"What the fuck was that about? I don't need her to find Buck's stupid ass," Eva said.

"But she needs you. What if it was me Buck was holding for two million?"

"But it's not."

"What if it was?"

Eva looked away.

"And you're wrong. You do need her. You're going to need someone to talk some sense into that thick-ass head of yours. I want Buck dead, but I don't want you dying in the process."

"As long as he's dead, I'll die happy."

"See? That's the type of shit I'm afraid of. I can't lose you." He tried to sit up. She threatened to mush him again.

"The doctor told you to lie still. Now lie still before I strap you to that bed."

"That sounds kinky." Bono winked.

"If I didn't love you so much, I would've killed you myself a long time ago."

"I love you too."

Two days later, Dawn pulled up to the building in Brooklyn where her and Bono went that day after Trini killed Chance. Julisa sat in the passenger seat with her hands in her lap.

"You okay?" Dawn asked her.

"Hell no. You got us in the middle of the hood with no backup."

"Here comes our backup."

Julisa stared in disbelief as a swarm of hoodies and Timbs poured out of the building's lobby. The spill was headed right for them. Julisa stepped on a imaginary gas pedal.

Dawn opened her door.

"Bitch is you crazy?" Julisa said.

Dawn ignored her and reached for the duffel bag in the backseat. As the wolf pack converge on the car, Julisa locked her door. One of the wolves removed their hood. It was Eva.

"How is he?" Dawn asked, as she looked up at the apartment window.

"Bono's fine."

"Is he—"

"Did you bring the money?"

Dawn handed her the duffel bag.

Eva opened it and inspected the cash. Satisfied that it was all there, she tossed the bag at Dawn's feet. "Call him." She was referring to Buck.

Dawn pulled out Lowe's cell and called Buck.

"Good news or bad news?" Buck said, as he answered his phone.

"I got the money."

"Bullshit!"

"I got it."

"I knew you would," Buck said with a chuckle.

"Where are they?"

"Bring the cash to Tompkins Square Park. When you get there, call me. Come alone or... I'll let you fill in the blank." He ended the call.

"He wants me to bring the money to Tompkins Square Park," Dawn said to Eva. "And he wants me to come alone."

"We both know that's not happening" Eva looked toward Monster-Sick. "Go get that."

He walked to the van and came back with a knapsack. Eva took it from him and tossed it at Dawn's feet. "You got your two mil. Get in your car and roll out. Don't worry about us, we won't be too far behind."

Dawn looked at Eva and then at the hungry wolves behind her before getting into her car.

"What's happening?" Julisa asked when Dawn closed her door.

"We're on our way."

When Dawn pulled up to the park, she called Buck. "I'm here. Where are you."

"I see you brought Julisa with you."

"Where are you?"

"I'm around. Just making sure you weren't followed."

"I'm tired of playing this game, Buck."

"This is far from a game, Honey. This is what I do. You ready?"

"Ready for what?"

"377 East 10th Street."

"What about it?"

"I'll be waiting in the lobby."

He ended the call.

"What did he say?" Julisa asked.

"He gave me an address. 377 East 10th Street." When Dawn pulled up to the building, she shook her head. "I should've known." She stared at the abandoned building, and then reached under her seat. She grabbed her .380 and shoved it in her waist.

Julisa grabbed her Mack 11 from under her seat.

"No, Julisa. You're staying here."

"No the hell I ain't."

"Don't' argue with me. I need you to slide over to the driver's seat and be ready to peel out of here, just in case."

"That's bullshit."

"Please, Julisa."

Julisa sucked her teeth. "I'm keeping my gun in my lap."

"Whatever." Dawn transferred the money from the knapsack into the duffel bag along with her money, and got out of the car. She looked around. Eva was good. Her nor Buck spotted Eva or the black van. She took a deep breath and headed into the abandoned building.

Buck was standing by the stairwell with a shotgun aimed at her. "Real slow, Honey, we don't' want any accidents."

Dawn stepped into the lobby with her hands in the air.

"Toss the bag over."

"Where's Dante and Whitty?"

"I count the money first, then I'll tell you where they are."

"You're going to count all of this money right here, right now?"

"You got somewhere to go? Toss the fucking bag."

Dawn tossed it to him.

Buck let it drop at his feet. He stood the shotgun against the wall and pulled out a handgun. "Walk over to that wall and put your hands on it."

Dawn did what he said.

"You move, I'll pop you." He stooped down and unzipped the duffel bag with his free hand while keeping an eye and his gun trained on her. He wasn't interested in counting all of the money; he just wanted to make sure the bag wasn't filled with telephone books or old shoes. He nodded and zipped the duffel bag back up.

Dawn looked over her shoulder. "You got the money. Where are they?"

"They're in apartment number—" He crouched and pointed his gun in the direction where he heard what sounded like a squeaky hinge. "Who's here with you?"

"Nobody's here with me. You saw that for yourself. Just tell me where they are and we're done."

Buck slung the duffel bag over his shoulder and grabbed up his shotgun. "They're on the third floor; apartment—"

Dawn dove to the floor as she heard bullets shattering the wall tiles behind Buck. She cringed when she heard the shotgun blast.

"You bitch! I'm going to kill them."

Hearing Buck's threat got Dawn off the floor and running toward the now empty stairwell entrance. She pulled out her gun. Eva walked up behind her and started to walk through the stairwell entrance. Dawn stopped her.

"Are you crazy? That's what he wants."

Eva pushed past her and stole a peek into the stairwell. Another shotgun blast echoed and pellets embedded themselves into the stairwell's entrance.

"They're dead, you hear me?" Buck shouted.

Eva stuck her arm through the stairwell entrance and held the trigger of the Uzi until the clip emptied.

"You didn't have to come in, he told me where they were," Dawn screamed.

Eva ignored her as she retrieved a clip from her hoodie and slid it into her gun.

"Did you hear me? He said they're on the third floor. We have to get up there before he kills them."

"They're already dead!" Eva said with no emotion.

They both looked up to the ceiling when they heard another shotgun blast.

"Talk to me," Eva said, as she took off her hood. That's when Dawn saw the headset in her ear.

"We got him pinned on the third floor landing," one of Eva's team said.

"Don't let him onto the third floor."

"Got cha."

"What?" Dawn said.

"He's pinned on the stairs by the third floor."

"That proves that they're alive. Why else would he be trying to get onto the third floor?"

"Monster, get in here," Eva said through her headset.

Monster-Sick and two team members walked through the doorway, guns first.

"Stay here. If he tries to come back down, hit with a flesh wound, understand?"

Monster-Sick nodded.

"Everybody listen up," Eva said through the headset. "Force him onto the roof." She exited the building with Dawn right behind her.

"How are we getting to the roof?"

"The same way my team got on the other floors."

"And how's that?" When Eva didn't answer, Dawn grabbed her by the arm.

Eva turned on her and shoved the muzzle of her Uzi under Dawn's chin. "You're really starting to piss me the fuck off."

"Likewise." Dawn poked Eva in the stomach with her .380 to let her know she wasn't the only one with a gun pointed at her.

"Go wait in the car," Eva commanded.

"I go where you go."

"I can't protect you up there."

"I don't need your protection."

"Fine." Eva ran to the fire escape with Dawn right behind her.

"He's on the move," A voice said through Eva's headset. "He's heading toward the roof," another voice said.

"We have to hurry," Eva said to Dawn.

Dawn stopped on the third floor. "You go ahead."

Eva looked down and saw what floor she stopped on. "Whatever." She kept climbing.

Dawn opened the window and crawled through. The apartment looked like it was hit by a tornado. Plaster, glass, and wood, were everywhere. There were stains on the rotted out furniture that she didn't even want to imagine what they were. The floor squeaked so bad, she started to tiptoe, afraid that it would cave in under her weight. "Dante!" She quickly checked every room and then went to the next apartment.

Eva made it to the roof just in time to see Buck busting through the roof's entrance. Their eyes locked for a moment before either of them reacted. Eva was first. She swung her gun up and opened fire. Buck ducked back inside. Eva ran toward the roof's entrance, firing in spurts to keep Buck for firing back. When she reached the door, he was nowhere in sight.

"Can anybody see him?" She said into her headset.

"Fourth floor," Eva heard before she heard the shotgun blast.

Buck stepped up to the man he just shot and pulled the headset out his ear. "Eva, I didn't expect to see you here. That shit with Bono wasn't personal, he shot me first."

"And I'm here to finish what he started," Eva responded.

"I got two million. How about we split it down the middle?"

"I much rather split you down the middle."

"You have to catch me first. Which I doubt you can do, because, this is what I do."

"You're not too good at it."

Buck caught a shadow in his peripheral and dove through an apartment. Eva's bullets missed him by inches. He scrambled to his feet and headed into one of the bedrooms.

Eva stuck her head in and then stepped into the apartment. She opened fire on anything that was big enough for Buck to hide behind. The bedroom was the last place she checked. The bedroom curtain moved; she fired at it. "Fuck!" She ran to the window and stuck her head out. "Anybody see where he went?" she said through the headset.

"He didn't come back down here," Monster-Sick said.

"All floors report," Eva said.

"Lobby," Monster-Sick said.

"Second floor clear," another voice said.

Eva waited for a moment. "Third floor? Crunk, you there?" No response.

"Everybody get to the third floor!"

Dawn kicked in the fourth apartment door. She was crying now. She didn't want to believe that Buck had already gotten to Dante and Whitty. She entered the apartment screaming Dante's name. She jumped when she heard a soft knock. "Dante?" She heard the knock again, only it had gotten weaker. She ran toward the back of the apartment where she thought she heard the sound. She cracked the bedroom door and peeped inside. Dante and Whitty were duct taped back to back. Dante wasn't moving. The sound was Whitty hitting her head against the wall. It was her only way to signal Dawn when she heard her voice.

Dawn ran into the room and hugged them both. Whitty slumped in her arms. "You okay?" Dawn whispered.

Whitty nodded.

Dawn shook Dante. His eyes fluttered. "Baby, it's me."

He blinked a couple times before realizing he wasn't dreaming. He leaned into Dawn.

She hugged him tight. "I love you so much." She put her gun down and looked around for a sharp object to cut through the duct tape. "I'll be right back," she said to Dante.

He shook his head violently.

"I have to find something to cut you free." She got off her knees and headed to the kitchen. She pulled out all the kitchen drawers, frantically looking for anything sharp. She spotted a shard of glass on the floor. She snatched it up and ran back into the bedroom. She hacked at the duct tape. When she freed Dante and Whitty's upper body, she started cutting apart their legs.

"I see you found them," Buck said from the doorway.

Dawn spun around. Buck kept his gun on her as she slowly stood.

"You got the money," Dawn said.

"I also got a psycho-bitch who's not going to let me leave this building alive. You set me up."

"No—"

"The fuck you didn't! Walk over to me slowly."

Dawn shook her head.

Buck pointed his gun at Dante.

"Wait!" She began walking toward him.

He grabbed her around the neck.

"Buck!"

He turned around, holding Dawn in front of him as a shield. Eva had her gun pointed at them.

"In order to shoot me, you got to shoot through her first."

"That won't be a problem."

Two shots rang out.

Buck arched his back as the two bullets bore into him. He pushed Dawn into Eva and spun around. Whitty saw the rage carved into his face and dropped the gun Dawn had laid beside her earlier.

"You bitch!" He raised his gun. Dante dived on top of her.

"Dante!" Dawn screamed.

Her scream was drowned out by the gunshots. Eva didn't stop firing until she was right up on Buck. She kicked him over onto his back.

He looked up at her with a sadistic smile. "Finish it."

"My pleasure." She shot him three more times in the chest.

Dawn looked over at Dante who was still on top of Whitty. Whitty was hugging him and sobbing in his arms. He looked up at Dawn, and then he looked at Eva, who was yanking the duffel bag strap from around Buck's neck.

"Dante," Dawn said, causing him to look back at her. She saw a flicker in his eyes. He looked down at Whitty in disgust and let her go. When she grabbed his arm, he pulled away from her. Dawn ran to him. He sidestepped her and kept walking.

"Dante." She ran in front of him. He pushed past her. She started to run in front of him again. Eva stopped her.

"Let him be."

When Dante got to the hallway, guns were aimed at him.

"Let him go," Eva said. The guns slowly came down.

Dawn watched him walk away.

"Honey." Whitty ran into her arms. "Thank you for coming for us."

Dawn held her at arm's distance. "I came for my husband. You come near him again, I will kill you."

"I'm so sorry."

Dawn spun on her and ran after Dante.

"The cops are on their way," Monster-Sick said through his headset.

"We're out," Eva said.

Dawn caught up with Dante outside. He was hugging Julisa and crying on her shoulder. Julisa was crying with him. Before Dawn had a chance to reach them, a cop car skidded to a halt. Two officers got out and drew their guns. Two more cars arrived at the scene, followed by an ambulance.

An hour later, they brought Buck's body down. Dawn, Dante, and Whitty were taken to the hospital and then to the precinct.

The official story was Buck had kidnapped Dante and Whitty and was holding them for ransom. Of course, there were holes in the story. Like where was the money? And where were the guns that were used on Buck? Nevertheless, they were released the next day.

Dawn took a hot shower when she reached the townhouse and cried herself to sleep. Her phone rang a little after midnight.

"What?" she answered.

"You're welcome," Bono said.

Dawn was silent.

"You there?"

"You know I'm here. Where's my money?"

"Gone."

"Gone?"

"Paying the police to turn a blind eye to what went down wasn't cheap."

"And that's what you used my money for?"

"I wasn't going to use mine."

"I'm really tired, Bono."

"Mr. Green said he owes you one."

"For what?"

"Lowe."

"I don't know what you're talking about."

"Funny. That's the same thing Julisa said."

"What a coincidence," Dawn said sarcastically.

"I bet. I talked with Mr. Green about a few things."

"Really?"

"I convinced him to sign The Bank over to Julisa, and I convinced him that I would kill you myself if you ever thought of opening your mouth to the Police, Press, or anyone else. So, you're a free woman."

"You finished?"

"Yes."

"Good bye," Bono.

"Good bye, Honey."

Monday morning, as soon as Dawn sat at her desk, Mr. Morgan stepped out of his office.

"Dawn, I need to see you."

"Here we go," Dawn mumbled. *I give up. If today is my last day, so be it.* She entered his office and closed the door.

"Have a seat," he said to her.

Dawn plopped down in the chair.

"You okay?" Mr. Morgan asked.

"No, I had a terrible week, and now I'm sitting in your office."

"I'm sorry to hear that."

"I bet."

"And me calling you into my office doesn't' have to be a bad thing, does it?"

"We're about to find out, aren't we?"

Mr. Morgan cracked a smile. "You are something else. Even when I want to be mad at you, I can't be. I'm not going to make this any longer than it has to be. I gave The Powers That Be an ultimatum. Either they give you back your full-time item number or they're going to have to fire me."

"So, you called me in here to tell me that they fired you?"

"As of this morning, you are full-time, with a raise."

Dawn blinked. "What's the catch?"

"Catch? You're my best secretary. I went to bat for you."

"Why?"

"Why? Because fair is fair. You deserve it."

Dawn stood up and walked around his desk and shook his hand. "Thank you, Mr. Morgan. Sometimes I forget that there are still some decent people in the world."

"It's the least I can do for an employee and... a friend."

Dawn left his office. When she got back to her cubicle, she was surprised to see a bouquet of roses on her desk. She looked around. "Who put these here?" she asked Susan.

Susan pointed over Dawn's shoulder.

Dawn turned around and almost fainted. "Dante?"

"Can we talk?"

"Of course." She led him into the break room and closed the door. She turned to him. "Dante—"

He held his hand up. "I don't want to hear anything you have to say; I came here to get something off my chest."

Dawn's eyes filled with tears, but she remained silent.

"For the past two weeks, I've tried to make sense of what happened and why. I confronted Julisa and she said she couldn't talk about it. I confronted Whitty and she apologized for what she did to me, and then almost turned white when I asked her to tell me what was really going on. So here I am, standing in front of you, and if I was a gambling man, I bet you will tell me you can't talk about it either."

"Dante. I love you. I will always love you. I swear to you that I never slept with men for money."

"Where'd the money come from, Dawn?"

She put her head down.

"Tell me or I'm walking."

"Please, Dante. It's over, I promised I would keep my mouth shut, I gave my word."

"And I gave you my life. When we got married, *I* no longer existed for me. There was only *we*. Now, you tell me. What's more important, me or you keeping your word?"

Dawn wiped her tears and looked up at him. "We needed money, so I started to work for a man. His name is—"

"Mr. Green."

"How did you—"

"You helped him launder money, you ran his carwash-slash-cocaine enterprise, and you gave him twenty percent of Lowe's loan sharking business."

Dawn stared at him in disbelief.

"That's the same look I had on my face when that woman came to the house and ran everything down to me."

"What woman?"

"She wouldn't tell me her name. She said she'd probably get in trouble for telling me everything, but she said I had a right to know what I almost died over." He grabbed her by the shoulders. "Damn, Dawn. You didn't have to do any of that shit. I told you we were going to be all right. Why couldn't you believe that?"

"I wanted to, but shit just kept getting worse and worse for us. You got fired, I got knocked down to part-time, the bank was foreclosing on our house. I couldn't just sit back and watch us lose everything. I didn't know what else to do. We were at the darkest moment in our lives."

"Baby, it's always darkest before dawn. I lost my job, but I found another one; one that I find more fulfilling and with more opportunities than I could've ever imagined. I got a two hundred thousand dollar book deal, a prominent position on the executive board, and there's talk about me having my own radio talk show. I didn't have to run to the streets to get all of that. All I had to do was keep working hard. Hard work *does* pay off."

"I'm happy for you. I should've listened to you, you're always right."

"I was wrong one time," Dante said.

"When?"

"The night I kicked you out and didn't give you a chance to explain the text messages. If I would've believed in you the way I asked you to believe in me when I said we were going to be all right, you wouldn't have slept with Andre or Gamble or that Chinese kid."

"Oh my God. How did—"

"What can I say, once that woman started spilling the beans, she didn't stop until I knew everything."

"I'm so ashamed."

"Don't be. I'm no saint. I only slept with Whitty, hoping that she would go back and tell you."

"So, where do we go from here?"

"You coming home tonight would be a start. And I'm not talking about the townhouse on Bethune Street."

"My God, is there anything that Eva didn't tell you?"

"Her name."

"Of course."

"She also gave me a message for you."

"What's that?"

"She told me to tell you that if you ever put my life in danger again, she's sending the wolf pack after you."

"I swear on my life, I will never put you in harm's way again. From this day forth, I'm as straight as an arrow. Nothing illegal. Just call me Miss Honesty."

"Well, Miss Honesty, what are you going to do with all that money you still have in the stash?"

"What money?"

"Come on now, Honey from Charlotte."

"Okay, I'm changing my name. I don't like being Miss Honesty."

Dante kissed her and held her in his arms. "I love you."

At that very moment, Dawn knew that everything was going to be okay. "I love you, too."

COMING SOON!

Brathwaite Publishing
P.O. Box 38205
Albany, NY 12203
Phone: (800) 476-1522
www.BrathwaitePublishing.com

Order Form

Title	Price	Quantity
Youngin' by Arlene Brathwaite	$15.00	_____
Ol 'Timer by Arlene Brathwaite	$15.00	_____
In the Cut by Arlene Brathwaite	$15.00	_____
Paper Trail by Arlene Brathwaite	$15.00	_____
Soul Dancing by Arlene Brathwaite	$15.00	_____
Shipping/handling (via U.S. Media Mail)	$ 3.95	_____
	Total:	_____

Purchaser Information

Name: _____ Reg. #: _____

Address: _____

_____

City: _____ State: _____ Zip: _____

Total Number of Books Ordered: _____

We accept Credit card payments, money orders and institutional checks.
No personal checks will be accepted.